THE LADY'S ROGUE

CONRAD LEGACY

BOOK THREE

C.K. MACKENZIE

EMELIA PUBLISHERS LLC

The Lady's Rogue

Forced Proximity, Fake Marriage, Road Trip Regency Romance

Conrad Legacy Book 3

Contact Information: ckmackenzieauthor@gmail.com

Cover Art by Graziana Masneri

Publishing History

First Edition, 2023

Paperback ISBN 979-8-9850526-9-5

Published in the United States of America

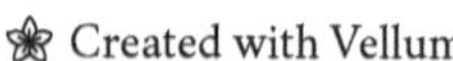 Created with Vellum

A special shoutout to Carmel, who came up with the name for Alec's horse! Thank you, Carmel, Alastor is an absolutely perfect name for an absolutely perfect horse. And he know it, too!

BRIGHTON, ENGLAND

APRIL 1810

"Oh, dear, you've run me into a dead end." The feminine voice sounded almost playful. Quite at odds with the words themselves.

"And Mr. Hartwell will pay handsomely for your return," came the sneering reply. That was most definitely not playful. "Even if you're a little roughed up."

Mr. Alexander Georg Ludwig von Stein growled. He paused just outside the alleyway and reigned in his temper. No easy feat these days. Honestly, he'd been minding his own business. Minding his own business, walking down a somewhat shady street in Brighton in the middle of yet another rainstorm on a frigid April day. Nonetheless, he hadn't bothered anyone, and no one bothered him.

He'd gone to Brighton in what now seemed a vain effort to escape his own thoughts, to escape all of London and the gossip swirling around him. After all, who went to the beach in early spring?

Apparently, a lady who was now being threatened with a definite kidnapping.

Alec scowled but didn't move away. No one was more

surprised than he at the realization there remained a part of him that wasn't a bitter rogue. He supposed that ought to cheer him immensely, but the rain dribbled down his face and chilled his nose.

He disliked the beach, but no one ventured to Brighton in early April, and he'd thought—mistakenly—that he'd enjoy the town in peace and quiet while he licked his wounds and planned his next move. Yes, he'd been quite clearly mistaken.

"We've bribed your servants," the man snarled. "No one will help you now, Miss Archibald."

Alec peered around the corner, a quick, assessing look. The scene played out much as he imagined: a lone woman, blond, well-dressed, taller than at least two of the men. She stood midway into the alley, surrounded by filthy walls and dirty puddles.

"Indeed." The woman lifted her chin. She looked quite unruffled for being surrounded by five ruffians in an alleyway just off where the bathing houses were stored for the winter. "Bribed my servants...yes, that does seem dire."

She didn't sound in dire straits, which was what had caught Alec's attention in the first place. Her stillness, her calmness, intrigued him. He supposed that utter stillness might've been from fear, but she didn't sound afraid. Not even frozen nor deadened inside from terror. No, her tone sounded almost...intrigued?

How utterly ridiculous. Perhaps when that beam hit him on the head he'd lost even more of his sense than he'd first thought.

"I hope you gave them a goodly amount." Intrigued? He suppressed a smile. She sounded absolutely indignant. "I'm certain I'm worth more than a quid or two. Twenty pounds each, at the very least."

Alec stifled a laugh. He tried to, at least. She must've heard him or saw a movement, for her gaze met his. Her clear, dark eyes gave nothing away, and she looked back at the gang as quickly as she'd met his gaze.

The gang didn't seem bothered by her mockery. They didn't even acknowledge it. Alec sighed and shed his greatcoat. He'd left his servants to their duties when he'd fled London, and he didn't fancy trying to repair or clean his clothing himself. And Godred certainly wouldn't volunteer.

Folding it so the inside didn't get wet in the downpour, he set it aside far more carefully than he had anything else in the last four months.

He wasn't much on rescuing damsels in distress, no matter how not-in-distress she seemed. A good brawl? Oh, yes. That tempted him.

Cracking his knuckles, he rounded the corner of the miserable little alleyway. Nothing had changed. But he felt it. That pulsing temptation to fight, to let loose his anger on a worthy opponent. Or not so worthy, as the case may be.

All that pent-up energy he'd prowled around Brighton with crackled to life here and now. Alec grinned.

"I'm afraid I'm going to have to decline this most intriguing offer," Miss Archibald said as Alec stepped more fully into the alleyway. "I've never been kidnapped before, but it's not one of those adventures I've any desire to endure. I do hope you understand."

He grinned wider now, unable to stop his amusement at her obvious disdain. Perhaps her servants weren't as bribable as this gang believed. He hadn't seen anyone else around, but that didn't mean they weren't waiting nearby.

"I'm afraid I must agree with the young lady. Kidnapping is so last season."

Where his own mocking humor came from, Alec had no idea. Not five minutes ago, he'd prowled the empty streets of Brighton, keeping his distance from everyone and trying to escape even himself. Now he stood in an alley, facing five men armed with knives and terrible hygiene, who didn't look like they were about to take no for an answer.

So be it. Perhaps a good fight over the lady's honor would shake him from the anger that had gripped him since the new year.

"Ah, her lover. Perfect. We'll get extra for him."

Miss Archibald laughed—definitely not a simpering little sound. Rather, a full, robust ridicule of a laugh. "I'm afraid you won't. As interesting as this little interlude has been, it's time for the grand finale."

Before Alec could blink, Miss Archibald had produced a truly wicked-looking dagger from somewhere on her person and sliced it along the arm of the man nearest her. The man yelped and stumbled backward, clutching his arm and staring at it in open-mouthed shock.

For one heartbeat, the others stilled in surprise. Then all hell broke loose in the narrow alleyway. Three of the men turned on Alec, which he considered a very bad choice, indeed. He wasn't the one wielding that dagger.

Turn on him they did, however, and he gratefully tackled the first, literally rushing headlong into the melee.

Keeping his attention on Miss Archibald, he easily knocked out the first man, stunning him, at least, even as the other two ganged up on him. The closeness of the brick walls allowed him to slam backward, shaking off one man with a nasty blow. Alec twisted toward the second man and landed a solid punch at his jaw.

"Ah, Bennett, has Augusta escaped?" Miss Archibald's voice cut through the ringing in Alec's ears as the final man slid down the wall.

"Aye, miss." The voice came from the mouth of the alleyway. "On the ship with Eabha and Bernard. And Una should be back at the townhouse by now in the second carriage. Captain

Hoffman has sworn he and the crew will escort Miss Augusta safely to Upper Canada."

The servants who weren't as bribable as these men thought. Breathing hard, Alec straightened from the wall and grimaced. He'd twisted a muscle in his back, one he hadn't even known could twist. The movement sucked the breath from him.

Not enough training, he supposed. Embracing the sedentary lifestyle and giving up all movement that didn't involve stalking the streets of Brighton. Too much feeling sorry for himself.

"Thank you, Bennett." Miss Archibald stepped daintily over the legs of the first man she'd cut. Poor man was looking in awe at his still-bleeding arm. Miss Archibald frowned down at him, then at his friend, who was also holding a long gash across his arm. "You really should run along now. You won't be getting paid, and that wound needs tending."

Alec swallowed another laugh. The men, both still stunned, stumbled to their feet and did as Miss Archibald bade. They disappeared down the street in the same direction.

Shaking her head, she dismissed the ruffians as if they were no more than lads playing a prank. She stopped directly before him. "Thank you, sir."

"Ah. Yes. You're welcome." He had no idea what had happened in the last half hour—not even that long, he'd wager. Frowning, Alec flexed his hands. "Been a while since I found a good fight."

Her head tiled. "Was that a good fight?" Her gaze flicked toward the bodies of the men sent to kidnap her. "I thought them rather inept, but they gave a rousing snarl."

Alec laughed. Somehow, that hurt his back, and he stilled. Damnation. "I have a feeling you didn't need my help, Miss Archibald."

"I never turn down help," she said. Her dark brown eyes twinkled in the miserable light, and her mouth turned upward in a faint smile. "Especially competent help such as yours."

When Alec had stepped into the alleyway, he hadn't realized how stunning she was. He'd focused on her situation, but now, watching her as the rain dripped down her wilting bonnet, he noticed. Indeed, he noticed.

"That makes you smarter than these men, Miss Archibald." He waved a dismissive hand toward them.

"Hmm." She ignored the men and turned for her footman and the open street. "It's Conrad."

"Miss Archibald Conrad," he corrected, wondering if he'd be able to climb into the tub for a hot soak for his back. He could climb in, perhaps, but he wouldn't wager on climbing back out. Not when even breathing hurt.

"No, just—" She frowned at his stilted movement and waved away whatever else she'd planned on saying with an impatient flick of her wrist. "Are you injured?"

"I'm quite well, thank you." That was a lie. Alec eyed the footman. "Is Brighton always like this, roving groups of men trying to kidnap women in alleyways?"

"Oh, no." She paused and shrugged. Her gaze watched his carefully; however, it was strong and direct. "Truthfully, this is my first time in Brighton, but I doubt it. The attempt was for the woman I intended them to kidnap." Miss Archibald grinned, a hard, knowing smile that intrigued him. "I'm indebted for your help, sir. If you'd care to accompany me back to my townhouse, we'll take a look at your back." She turned but stopped in the mouth of the alleyway. "Would you also care to enjoy luncheon with me?"

"My back is perfectly fine," Alec said, quite certain he'd never had control of this conversation at all.

Miss Archibald snorted in a most unladylike way and nodded at Bennett. Apparently, the footman agreed with her, and he picked up Alec's greatcoat and held it out as if they all stood around a salon.

"Sir." Bennett, who looked quite capable of holding off a

gang of would-be kidnappers, no matter their level of ineptitude, merely waited.

"Luncheon, however, sounds lovely. Thank you." Alec had no idea what had happened to this conversation. Nor what had happened in the alleyway. He blinked and searched for his hat, but Bennett had already liberated it from beside a puddle and was holding it out for him. He nodded in thanks, not entirely certain what else the situation called for.

He'd never stopped an attempted kidnapping.

There was a first for everything, he supposed.

GRATEFUL TO BE out of the rain, Miss Yara Hannah Teresa Conrad settled into her carriage opposite her handsome rescuer. Bennett had eyed her once before nodding and climbing into the driver's seat. The arrangement might've been highly unusual, but then, Yara hadn't planned on actually having a rescuer.

"You'll excuse the impropriety of the carriage ride, I hope." She eyed the man across from her as the carriage jolted forward. "I wasn't prepared for guests."

He snorted. Yara's lips twitched in amusement. "What were you prepared for then?"

His modulated tone intrigued her. It was as if he carefully spoke every syllable of each word. Perhaps he'd injured himself more than he let on. His clothing looked well-cut and expertly tailored, but then, even the most corrupt of men looked well-tailored.

Money could, indeed, purchase illusion. And illusion was all most people saw anyway. However, this man had taken on three of those five ruffians with ease, which fascinated her more than his wealth, real or perceived.

"Oh, I prepared for exactly that." She folded her hands primly over her lap—her own illusion.

Her khanjar, a specially made Egyptian dagger, rested on her lap should she need it. Yara hadn't bothered to hide it again once the gang made their move against her. Though she doubted she'd need it here, with the man who'd rescued her.

"You prepared for your own kidnapping?" The man's eyebrows shot upward, but his mouth curved in the slightest of smiles.

"Not my own, no." Yara frowned. Had he said his name? She didn't think so, but she couldn't remember, what with all the fuss. "Mr....?"

"Von Stein," he said promptly. "Alexander von Stein."

"Prussian?"

"My family was, yes." He grimaced slightly. If Yara hadn't been studying him so intently, she might've missed it. She supposed the scowl might have been from his back pain, but she also suspected it had more to do with his family. Interesting.

Perhaps Mama or Auntie Hannah might know more about him. They both knew a great many people.

Dropping the subject, she nodded. "Mr. von Stein." What had she been saying? "While I'm always prepared to defend myself, this kidnapping was not my own. They merely believed as much."

He looked confused, poor man. His gaze flicked to her dagger in her lap and then back to hers. "You orchestrated someone else's kidnapping?"

"I...yes. Yes, I did," Yara decided. It was the easier explanation, though von Stein looked more interested than placated. "I made it so those men, sent by the odious Mr. Hartwell, believed I was Augusta, my friend. They didn't know any better."

Men were easily fooled by a change of clothing and a wig. And easier fooled by a lone woman walking down the street.

Honestly, those men should've known better. Alas, Hartwell's stinginess had been his downfall.

Von Stein frowned, and Yara knew it had nothing to do with his back pain. "They didn't know who they'd been sent to kidnap?" He snorted again. "Sloppy."

"Indeed. Lucky for Augusta."

"I'd say it was luckier that she had a friend like you who was willing to take her place." The carriage slowed around a corner, and Yara knew they'd arrived on her street. "What would you have done if they'd actually been successful?"

"Successful?" The thought hadn't even occurred to her. She laughed at the very notion. "They hadn't bribed my servants; I never worried over that. Well, I suppose they offered Bennett money, but that was as far as the exchange went. If you hadn't come along, I'm certain Bennett and I could've taken all five."

Von Stein didn't look convinced, but Yara expected that. She ignored his skepticism, just as she had ignored such skepticism all her life. Other people's opinions might've dictated her future, but they didn't shape her life.

That was a hard-won realization she kept close.

"You believe servants are all bribable? Rather, all servants are bribable?" She shrugged as the carriage rolled to a stop. Some, perhaps. She'd grant him that. "Or that Bennett and I wouldn't have been successful?"

"I'm not certain I should answer either of those questions," he said truthfully.

Yara swallowed a chuckle. "You're a smart man, Mr. von Stein. We've arrived. I'll have Bennett run ahead, and he'll have hot water drawn." She paused and tilted her head. "Perhaps a cold pack instead?"

"I'm perfectly fine," he insisted. "I agreed to luncheon, remember." He offered a smile that hid his back pain well enough. Hid something else, too, she'd wager. He'd fought with a barely suppressed fury Yara understood all too well.

She was unconvinced as to his "perfectly fine" statement, but she let it go as she felt the carriage rock. Bennett jumped from the driver's seat and opened the door. "Thank you, Bennett. Out of curiosity, how much did those men offer you as a bribe?"

"Five pounds, miss."

"Only five?" Yara couldn't hide her outrage. She huffed, much to Bennett's amusement and von Stein's choked laughter. "I'm worth more than that." She shared his grin. "You as well, Bennett."

"Thank you, miss," he laughed.

"Mr. von Stein insists he's perfectly fine and does not require either a hot or cold bath." She glanced at the tall, handsome man out of the corner of her eye. Perhaps she ought not to have thought that last—"handsome" was far too insipid a word for him. Fierce. Towering. Muscled—very well-muscled, indeed. Singular. All those words fit him far better than *handsome.* "Please have Charlesworth see to him just in case."

"Yes, miss."

"Thank you," she repeated absently, her mind already returning to her description of Mr. von Stein.

Rugged, she supposed, was also a good word as she detoured for the pair of horses and petted them fondly. All sharp angles and haughtiness. Well, his looks screamed haughty, but that nose—it had definitely been broken, and more than once. His eyes, a most interesting blue, reminded her of the Irish Sea.

"And you as well, my dears, thank you." She petted each horse in turn, lavishing warmth and praise on the pair. "We couldn't have done it without you." They whinnied in reply and nuzzled her affectionately. "I haven't anything for you, but I promise Bennett will give you an extra apple."

"Of course, miss!" Bennett took the horses' reins and petted them each.

She turned for the house and waited for von Stein at the gate. Danvers, their butler, had already opened the door and was standing just inside. Smiling at him so he knew all was well, Yara turned as von Stein exited the carriage. Though "exited" might have been a misnomer.

Half slid down the steps, spine straight and stiff, stifling a gasp—that was the more accurate description of how the poor man withdrew from the carriage.

"I'll have the boys tend to the horses, miss," Bennett promised as von Stein straightened with another pained gasp. "But maybe hitch another pair."

"For the best," she agreed.

"It's nothing," von Stein insisted as they walked up the path to the townhouse. "Nothing a good glass of wine or two won't solve. I don't need your carriage." That last was growled more than spoken.

Oh, dear. Well, one thing at a time. "Danvers, is Mama home?"

"No, miss, not yet."

Stepping out of the rain, she embraced the warmth of the house. Oh, but she detested the cold and wet. Tugging off her gloves, she flexed her fingers and longed for the heat of the fire.

"This is Mr. von Stein; he'll be joining us for luncheon." Yara tugged at her bonnet's ties, but they were soaked through and knotted tight. "He injured his back while fighting off the ruffians Hartwell sent after Augusta."

"And has Miss Augusta safely boarded *The Persephone*?" Danvers asked, taking von Stein's outerwear as well as Yara's— minus the hat, which still refused her efforts.

"She's well away from here," Yara promised. "Though I'm certain Hartwell will try to find her."

Danvers gave a very un-butler-like snort as he disappeared down the hall.

"Indeed." Yara grinned.

"You have the most unusual household," von Stein observed.

Then he shook himself, paused, and straightened carefully with a pained grimace.

Not the first time she'd heard that. She'd seen other households, where they treated their staff like inanimate objects and paid them even less. Where they didn't bother helping anyone because it inconvenienced them. Or, worse, didn't even notice them.

That was not how she'd been raised, and she couldn't imagine any other life. Yara refused to fall into the trap of not caring. Of being one of those people more interested in herself than in helping others.

"We'll lunch in the morning room," she said instead. "There should be a lovely fire there. Oh, this knot!"

"Allow me." His deep voice reached her a moment before his fingers did.

Yara stilled as von Stein's large hands grasped for the knot that secured her hat. How had she not noticed his hands before now? They were large and strong, strong enough for the brawl he'd engaged in earlier. Capable.

All the breath left her, and Yara forgot why he was standing so close, frowning down at her. Before her scrambled mind could grasp a coherent thought, von Stein tugged the strings of her bonnet and deftly untied it. Struggling to regain her breath, she watched his face, which was set in concentration. His eyes, that deep blue, focused on his task, crinkling at the corners. What might it be like to kiss him?

Yara stumbled backward just as the knot released and her hat tumbled to the floor, and she blinked down at it. Kissing him? Where had that thought come from? Had she lost her mind? Clearly.

"*Oomph.*" He'd bent and retrieved her hat, and she silently accepted it.

"Thank you," she whispered, still grappling with this stunning and unwelcome realization. Her fingers tightened around the hat, crushing the sopping material. "You shouldn't have."

"I'm fine," he insisted with a lopsided grin. "However, I won't say no to luncheon."

"Yes, right." Yara looked down at the poor thing in her hand and set it on the side table. "I'm afraid we haven't any—"

The quick tapping of paws on the floor caused her to break off midsentence. Before she could warn her guest, Micki bounded into the foyer with an energetic yelp and slammed into her legs.

TWO

Alec wasn't prepared for the attraction that overtook him. Standing in the pristine marble foyer with a dozen different doorways, his trousers still sopping wet from the alleyway brawl, Miss Archibald's charm smashed through every single wall he'd built over the years.

A fun dalliance was never a problem. A quick smile and a good flirtation were in his bones, a part of him. Kissing a maiden? Alec wasn't certain he'd ever felt such a visceral need. Yet here he was, trying not to stare at her lips and wonder what they'd taste like.

They'd taste like all the passion she'd displayed in that alley, he'd wager. Hot fire beneath her cool exterior and sharp wit.

Miss Archibald was beautiful with her blond hair and deep brown eyes. She was obviously caring, given the way she looked after her friends, and clearly capable. He wouldn't have a go against that dagger of hers, no matter his confidence in his own skills.

Standing before her, so close he could kiss her, Alec hadn't anticipated the arousal that punched through him.

"There you are, my sweet girl." Miss Archibald crouched in

front of the yipping collie, who bumped her nose against Miss Archibald's chin until she laughed and opened her arms.

"Are you going to greet our guest?" She straightened just as the dog realized there was another person in the room and turned her exuberant attention on him. "Mr. von Stein, I should warn you, Micki is a bit exuberant. I hope you like dogs."

Then there was the dog. The border collie, with her beautiful black and white coat and effervescent greeting—which nearly sent him to his knees. Damn this pain.

"Careful, Micki; Mr. von Stein injured himself helping me." She wrestled Micki from around Alec's legs, where he was scratching her ears.

"No, no, it's quite all right." He grimaced and straightened. Alec tried to repress the groan at the movement—he didn't want another offer of a bath—but he couldn't quite manage it. "I like dogs."

Micki, who didn't care about his injuries, his past, or his reasons for being here, continued nudging his hand. Alec wasn't certain he could bend again, and just what the hell had he done to cause this unholy pain?

Getting old.

Images of that last blockade run tried to crowd his mind, tried to push through the barriers he'd erected around his past. Growling, he stepped back, as if doing so might physically distance him from his actions. Instead, he knocked into poor Micki. She yelped as he trod on her toes, and Alec crashed onto the floor.

"Bloody hell," he muttered, the wind knocked from him. But he reached out for Micki and scratched behind her ears. "Are you injured?"

She merely licked his hand. At least someone accepted his apology.

"Micki!" Miss Archibald huffed. "I do apologize; she's a bit, ah, lively. She means well." She peered down at him even as she once more wrestled Micki, who was still trying to lick his face, away from him. "Do you require assistance in standing?"

"I do not," he snapped. He probably did, but this was embarrassing enough without the help of the household staff.

Alec sighed. Wasn't that what had gotten him into trouble in the first place? His damnable pride? Nonetheless, he pushed upward, jaw clenched. Somehow, no doubt through sheer stubbornness, he managed an upright position with minimal groaning and grimacing.

Miss Archibald watched him quizzically, eyebrows raised, face set in condescending expectation. Alec wasn't at all certain he liked that look, but he was far too busy regaining his breath.

"Men." She turned, called to Micki, and started down the hallway. "Come along then, since you don't require any help."

Why did she make refusing help sound like a weakness? Alec strode down the hall after her, back on fire, his tailbone aching and his pride mortally wounded. For a moment, he worried about the impropriety of the situation, but the instant he thought that, he noticed the footmen.

They stood at each doorway, dressed like typical footmen. Except they all watched him carefully. No disinterest here; rather, each man was a vigilant sentry ready to protect his mistress. As he stepped into the morning room, Alec decided this was the most unusual household he'd ever set foot in. And he'd graced everything from the most opulent manor houses of the ton, with their maiden daughters eager for a good flirt and the hope of more, to the most hidden of brothels, with women who weren't shy about wanting his body or his coin.

"Are you certain your mother won't mind this, ah..." He searched for the proper word for a most improper situation. He also wondered about this newfound need for decorum. "Intrusion?"

Miss Archibald merely laughed. "She'd have been more

annoyed if I hadn't looked after you, especially since you came to my rescue."

A rescue he was certain she hadn't needed. "I see." But he did not. "Miss Archibald—"

"Conrad." She frowned. "My name is Yara Conrad."

"Miss Conrad?" He had no idea what she was talking about. Perhaps he'd hit his head as well as twisted his back. "Then who is Miss Archibald?"

"My friend," she explained as their meal was served. "Thank you, Edna. And please tell Cook I'm most grateful for her speedy preparations."

"Yes, miss." Edna smiled, bobbed, then stepped back.

Alec felt as if the world were spinning out of control. To make matters worse, he didn't see any wineglasses. His head pounded.

"My friend," Miss Conrad said again. "Miss Augusta Archibald. She's the one those ruffians believed me to be. I thought we cleared this up in the alleyway?"

Alec rubbed his forehead. Had they? He didn't remember, but his day hadn't progressed in the manner in which he thought it would. Then again, he preferred the excitement to the constant recriminations racing round his head.

"I don't remember," he admitted. "Have you any wine?"

"We do not," Yara Conrad said in that same even voice that bordered on vivacious. She said everything in the same tone, from her faux regret when speaking to her would-be kidnappers to her questioning his fitness and health. "We can offer the finest Chinese tea, some strong Egyptian coffee, and a variety of juices, including carob and orange. Even a pot of chocolate, if you so choose."

"Coffee." Alec paused. He had questions, but not about the lack of wine. Why did her surname sound so familiar? It wasn't uncommon. "Conrad. Conrad...I know that name."

"Possibly." She waved the comment away with a flick of her wrist. "My sister married the Marquess of Strachan."

"No." He drew the word out. Strachan, he recognized—not the current marquess, of course. His father, vile bastard that he was. May his soul rot in hell. "Conrad Shipping." His eyes narrowed. "You're the daughter of Conrad Shipping?"

———

YARA COULDN'T STIFLE the laugh. It felt good, this release of her long-held anger, and she basked in this moment. She had hoped Brighton might ease her constant anger. Of course, Augusta had needed an escape, and Yara had already agreed to travel to Brighton with a pouch of papers for the commander at Preston Barracks. Plus, it had been easier to send Augusta from Brighton, as Mama had business here.

Yara hadn't expected this pleasant interlude. Nor the way Mr. von Stein made her skin tingle with anticipation. That was most unexpected.

"I assure you, I'm not the daughter of the company." She grinned wider, enjoying their tête-à-tête. When was the last time she'd so enjoyed a conversation with someone outside her family? Her rather large extended family.

"No." His own lips curved into a smile, and his eyes sparkled. "I didn't mean to imply that—as if you were born from the company like Athena from the forehead of Zeus." He paused as Edna returned with his coffee. "It's been a most interesting day."

Yara chuckled and sipped her carob juice. Amusing *and* well-read? Her day looked brighter. "Let's begin again, shall we? I'm Miss Yara Conrad of Nelda Hall, not of Conrad Shipping. This is my beloved dog, Lady Michaela. I admit," she added with a fond glance at Micki, who now lay on her feet, "my day isn't going as I planned either." She tilted her head and smiled at him. "It's going better."

He raised his coffee cup in salute. "I'm most pleased to hear that." Chuckling, he sipped the hot brew, then did a double take. "This is delicious."

"I'm glad you approve." Yara grasped for anything else to say. Unfortunately, her skills at small talk extended to the Peninsular War, animals, her family's shipping business, and the beauty cream business she was set to inherit, Conrad Creams. She wanted to ask why he'd chosen Brighton in the middle of the April rains, but something told her that was the absolute wrong question.

"Tell me about your planned fake kidnapping," he said, saving her the trouble of searching for some other topic. "And why Brighton. I'd have thought Portsmouth or one of the dozen or so wharves in London might be easier."

"Easier for whom?" Yara tilted her head and deliberately and delicately speared a chunk of cheese with her fork. "For Hartwell, no doubt. He's an odious man—I mentioned that, did I not?"

Von Stein grinned and chewed a piece of chicken. "I believe you did, yes. So you settled on Brighton, but he still found you?" He paused then laughed. Yara most certainly did not stare as his lips curved upward and that lovely, deep laugh settled within her in ways she'd certainly ponder later tonight.

His laugh was not all sharp angles, but a deep mirth that danced down her arms and skidded over her heart.

"No," he added on an amused smile. "You ensured he knew where you were headed. Clever."

"Indeed." She tilted her head in acceptance. *Stop thinking about his laugh. And his eyes. And his hands.* "Portsmouth was the obvious location, true, and I admit Brighton might've made things a tad more difficult, for me as well as Hartwell, given its closeness to France and the ships departing for the Peninsula."

No one ever said she took the easy path. But Alexander von Stein knew nothing about her save her name, and that was perfectly fine with Yara. Explaining her plan in no way jeopardized any *other* plans she had in Brighton. Not even Mama knew the specifics of those.

"You chose Brighton to make things as difficult for Hartwell as possible?" He laughed again, and Yara decided she could listen to that sound all day and half the night. "I applaud your spite."

She returned his smile and stared down at the small bit of bread left on her plate. Spite, yes. Pettiness, perhaps, though she supposed there was a fine line between the two. Yara swallowed her last bit of carob juice, but it didn't wash away her bitterness.

"Edna, please bring another cup of coffee." Edna nodded and disappeared. "Anyway, Augusta pretended she was me and boarded a carriage with my lady's maid, Una. All the servants called her Miss Conrad; the ship's captain did as well, to ensure the ruse."

"And you," von Stein said, clearly picking up on the rest of the tale. "Your servants called you Miss Archibald and drew out the gang of kidnappers."

"It was easy enough." But Yara was quite proud of her deception. "Though why they supposed a young woman would walk the streets in the middle of a rainstorm quite unchaperoned, I do not know."

"The better for them to think they bribed your servants."

"It worked," she agreed. "And now Augusta is well away from Britain, Hartwell, and the scheme he had for her fortune." Yara waved it away. No sense in going into details Mr. von Stein didn't need to know.

He didn't need to know how they'd stolen a goodly portion of what little remained of Augusta's father's wealth to fund her new life in Kingston. Nor that her father was just as odious as Hartwell and in on the scheme to marry her off to pay his gambling debts.

"Is he being investigated?"

She paused. He'd asked so casually, Yara wondered if he knew something about Bartholomew Hartwell. "I'm sure he is," she said with a carefree smile. She had, after all, perfected such smiles. "Ah, Danvers. Is Charlesworth ready?"

Danvers nodded. "He's in the downstairs bedroom, miss. Should his efforts prove inefficient, we'll bring in hot water for Mr. von Stein."

"Excellent." She stood, oddly bothered that her time with von Stein was at an end. She doubted she'd see him again; men rarely visited her a second time. Unfortunately, she expected such things. Pushing away that depressing thought, Yara smiled at her handsome rescuer and gestured for him to follow Danvers.

"You're in capable hands, I assure you. Charlesworth was once apprenticed to the best healer in India."

Von Stein stood and bowed, but he paused halfway and grimaced. "Thank you. I was going to say it was unnecessary; however, I'm afraid my back feels otherwise."

She giggled. She liked his sense of humor; it matched hers. "Take as long as Charlesworth feels you need. And thank you again for aiding me this morning."

He looked at her oddly but left with Danvers.

Yara waited until his steps echoed down the hallway. "Shame, Micki." She settled on the floor with her dog, who didn't bother to sit fully upright but rather inched her way across the short distance. "I liked him. He made me laugh, and when was the last time a man made me laugh?"

Micki settled her head on Yara's lap, and she dutifully stroked her hand through the dog's fur. The floor was cold, though the fire heated the room enough that she stayed where she sat.

Edna returned with the coffee and handed it to Yara, who was still sitting on the floor. "You all right, Miss Yara?" She peered down at her. "Is Micki all right? She seemed happy enough when you returned. Even greeted your handsome stranger."

"He's not mine," Yara insisted, and why oh why had she led with that? "He stepped in when Hartwell's gang thought they'd forced me into that alleyway. Took on three of them himself."

"Impressive." Edna made a low sound in the back of her throat as she cleared the table. "Handsome and adept at fisticuffs."

Yes. Yes, he was. Yara gently moved Micki's head and stood, shaking out her shirts. "Mama should be back shortly." She set the empty cup on Edna's tray with a smile. "I'll be in my rooms, removing this wig." She pouted and gingerly scratched her hairline. "It itches."

"Una is waiting with a fresh gown," Edna added.

Yara ignored Edna's knowing smile, whatever it might have implied, and tossed Micki the last piece of chicken from her plate. Then she hurried upstairs and let Una pull the pins from the wig. "Something simple, Una, please. I won't be leaving the house again today."

Yara ignored the surprised look on her lady's maid's face and stared straight ahead. She pushed Alexander von Stein from her mind, burying him along with all the other disappointments she carried.

It wasn't his fault, of course. He'd offered nothing more than his help. Still, better she embraced such disappointment now than harbor any hope for...well, anything.

Besides, she had work here in Brighton. Work that most certainly did not include handsome men who leaped into fights with barely a hesitation. Men with incredible eyes she thought she might drown in. Or laughs that still made her skin tingle.

The letter from Lieutenant Colonel Marcus Hilton of Horse Guards remained secreted in her inner pocket, a precaution she probably didn't need. With French spies hidden amongst the populace and what remained of the French navy threatening

Britain's shores, Yara hadn't wanted to chance anything. Hilton insisted she was only to exchange letters—hand over her pouch containing directives from both Hilton and the Duke of York and Albany and take whatever missives the captain of the barracks wished to send.

Her meeting with Sergeant Armstrong was the more clandestine of the two. As far as Yara knew, he didn't know her identity but supposedly had information about infiltrators within the barracks.

Yara had a feeling tomorrow might yield far less than even that. If this were a simple exchange of clandestine information, Hilton could've sent anyone.

No, as much as it pained and angered her, she had a feeling Hilton felt sorry for her. Yara pushed that thought away, too. Buried it with her anger and disappointments. She *knew* acceptance into the Royal Veterinary College was for men only. The fact she could do very little with all her knowledge infuriated her as much as it incapacitated her.

As a woman, her choices were limited to marriage and spinsterhood. According to society, she wasn't even allowed the burning anger that went along with such limitations.

"Miss?" Una's concerned voice broke through her thoughts. "I believe your mother has returned."

"Thank you." She swallowed the lump in her throat and plastered on the smile she'd honed these last years.

Racing down the steps, her smile turned more genuine when she spotted her mother. Micki greeted Kaya Conrad as exuberantly as she did everyone, though she was far more respectful with her kisses. Everyone was respectful around Lady Conrad.

"Mama."

"Ah, there you are." Kaya kissed Yara's cheeks and smoothed a hand over hers. "Augusta off safely, I presume?"

"As planned. Did Danvers tell you of our guest?"

"He rescued you?" Her mother's eyebrows shot upward, and Yara swallowed a laugh.

"He came *to* my rescue," she corrected. "He had no idea what was happening, other than that gang had cornered me in an alleyway. In the process, he injured his back." She ignored the flutter of excitement at the memory of Alexander von Stein stepping into the fray and tackling two men at once. "Charlesworth is seeing to him now."

"Lady Conrad," Danvers interrupted. "Your coffee is ready in the morning room."

"Ah, thank you Danvers." Her mother glanced at her from the corner of her eye. "And our guest?"

Yara did not roll her eyes at her mother's obviousness, but turned toward Danvers with a polite, expectant expression. "Has Charlesworth seen to his back?" She already knew the answer.

"I believe Mr. von Stein has departed, miss. He expressed his sincere thanks both to yourself and Charlesworth."

Without even a goodbye? Yara merely nodded. She'd expected that. Her disappointment hurt but wasn't a surprise. "Thank you, Danvers."

She swallowed that disappointment. Another useless emotion. Meeting handsome men who engaged in fisticuffs at the drop of a hat—or a greatcoat—was not on her list of reasons for being here. She'd do well to remember that.

Kaya linked her arm through Yara's and led her toward the room. "I detest this weather." She sighed with a forlorn look out the windows. "So much rain. I miss the desert."

"We definitely live in the wrong country," Yara commiserated. She'd never had the opportunity to visit Egypt, where her mother was from. The war prevented such things. Perhaps one day.

"Tell me of your Mr. von Stein," Kaya said in an abrupt change of subject Yara should've anticipated.

"He's not mine." Exasperated, Yara rolled her eyes, mostly at herself for once more leading with that.

Kaya merely watched her. Yara sighed again and told her mother what happened in more detail. But she left out the parts about von Stein's eyes, his capable hands, and his magnificent laugh. "I thought it rude to leave him in the rain after he came to my aid."

"Yes, of course." Kaya dismissed any other notion with a wave of her hand and smiled at Danvers as he served their coffee. "I'm sorry I won't get to meet him. Perhaps we'll run into him again."

"I doubt that," Yara said before she remembered to moderate her words. And her tone. That wistfulness would never do. And her mother's eyes were as sharp as her hearing—Kaya Conrad never missed a thing. "We're not here for socializing," Yara hurriedly added as her mother narrowed her dark eyes in patient watchfulness.

"Hmm," Kaya said. "No, we are not, are we."

Yara had a feeling that acceptance wasn't as accepting as her mother made it seem.

THREE

$\mathcal{Y}$ara worked through her morning exercises, eyes closed, breath calm. She gripped her khanjar as her mother taught her, the bone handle an extension of her hand, slipping around her palm in a single, controlled movement.

Outside, the dreary April weather continued, the rain a slip of a whisper as it ran down the panes. The sun had risen not long ago, but it barely dented the unending gray of the seaside town. The household had woken by now and was moving about in their normal animated fashion, though that was mere background noise.

Yara slowed her arm movements, even as her mind raced. No matter how she controlled her breath or the sweeping arch of her arm, her mind refused any focus whatsoever.

Alexander von Stein occupied her thoughts, and she honestly couldn't offer any reason—good or otherwise—for such a thing.

Perhaps it was his unexpected help in the alleyway yesterday. Or his interest in her explanation as he clearly (and far too easily) followed her line of thought when it came to

Augusta's faux kidnapping. Not that it had been a complicated plan.

Perhaps it'd been the way his blue eyes, sharp and intelligent and so very focused on her, had watched her. And his laugh—even now, the memory of that sound settled in her.

Yara opened her eyes, breathing hard. She dropped her hands and stared at them. Worn and rough from years of practicing with her dagger and tending to her family's estate animals. They were certainly not a lady's hands. Which had never bothered her before. Only yesterday, with the handsome and intriguing von Stein. But he'd certainly seen her at her most unusual.

"*Woof?*" Micki asked in a hopeful bark from where she lay curled up on the center rug.

"There you are, darling." Her mother breezed in, the most graceful person Yara had ever known. Kaya stopped beside her and kissed her cheek before scratching Micki behind her ears. "Would you like to spar, Yara?"

Kaya's dark eyes held hers—nothing but love and understanding there. For one inexplicable moment, Yara felt her throat close, and tears pricked her eyes. Horrified, confused, she smiled instead of letting them fall.

"Perhaps later, Mama. I'm famished." In truth, exhaustion tugged her limbs and unsettled her stomach. Food was the last thing on her mind.

Though Yara had long grown used to interrupted sleep as she oversaw the farm animals, last night had been different. Strange dreams kept her tossing and turning, images she couldn't remember once she woke. Though she knew she'd slept somewhat, come morning, it hadn't felt so.

"Hmm." Kaya merely nodded and gestured with one hand. She'd hummed that far too often lately, that noncommittal sound of…something.

As if she knew Yara lied (of course she did) but wouldn't

outright call her on it. Then again, Kaya knew all about disappointment. England was certainly not where she'd intended her life to lead her. But her debilitating seasickness, and this lengthy war, prevented the sort of travel she'd long dreamt about.

Though Yara didn't suffer that same sickness, the war had prevented her travel adventures from seeing fruition.

As Yara twined her arm with her mother's, she pushed down the unreasonable resentment she harbored. How many young ladies had the opportunities for such freedoms as she'd enjoyed? She'd lived her life on her own terms, doing as she pleased with the full backing of her parents and extended family. And a rather extensive inheritance.

"Cook has made a fresh batch of yogurt," Kaya was saying as the three of them—Yara, her mother, and Micki—entered the back salon overlooking what promised to be an amazing garden. Once the sun came out again. "And there are fresh strawberries and cherries."

"That sounds delicious." Yara forced a smile, one that turned very real as they entered. "Oh, Danvers, thank you."

The butler bowed at the compliment. But he deserved that and more for arranging the candles and mirrors now illuminating the small room. Despite the early hour and the constant rain, the salon looked like it sat in open air at midday during the height of summer. The fireplace burned at one end, warming the room and thawing Yara's heart.

"This is wonderful," she sighed as she sank into the chair. And it was just what she needed, though of course she'd never have asked.

"Miss Yara." Danvers nodded. "Lady Conrad." He bowed and left. Micki settled beneath the table, ever hopeful despite having finished the breakfast the kitchen staff had already provided her.

"I recalled where I've heard the name von Stein," Kaya began before Yara had a chance to spoon the first bite of yogurt into her mouth.

"And here I'd hoped for at least a small respite," she sighed. "All right. I'm listening. Will it upset my meal?"

"Not any more than a restless night already has," her mother shot back.

Yara made a face at her, which Kaya returned. "At least let me enjoy my coffee first."

"There's nothing to spoil, darling." Kaya held her own cup with both hands and watched her over the rim. "You make it sound as if the pair of you were thinking of eloping to Scotland after a single meeting."

Yara snorted and choked on a berry. "Hardly." She sipped her coffee and settled in, already feeling better—perhaps not up to matching wits with her mother, but more herself at least. "He came to my rescue, which surprised me. Then we enjoyed a pleasant carriage ride, an enjoyable luncheon, and naught more. I assure you; elopement never came up nor entered my mind."

"I am most grateful." Kaya sighed and shook her head. "I promised your father we wouldn't find any trouble in Brighton." A small, fond smile tilted her lips. "He didn't believe me."

Yara laughed. Oh, but it felt so freeing to let loose and laugh like this. As if nothing had changed in the previous months, as if all her dreams hadn't vanished beneath the harsh boot of reality.

"I'm surprised he didn't join us," Yara admitted. "Then again, I'd have been equally surprised if we hadn't found even more trouble with all three of us here."

"It does seem to follow us," her mother admitted. "Now then. Since you aren't eloping with Mr. von Stein—"

"I can't believe you'd even think that," she muttered.

Eloping with a man after a single meeting? Not at all her, and yet here they were, talking about it as if it were an actual possibility. Yara rolled her eyes.

"I've recalled where I heard his name. He owns a string of,

well, many things. Boxing clubs, fencing clubs, and horse stables." Yara perked up. "Yes, I knew that'd catch your attention. He also owns several ships, and from what Stokes has said—"

"You asked Stokes?" Yara yelped.

"Stokes is a trusted member of this household," Kaya reminded her with that haughty rise of her eyebrow, the one Yara could never emulate no matter how often she practiced. Then Kaya smiled and finished her bowl of yogurt and fruit. "He's also an amazing font of information and gossip."

"And what has Stokes said about Mr. von Stein?" Yara didn't acknowledge her own burning curiosity. Nor the pounding of her heart at discovering more about the handsome man.

And, truly, she needed to refer to him another way. Any other way might do.

"He's a blockade runner," Kaya added with a hint of understanding. Yara hid her smile behind her food. The Conrads had started their shipping empire by smuggling—it was a very profitable business. "Very wealthy, very connected, and, unfortunately, currently disgraced."

Yara frowned around her toast. "How so?"

"Stokes didn't say." Kaya waved a hand. "But, as you aren't interested in him, I suppose it doesn't matter."

Of course it didn't matter. Yara could ask Stokes herself, but why? For her own satisfaction? No. As the chances of ever seeing Mr. von Stein again were nil, Yara had no reason for more information. She mentally repeated that. Twice. But curiosity still burned through her.

Yara pushed all that aside and purposely changed the subject. "I'll need Bennett today," she reminded her mother. "I've a meeting."

Kaya nodded in acceptance. Yara didn't have the heart to tell her mother it wasn't that *she* wasn't interested in Alexander von Stein—it was that, in general, men weren't interested in *her*. Her money, her dowry, her business, even her understanding of horses, yes. Always yes to those parts of her.

Never her herself.

Even if Kaya did realize that nasty little tidbit, she was still her mother. And Yara didn't need useless, banal platitudes of reassurance.

"I'll be back by luncheon; will you be here?" Yara asked as she sipped the last of her coffee.

"No. I'm meeting with the captains of *The Lady Marta*, *The Queen Theresa*, and *The Lady Olivia*."

All named for women who had helped Kaya in Calabria. Before the war. Before Napoleon invaded. Before all contact had been cut off. There'd been no word in over a decade, though they tried through the usual postal methods and by blockade running. Nothing.

Squeezing her mother's hand, Yara kissed her cheek. "Have a prosperous meeting. You can tell me about it over supper."

She scratched Micki's head and promised they'd lunch together, then she hurried from the room. Her first meeting, the far more open and expectant of the two, was with Captain Martin Blackwood.

The hour was early enough that she would probably not be noticed, but with the area swarming with troops, best to plan ahead. And Yara always planned ahead. She had her cover story about Conrad Shipping offering supplies for the army, made all the more plausible with her mother's meetings in Brighton.

If that failed, at least with Captain Blackwood she could always mention the duke or even Hilton. People were so easily impressed. Another part of her illusion.

Settling into the carriage, she rested her hand over the bundle of letters and instructions hidden in the inside pocket of her cloak. Simple and easy—truly, anyone could've delivered them. One of Hilton's trusted assistants could've accomplished it. But, whatever Hilton's reasons for entrusting her, Yara would see it through.

She'd accept the offer of meaningful work in her effort to escape her own heartbreak.

Her later meeting with Sergeant Armstrong in Preston proper, needed more planning. That one required stealth and preparation. That was the meeting that counted.

ALEC CLIMBED from his bed into the chilly morning air, gingerly swinging his legs over the side. His back didn't ache. Nothing ached. True to the praise heaped upon him, the incredible Charlesworth's steady hands had manipulated Alec's back and remedied all pain.

Alec didn't know how the man had accomplished such a thing with a simple massage of his muscles, but he was grateful.

His back had never felt so good. Still, the twisted muscle itself reminded him of the need to remain ready. Other than prowling the rainy streets of Brighton, Alec hadn't done one bit of physical exercise in the four or so months he'd been here.

He also hadn't had such a good night's sleep in months. Not since the accident.

Scowling at his own constant need to remind himself of what happened, Alec stood and stretched, but the memories once more crowded his mind. Damn him!

"You're moving much better," Godred said as he held out Alec's dressing gown. "I brought breakfast," he added, though Alec already knew he had.

Every morning since they'd arrived in this miserably cold and wet town, Godred came in just as Alec woke. It was as if he stood just outside the door, listening for movement. He bore a tray of breads, meats, and coffee, lit the fire, held out Alec's dressing gown, and listed all the letters that had arrived that morning.

Better than having a true valet. Or a butler.

"Do you know of any Conrads, Godred?" Alec asked, forestalling the litany of correspondence that awaited him. The avalanche he planned to ignore, just as he had all the correspondence that arrived in Brighton. How anyone found him, Alec didn't know. Damn gossip. Even hiding away in the offseason didn't shield him from that.

"Of Brighton?" Godred paused in breaking the thin layer of ice that coated the wash bin. "I've heard a Lady Conrad is here. The kitchen staff is full of stories about her, each one as improbable as the last."

Curious, Alec frowned into the cold water as he washed, but he resisted asking about those stories. He'd had his fill of gossip. For as much as he'd needed the swirling sea of rumors for his own missions, gossip never did anyone any good.

Scrubbing the towel over his face, he turned for his breakfast tray. "Any others? I met a Miss Yara Conrad yesterday, of Conrad Shipping."

"Ah, the young lady who caused the pained muscle?" Godred peered over the morning jacket he was brushing with more vigor than it was worth, especially considering Alec didn't plan on entertaining today. Or any day.

"She didn't cause it," Alec protested, ignoring Godred's knowing look. He snarled at his acting valet, who ignored it as he had all Alec's scowls for the last months. Just as well; Godred was the only person Alec hadn't fired.

Well, he'd fired Godred, along with all his household staff and ship's crew, in a fit of fury and pain. But Godred hadn't listened. Godred never listened.

"You leaped into the fray, so to speak, for the fun of it?" Godred handed him the morning paper, which Alec didn't care to read but took anyway with another scowl. "That doesn't sound like you." He paused. "It *does* sound like you, but not the new you."

The new him. The new him who hid away in Brighton, of all the damnable places. Scowling at everyone who came within five feet. The new him who didn't involve himself in anything—social activities, gaming, horse races, sailing, smuggling, flirting. Alleyway brawls. Nothing.

No wonder he'd needed the fight yesterday. And, apparently, human interaction.

It'd been nice, speaking with Yara Conrad. Nice wasn't the word—entertaining. Eye-opening. Pleasant—no, not pleasant. Satisfying, perhaps, or enjoyable. Pleasurable?

Fun. Exciting. Stimulating—very stimulating. He'd forgotten he could laugh like that, forgotten he could laugh at all. Forgotten that the memories and screams and recriminations could, indeed, fade far enough into the background and that he remembered how to enjoy simple pleasures.

"I'm certain there's a boxing club nearby," Alec said rather than dignify Godred's comment with a reply. Not that he had one, which irritated him even more. His fingers curled around the newspaper, and he barely resisted smashing his hands onto the table. "I'll spend the afternoon there."

"There's Sholot's," Godred offered in a tone that said he was surprised Alec didn't know of it.

Reining in his temper, a feat that wasn't as easy as it once was, Alec finished his breakfast. All snapping at Godred would get him was more sarcasm in return. He'd known that from the moment they met, but it hadn't bothered him until recently. Why Alec allowed it, and why Godred stayed on, he didn't know.

He also didn't ask. Because a small, tucked-away part of him was grateful Godred stayed.

"And will you be calling on Miss Conrad, of the enviable Conrad Shipping, later?"

Alec's hand jerked at the question, spilling lukewarm and mediocre coffee all over him. The coffee was not at all up to the standards he'd enjoyed yesterday. "I will not." Scowling, he grabbed the linen napkin and mopped up his mess.

"If you keep scowling like that, your face will freeze," Godred said in that unconcerned, breezy tone that provoked Alec all the more. "Why not?"

"Call on her?" He laughed, a harsh, rough sound of broken glass. "I'm not calling on anyone."

"She's not anyone." Godred snorted and sat beside him, snatching a piece of meat from his plate. "I haven't seen you speak with anyone since we've arrived in this godforsaken town."

Alec had arrived, and then Godred had appeared within hours, breezily sweeping into his nearly empty house as if that last voyage hadn't happened.

"What's your interest in this?" Alec demanded, dropping the unread paper onto the table.

"She's the first person you've spoken with since arriving here." Godred paused dramatically. "Besides me, of course. And I thought I saw a smile yesterday."

The damned man probably had. Alec had enjoyed his luncheon with Miss Yara Conrad, and she had, indeed, made him laugh. That wasn't anything to do with anything, however. A simple meal of thanks after he'd helped her.

He could still hear her laugh, bright and animated, as she spoke of her plan. It'd been a good plan, too, just complicated enough to throw off even the keenest of trackers, yet easy to execute. He could see her sparkling brown eyes from across the table. The way her lush mouth curved. A temptation he wanted very much to indulge in—and one he never would.

After Charlesworth had manipulated his back, Alec had disappeared from the house with a quick note of thanks.

"You didn't, did you?" Godred accused with a very sincere

frown of displeasure. The damned man had an uncanny way of reading his mind. On the ship, as they ran blockades and amassed wealth. In the gaming halls, as they charmed customers and flirted with the ladies. Back then, it'd been all well and good for his first mate and closest friend to read his mind. Here and now, Alec detested it. "You didn't even thank her."

He had not. He'd thanked Charlesworth, whose laugh he didn't dream of, and he'd offered Danvers a heartfelt thanks to pass along as he slipped out the door and into the constant drizzle and brisk sea wind. He'd declined the carriage and ignored the driver's knowing look—and probable eyeroll—and walked the several blocks back to his own townhouse.

"If I didn't think you'd take me in half a round, I'd punch you myself," Godred muttered.

"Don't start," Alec warned and stalked for the door.

His grand plans for the day only included getting in some exercise at Sholot's, perhaps a pint or three, and then heading back home. His day most certainly did not include a stop at the Conrad townhouse.

FOUR

Of course, his day included a stop at the Conrad townhouse.

He'd been a fool to think otherwise, considering he hadn't stopped thinking about Yara Conrad since meeting her yesterday afternoon.

Stripped to his waist, breathing hard, and still angry with himself, Alec dunked the towel into the bucket of water and washed off. The hours he spent in Sholot's had helped, he supposed. At least his mind no longer screamed at him, and his gaze no longer turned inward. The physical activity expelled some of his restless anger, but then he'd known that it would.

One of the reasons he hadn't bothered to expend it before. Because exorcizing his anger might have made him feel better. He didn't deserve to forget. He didn't deserve absolution. And he sure as hell didn't deserve to feel better.

He had, however, needed the exercise. He'd become woefully out of shape, as evidenced by the twisted muscle in his back during yesterday's brawl. And now, here he was, seriously debating a return trip to the Conrad townhouse and a visit with Miss Yara Conrad.

Debating? Ha. He'd known from the moment he woke this morning he'd visit her. He didn't deserve that, either, but something in her drew him.

Her dagger? Perhaps, though Alec never envied such trivialities. Even if her dagger was unlike anything he'd ever seen and she used it with deadly precision. It moved like a natural extension of her hand, and she handled it confidently. Her laugh? He did enjoy the way her entire face lit up when she spoke of her plan. Still, that, too, seemed trivial compared to—what?

The sense of calmness that had settled over him when they'd lunched together.

That, Alec couldn't explain, and it worried him—well, concerned him, at least. He'd never felt such stillness, such peace in the presence of another. It made no sense. The only explanation was that Yara had captivated him so absolutely, nothing else mattered.

His memories hadn't crowded his mind, the screams of his men hadn't haunted him until he punched something. Oh, he tried to justify that the brawl had helped, but that nagged at him like a lie, unsettled and sour.

Alec stared at himself in the dirty windowpane. For the last few hours, as he'd worked through muscle routines he'd forgotten and reawakened his enjoyment of physical activity, he'd tried to pinpoint this draw to Yara Conrad.

He had nothing.

Nothing except the need to see her again. Once, he'd have done so without a second thought. Knocked on her door, bowed with a smile that bordered on salacious, and seen where it would take them. Now he—well, Alec didn't know what now.

Caution beckoned him in a way he'd never fully appreciated before. But then, caution hadn't earned him a fortune worthy of the crown's.

"Had enough?" Sholot's manager, Dickens, watched from the side of the changing room. Since he entered, Dickens had watched Alec like a hawk hunting its prey. Alec had a feeling the man knew of his past. A port town like Brighton? He'd heard rumors of his exploits, at least, but he hadn't said a word about it.

Just as well. He'd prefer to return, not beat up the manager.

"You want to come back any time, I'll arrange a bout with one of my best."

"I'm finished with that," Alec said before he thought better of it.

He wouldn't fight in the ring again, in a formal or informal match. That rush no longer interested him. In the beginning, when he'd first bought several businesses in an effort to diversify his income, he'd been the main draw.

The captain of *The Argo*? Tall, rough Alec von Stein? Men came from miles around, looking for a fight. He'd obliged, mostly for the money, partly to literally punch out the restlessness he'd felt then.

"I wouldn't mind another few hours of exercise," he added now, twisting this way and that. Whatever Charlesworth had done had worked miracles.

Dickens merely shrugged. "We have whatever you need."

For a price, most people did. Alec merely laughed, tossed his used towel at the waiting boy, along with a small purse for the lad, who'd followed him around all day, and left.

He absolutely was not going to the Conrad townhouse. No. Not after hours at the gym, not after anything. He forced himself in the opposite direction, planning to walk the long way around to his own townhouse. Somehow, not long after leaving Sholot's, he found himself standing in front of the door he certainly hadn't sneaked out of yesterday.

Of course he had, and of course he did.

Before he convinced himself to turn, leave, and disappear from her life as he should, Alec knocked on the door. Bloody fool.

Danvers didn't open it but Yara herself, looking as vivacious and beautiful as she had yesterday. Wearing a smile that brightened his entire day and made her eyes sparkle.

"Mr. von Stein!" She sounded as surprised as Alec was that he actually stood before her door.

"You're not blond." Smooth, suave. Yes, wonderful. He used to be so good at this.

She laughed, that sound that washed over him and settled deep inside his soul. Once more, that strange sense of calm burrowed beneath his skin, and the tension that even the boxing ring couldn't expel slowly vanished.

"I'm not, no." She stepped back and motioned him inside. "That was part of my disguise, to fool the gang into following me and not Augusta."

Alec chuckled, stepping into the dry, empty foyer. Despite yet another dreary April day, the house retained significant warmth. For a fleeting moment, he thought maybe it was his imagination, the warmth of a welcome, but he'd never been that fanciful.

No, the house itself was warm, preserving the heat of however many fires that burned in various rooms. He liked that; it thawed the constant presence of ice in his bones.

"Clever." He shook his head. "Very clever, Miss Conrad."

"One never knows what to expect with one's kidnappers. Hmm." She grimaced but waved away the sentence. "I didn't wish for any mistakes, but that wig itched."

"It was convincing, however." Now that he stood before her, in the deserted foyer, he had no idea what to say next. A problem Alec couldn't remember ever having, and it annoyed him.

That's when he realized she was dressed for an outing. For all her vivaciousness, her clothing was on the drab side. Muted colors, browns and grays, in a simple style. Well-tailored against her tall, lush frame, but not expensive. The colors and style didn't seem to suit her, though Alec wasn't an expert on ladies' fashion.

"I've delayed you," he said, that awkwardness returning. He shouldn't have come anyway. What did he have to offer her—to anyone? What did he expect from this acquaintance?

"Nonsense. I was merely, ah…" She trailed off, looking perplexed, and she waved that away, too. She paused again, as if debating her next words. Head tilted, she bit her lip. A plump lip he wanted to lean down and taste. "All right, yes, I was off."

"I'll leave you to your day then, Miss Conrad." He bowed, a strange, unnamable emotion twisting through his gut.

"No, it was nothing, I mean, well…" She sighed. "I do have a business errand," she admitted, sounding sincerely disappointed. "However, I shouldn't be long. Perhaps after tea?" She hesitated. "If you have no other plans?"

"Business?" He felt the fool. She'd just asked him to spend more time with her, and he was questioning her? Definitely a fool. He could practically hear Godred's laugh. "I'd be glad to."

"Excellent." She smiled up at him, eyes bright. "I'll just… hmm, no." She frowned. "She's business elsewhere. Una, then. Oh, I promised her—one moment."

In a whirlwind of skirts and a subtle rose scent, she turned and disappeared. Before his thoughts could crowd his head, Micki's paws tapped on the marble flooring. Where she'd been, he had no idea, but she suddenly nudged his leg as if she'd stood in the foyer the entire time.

"Hello there." He bent to properly scratch behind her ears. She melted onto the floor, happily smiling up at him as he crouched beside her. "I'm happy to see you, too," he promised the collie. "Are you accompanying your mistress on her business trip?"

"No, unfortunately not." Yara returned, still alone.

Confused, Alec stood. For all her forthright mannerisms, she held her secrets close to her chest. He supposed everyone did—

that was the very nature of secrets. Too many years keeping his own while ferreting out others'.

Crouching down, Yara accepted the dog's exuberant kisses. "She'd like to come, wouldn't you, Micki? But she'll stay here. Perhaps go for a nice walk while I'm gone, hmm?"

Yara straightened, turned, and motioned for the door. He didn't know where her butler was; the man had been ubiquitous yesterday but was oddly absent now. Was Yara sneaking out of the house?

The more time Alec spent with her, the more questions he had. But then she settled beside him as they walked down the short path toward the waiting carriage, and he felt as if she belonged there. Or as if he belonged beside her, perhaps.

The driver from yesterday eyed him before nodding just enough to convey politeness. Her household was an odd one, indeed. She smiled at the man as if nothing was amiss and climbed into the carriage.

Shaking his head and ridding himself of those thoughts, Alec helped her inside and tried to remember his manners.

"Thank you." She smiled from inside the carriage, where she was sitting quite properly, as if they met along the street for a brief chat. "I look forward to seeing you later."

"Until later, then." Alec closed the door. He hadn't seen her dagger, and the small reticule she wore on one wrist certainly wasn't large enough—or sturdy enough—for such a knife.

This was a sharp contrast to the woman who cut two men just yesterday in a back alleyway while pretending she was someone else. Alec shook his head and watched the carriage disappear around a corner, trying to decipher the woman who fascinated him so.

THE RIDE to Preston wasn't long, but Yara found herself bored. Giddy and bored.

She'd planned on riding alone, with only Bennett for company. Faster that way. Safer, too, given the nature of her visit. Clandestine? That sounded more than a bit melodramatic. This trip was necessary, if only to satisfy Hilton's concern about a spy in the barracks.

Now, with the promise of spending more time with Alexander, she wanted this trip finished. Whereas before she'd been more than happy to accept her mission—which was also too dramatic a word for couriering papers from London—now she wanted nothing more than to spend time with Alexander.

What could they plan for later? What did one plan for such engagements? Meeting an informant suddenly seemed far easier than arranging an excursion with a gentleman she had far too much interest in.

This would be Yara's first time doing so. Brighton seemed full of new experiences.

Tapping her fingers on her leg, she fidgeted in the seat. Being so active on the estate's farm had made her ill-equipped for sitting still in a carriage, even for the short drive from Brighton. She'd barely managed the days-long drive from The Hall and had forced the carriage to stop far more often than necessary so she could walk around.

Una, her lady's maid, had agreed to accompany her for her meeting—rendezvous?—with Alexander, even though Yara had promised her the rest of today off, what with her meeting in Preston Sergeant Armstrong.

Yara hadn't been able to stifle the happy smile or the slight plea in her voice when she'd found Una upstairs tidying the bedroom. Which might've been why Una had instantly agreed, despite the promised time off.

The vehicle rocked as Bennett jumped down.

"You sure about this, miss?" He didn't look pleased.

The heavy gray clouds sat ominous above them, casting everything in strange shadows. Even with the cluster of buildings down the main street, the wind whipped viciously, as if they stood on the wharves.

"I shan't be long," she promised, pulling her scarf more securely around her. Yara hated the cold. "I'll be two streets off Market." She lowered her voice, barely heard over the wind. "If I'm not back in a half hour."

Bennett still didn't look pleased, but he nodded and stepped back to tend the horses. "Miss Yara," he began.

"I'm afraid I must do this alone." It's what she agreed when Hilton asked.

Sergeant Armstrong waited for her at the edge of town. Two streets off Market, just beyond a field south of the barracks. Stepping toward a side street, she instantly spotted the barracks and the field. No one stood on the grassy meadow; from her quick glance it looked empty. But then, she hoped Sergeant Armstrong wouldn't be so obvious.

Suddenly, the single letter she carried in her pocket weighed heavier than a handful of rocks.

No doubt Armstrong had seen her arrive, if he was as good as Hilton claimed. Fighting her own giddiness, not at this covert meeting but at the prospect of another meeting with Alexander, she slipped around corners and made her circumspect way toward their meeting point. One thing at a time.

Sneaking around a village, hiding from curious onlookers, that was easy. She'd been doing that since she could walk. The weather helped. The rain kept many inside, away from the puddles and the muddy ground.

"Excuse me," she said as she approached the man. "I'm looking for a horse."

The man, medium height, stout and strong, with an impressive black mustache that did little to hide his frown, blinked at her. His hands clasped behind his back, doing nothing to hide his military bearing, though he wore plain trousers and a heavy greatcoat.

"Aye," he said slowly and looked around, as if someone might pop out of the ground. She didn't sigh or roll her eyes; she'd expected that reaction, even if it annoyed her. "I've seen one just yonder, eating the flowers."

As code phrases went, Yara thought it was odd. But Hilton, who had the trust of several members of her family, had insisted on it. He'd given her a list of a dozen of those phrases, one for each meeting, though he'd insisted she'd need only two or three, depending on what information Armstrong offered.

"Excellent." Yara nodded and dug out the single letter Hilton had given her for the initial encounter. "I trust he's healthy and happy."

"Hilton sent you?" Armstrong was in clear disbelief, even as he took the letter. "A girl?"

Once more, she tried to keep from rolling her eyes. Honestly, she did. She'd heard such things all her life, and they always irritated her to the point of snappishness. "Were you expecting the Prince of Wales, perhaps?"

"Might have been less surprised," Armstrong muttered. "Who's your entourage?"

Entourage? Bennett? Yara ignored his question. She had copious practice in ignoring questions she didn't wish to answer. "I'll see you again tomorrow." She didn't ask; rather, she stated.

"Aye," he grumbled, tucking the letter into his inside pocket. "Just at the edge of town, opposite side, end of High Street. About four. If you can tear yourself from your following. I was told you'd come alone."

Yara spread her hands at her sides. Voice even, she held his gaze. "As you can see, Sergeant, we're quite alone. A woman alone on horseback would cause even more notice."

"This isn't a game," he growled.

Calmly meeting his gaze, she lifted her chin. "No, Sergeant, it is not. I'm here because Colonel Hilton trusts me. You honestly believe a man who commands the ear of the Duke of York and Albany would place his trust in just anyone?"

Armstrong frowned. "People are talking about your visit earlier. Not exactly careful, was it?"

"Colonel Hilton entrusted me with several errands." Had Blackwood not taken her ready-made excuse and spread it amongst his aides? Yara sighed. "I'll tell you what I told Captain Blackwood when I saw him this morning. I did offer him a simple reason for my being there, but I see he didn't utilize it. Conrad Shipping has offered whatever help the army needs to end this war and topple Napoleon. I was merely there to extend our offer as an ambassador of the company. Feel free to share *that* with the men."

Armstrong snorted. "Blackwood is a fool. And he's one of the men on my list of suspected spies."

Yara tilted her head and gave a slow nod. "I noticed this morning that he does seem to spend a lot of time writing correspondence." She held up one gloved hand and wiggled her fingers in reference to Blackwood's ink-stained fingers. That fact bothered her this morning. "Or he's a terribly messy writer."

The sergeant's eyes sharpened, and his frown lifted. She wanted to quip about being smarter than she looked, but she held her tongue. She didn't care what Armstrong thought of her, only that he trusted Hilton's trust in her.

"Aye," he said slowly. He shook his head and offered the barest ghost of a smile. "Well spotted. How long are you in town?"

"Until early next week," she admitted, curious about this change in topic. "Unless you need me here longer. Depends on the information."

"Should be enough time." He nodded. "Hilton trusts you, so I shall as well. But this isn't a game," he repeated. "Be careful."

"You as well, Sergeant." Nodding, she turned as the rain started in earnest. "Good day."

Mission accomplished, she walked back into the center of town, her strides confident despite the wet ground. Brighton needed better drainage; this field was a mess and ill-suited for anything the way it lay now. Once she was back on the cobblestones of Preston, she turned for the carriage.

She had an even more important rendezvous to get to.

FIVE

"Change?" Alec scowled at Godred, who looked back with a suspiciously smooth smile. "Whatever for?"

Now Godred huffed and rolled his eyes. "You're a fool. I've called you a great many things over the years, but never a fool." He held out a freshly pressed evening jacket with a sharp snap. "You're a bloody idiot and a fool."

Alec couldn't deny that. He'd made excuses all day for why he shouldn't have asked her in the first place, had thought up reasons why he might need to cancel. The simple fact was: Yara captivated him. She sparked a sense of curiosity in him no other woman—no other person—had ever done. She made him laugh, made him wonder what she held behind that bright smile.

And where she'd gone this afternoon.

He'd also berated himself for wanting more. Getting involved with her was sheer stupidity. Especially after he'd promised himself he wouldn't taint anyone else's life after what happened last year. Just because Yara intrigued him, with her mad schemes and warm smile, didn't change that.

As if he read his mind—bloody man—Godred's frown eased. "It wasn't your fault, Alec." He rarely called him Alec, usually

Cap or a mocking *sir*. "I'm not sure it was anyone's; it was an accident. You did all you could—more than. The storm took us all by surprise."

Jaw clenched, hands balled into tight fists, Alec willed his friend to shut the hell up. Temper far too close to boiling over, he kept his mouth closed and the spew of recriminations and retorts locked tightly behind his teeth.

"You can hit me if you'd like." Godred warily eyed Alec's balled-up fists. To his credit, Godred didn't back away. "But it won't change the facts. All it'll do is injure me and make you angrier."

Which was true, and that made Alec all the angrier. He hated this out-of-control feeling, as if he were a child and had forgotten how to control his temper. He'd never been like this, so volatile.

"Chloe blames me." The words slipped out, scraping along his throat like a thousand knives. "And I'm sure the children will, too. Holly blames me, as do Walter and Ian."

"Aye." Godred shook his head and looked sickened. No doubt at the memory of the vicious words that had been spat at him in the wake of the wreck. "Living is the hardest part of all, Alec. We're the ones who have to remember the past, pay tribute to the dead. And somehow still go on."

That was the problem. Alec didn't want to go on. He couldn't change the past; that was impossible. And he didn't know how to fix the present. For a bit there, he hadn't been certain he even wanted this present, but he'd not done anything permanent, either. One day at a time, one walk around Brighton, one litany of blame he heaped upon himself.

Until Yara.

"She makes you smile."

"She's young and innocent." Which was a stupid saying, one he didn't truly believe. In his experience, the past shaped everyone; every experience and every harsh word cast a person a certain way. Even the sweetest, most innocent young ladies shrouded themselves in a veneer for the masses.

Godred shrugged and held out the evening jacket again. "You know better than most that what we show the world is mere fantasy. A mirage for polite—and not so polite—society."

Alec scowled, suddenly unsure of his next move. He hated being unsure. More than that, he hated the knowing smirk playing around Godred's lips. Scowl deepening, he turned and let Godred slip on the ridiculous jacket.

"Nothing can come of us," he insisted. "It was a mistake, letting this progress."

"Was it?" Godred asked as he left the room.

"Yes," Alec growled into nothingness. Yet here he was, dressed for an engagement with an animated woman who made him smile. Made him burn with need and wonder what more life had to offer.

Idiot.

YARA ACCEPTED Alexander's help as she stepped down from the coach and onto the sandy cobblestones that lined the beach. The sun cast long shadows over the empty shoreline, only the gulls and terns to witness their…appointment? Meeting?

She'd never been on such an engagement, so she was quite uncertain how to classify it.

"I hope you enjoy the water," he said as they wandered along the path toward the ocean's edge.

"I adore animals, but spent much of my childhood on a ship," she confided. "Not much sailing, given the wars, but enough. I love the water."

"It's a mind of its own," he whispered. Shaking his head, he offered an absent grin and gestured for the expanse of sand.

There it was again, that secret he hid. She wasn't inconsiderate enough to ask, but it weighed heavily on him despite his attempts at hiding it.

The wind whipped along the beach, but she didn't care. It could take her hat, muss her hair, and chill her fingers, but she loved the water. A quick look behind them assured her Una was all right, with Bennett beside her.

Yara didn't think she'd need a chaperone nor an armed footman, but they'd insisted.

"How long are you in Brighton?" she asked, calling on years of forgotten small talk lessons, which her governesses had done their best to instill.

"I'm undecided," Alexander said, those beautiful blue eyes focused entirely on her. It made Yara feel something she'd never experienced before, and she was woefully unprepared to describe it.

Safe. Precious. Wanted. Definitely wanted. That want ran along her skin and pooled between her legs.

"At present, my plans include the races and naught more."

Yara perked up. "Horse racing?" She probably should've quieted her enthusiasm, but she did so love horses. "I hadn't even looked into such things. When are the races?"

"Do you enjoy the races?" He nodded at her grin. Even with the setting sun backlighting him, his sharp features mirrored her interest. "I'd be happy to accompany you. I believe they're the day after tomorrow."

"I enjoy the horses," Yara clarified. There was no help for it; either he still wished to accompany her or not, but she didn't know how to be anyone other than herself. She'd tried that. And failed. "Horses are magnificent creatures, and many of the jockeys are knowledgeable about their animals." She scowled. "Not all the owners are as kind, and far too many owners and jockeys alike care only for the purse at the end."

She hadn't expected the sudden interest in his sharp blue gaze. The keen watchfulness. Alexander stood straighter, though his posture before had been impeccable. "Indeed. I am familiar with horses, Miss Conrad, and they are intelligent creatures."

"Oh, yes!" She felt the threads of proper small talk slipping away one by one. How was she to know he'd show such interest in something she held so dear?

"Horses are incredibly intelligent, and very kind. Kind," she amended, "to those who show kindness. There are many in this world who do not, especially to animals."

"I have several stables in London," he said slowly, as if that might scare her off. Or perhaps he was more concerned with her profuse excitement. "I'd be most pleased to show you sometime."

Yara's hands clenched her skirts, less for holding them away from the sand and more so she wouldn't forget her manners. She consciously took a moment to swallow her far-too-eager shout of *Yes, please!* "I'd enjoy that very much, Mr. von Stein." Her smile refused to abate. "Yes, very much."

It wasn't often—or ever—that she had the opportunity to speak with someone about her passion. And horses—well, all animals—were her passion. The Royal Veterinary College's loss.

"My family has a large stable, and I enjoy riding. Perhaps we can enjoy a ride together?" Was that too forward? It was, wasn't it. Yara sighed, but it was too late. She couldn't take back the words, no matter how inappropriate they might have been.

His smile changed his face. Transformed it from that sharp handsomeness that so intrigued her into something...more. From the intense watchfulness of before into sheer enjoyment. The transformation sent a rush through her, a warm giddiness that made the hairs on her arms stand upright.

"I'd like that very much."

Yara's heart flipped, and she grinned with a happiness she hadn't felt in months. The wind blew cold off the ocean. The rapidly setting sun did naught to stave off the chill, and yet she felt warm from the inside out.

They turned, walking toward the setting sun and back toward the carriage. She wasn't sure what sort of conversation to have now. They'd exhausted her explanation about her plan to foil Augusta's kidnappers. Horses again? She could talk about horses for hours, but most people didn't listen beyond the first few moments.

Perhaps she should've listened to her governesses rather than hiding away and reading all the veterinary journals Landon—now the Marquess of Strachan and her brother-in-law—had obtained for her. Question about an animal? She was the county's expert. Anything else? She floundered.

The silence was broken only by the call of the gulls. Then Alexander said, "You know much about horses. Have you always been interested in them?"

"Yes." Moderation—a lesson Yara had learned the hard way. It was also a lesson she often forgot. "All animals fascinate me," she admitted. "I enjoy my family's farm and tending to the animals. But horses, they're top on my list."

"List?" His lips quirked upward. "You've a list?"

"Of my favorite animals." She laughed. "It changes, I admit. When the kids and lambs are born, goats and sheep are my favorite. But horses are always in the top five. Dogs, of course." She gestured beside her, where Micki usually walked. "Well, you've seen Lady Michaela."

He grinned wider. It really did change his whole face. From aloof and standoffish to welcoming. She liked seeing that smile, liked being the one who made it appear. And she very much enjoyed the way her heart did that slow flip in her chest at the sight of it. "Dogs are definitely in my top five as well."

"As they should be. I half expected her to accompany us tonight."

"I debated, but I decided she'd be happier in front of the fire."

In truth, as much as she enjoyed Micki's company, Yara had wanted tonight with Alexander. Just the two of them—the two of them and her pair of chaperones, but they walked farther and farther behind them.

"I think you're right." He laughed again.

She had grown so used to that laugh in a terribly short amount of time. It sent shivers down her spine. Yara licked her lips and pushed away all thoughts of kissing him.

Von Stein slowed beside her as they neared the carriage. Yara relaxed. For the first time in forever, she stilled her tongue about horses and dogs and let the silence stretch between them. It was nice. Still, she had questions about him.

Most of which probably weren't polite.

"I'm sure there's something well-mannered I should offer," she admitted. "However, I'm more interested in your stables."

He grunted, still so closed off. She met his gaze and waited, curious about his reaction. He hid something, but Yara had no idea what it could possibly be. Most people hid parts of themselves. She understood that better than most.

He had secrets. She could ask around, she supposed. But that didn't sit well with her.

"As I said, I like horses." He shot her that grin again. "And I detest the way most people treat them."

"They treat others the same way." Yara sighed. "People can be very cruel."

She hadn't meant to say those words, and certainly not with such emotion. Yara felt more than saw his sharp look, but she couldn't quite meet his gaze.

"Yes. They can be." He offered his arm. Surprised at the gesture, she took it without hesitation, slipping her hand into the crook of his elbow.

He wasn't a talker, she realized as they closed in on the carriage. He listened, which was more than most men offered her. But he rarely said more than a sentence or two in response.

Yara liked that. She liked their slow pace and the closeness with which they walked. She liked knowing she could talk about horses and dogs as much as she wished, and he had offered more than the typical bits about hunting.

"I'll be in Brighton through early next week," she said as they approached the carriage. "And this may be most forward of me; however, I very much wish to visit your stables."

He offered another quiet chuckle. "Are you angling for an invitation?"

"I believe I asked outright." She grinned and stopped just out of earshot of her staff. "And you did offer."

"You are a very interesting woman, Miss Conrad."

His hand covered hers for a moment, warm and strong. Her heart stuttered then raced. Oh. She hadn't ever thought herself that sort of woman, the sort who placed so much credence on something as simple as a man's hand on hers. But Alexander's touch made her wonder.

She also hadn't ever speculated what it might be like to kiss a man. In general, yes, of course she'd wondered. But this wasn't a general first kiss.

Well, a first real kiss. John Brandt's fumbling try two years ago didn't count. Plus, he'd been trying to get into her skirts, trying to trap her into a marriage she definitely did not want.

No, Alexander von Stein made her fantasize about kissing *him*, specifically. She had a deep need to know what his lips felt like against hers.

"Good interesting?" she asked, head tilted as she puzzled out his comment. "Or bad interesting?"

"Good." He walked her the few remaining steps to the carriage and helped her inside. "Most definitely good."

Once she was settled in the carriage, he stepped back and bowed. "I'll send word for the races." His smile played at the corners of his lips, capturing her attention and her imagination. "I look forward to seeing you again."

"Until then," she agreed, quite at a loss about a reply. What did one say? Thank you? Me too? She had no idea, but as the carriage started back toward the townhouse, she didn't think of her reply, but rather about kissing Alexander. The idea occupied her imagination the entire return trip. Una didn't say a word, merely sat in smirking silence, a silence Yara decided she could safely ignore.

"Has Mama returned?" she asked Danvers as she handed him her outerwear.

"Yes, miss. She's in her sitting room. Shall I have a tray sent up?"

"Thank you, yes." Yara turned for the stairs. She found her mother sitting at her writing desk with a pile of letters at her elbow.

"Was your meeting fruitful?"

"You're back later than I thought." Kaya stood and kissed her cheek, gesturing toward the small table. "Are you hungry?"

"Yes." She sat and picked up a scone. "Mr. von Stein arrived as I was leaving. I couldn't very well invite him along, but he agreed to a later engagement. We ended up walking the beach."

"And your business in Preston?" Her mother's dark eyes watched her with a curious light Yara had never seen before.

"All is well."

She might've needed a chaperone in Brighton, but she'd never shared her reasons why. And Kaya would never ask. Her mother knew of Hilton, of course. He'd stayed with them on several occasions, and Yara's Uncle James knew him well despite being in a different branch of the army.

"You and Mr. von Stein enjoyed a nice afternoon then?" Kaya picked up her quill and twirled it between her fingers.

Yara watched the movement and frowned. "I might've overstepped my bounds," she admitted, nibbling on the scone. "I think I should've paid better attention to those etiquette lessons you made Esme and me sit through."

Kaya laughed, a warm sound that set Yara at ease. Then the maid entered through the open door, hovering just inside the room.

"Thank you, Edna," Yara said, and she motioned her to the small table.

"Propriety is important," Kaya said, piling a plate high with cheese, bread, and berries. "But so is being yourself. Imagine if I forced my children into some proper mold ill-suited for all of you."

Yara shuddered and accepted the plate, sipping her carob juice. "If you don't mind, on our way back from Brighton, I'd like to stop in London and see his stables."

That eyebrow shot up. "Is inviting you to see his stables a euphemism I'm unaware of?"

"What?" Yara gasped at the suggestion, then giggled. "No!"

"Still no plans for an elopement?" Her mother did a poor job of stifling her grin, and Yara made a face at her.

"It's worse than that; I'm afraid I invited myself, Mama." Yara sighed and frowned. "As I said, most improper."

"He's agreed, though?" Her mother hummed that noncommittal sound that made Yara narrow her eyes. "I'm certain we can make a stop. Perhaps see Nadia and James as well."

"That would be nice." Yara stood and kissed her mother's cheek. "Day after tomorrow, he's also agreed to take me to the racecourse. Are you free?"

"Yes." Kaya said the word so fast, Yara blinked. Usually, she had appointments of her own, shipping business, contacts to meet with. But she hadn't even consulted her calendar.

"All right." Yara narrowed her eyes at the strange turn. "Thank you."

Leaving her mother to her letters, Yara returned to her own room. She had no additional plans for the evening, except her very solid plan of sitting with Micki by the fire.

"I'm afraid I'm going to ruin this," she whispered. Running

her fingers through Micki's fur soothed her as much as the dog. "I'm not used to a man showing interest in my interests, Micki. Only in my money."

Sighing, she tried not to think the worst. When it came to men, she had little experience. John Brandt, the local squire's son, had tried forcing her into marriage for her dowry. And George Whitehead, an otherwise nice man five or so years older than she, had tried to court her. However, he'd never once paid any attention when she spoke.

Yara had stopped trying. After all, marriage wasn't necessary when she had a very extensive dowry and the Conrad Creams beauty business. She'd planned on having a house all to herself, one that boasted an impressive number of animals.

She had never expected anyone like Alexander von Stein. Anyone who made her want more—maybe not more, but something else. She still wanted that house and the animals. Now she wondered what it'd be like to have someone who shared her passion.

And that made her imagine a different sort of passion.

SIX

"Ou're going to be late." Godred sighed, a deep sound of exasperation.

Alec ignored Godred's harping—the bloody man was good at it—and returned to the pile of letters he'd ignored for weeks. He still ignored them, but they were a good excuse for also ignoring Godred.

He'd visited Sholot's again yesterday and spent far too much time exorcising demons that would never be fully exorcised. Then he'd finally visited his own horse, Alastor, who was not thrilled at the visit. But then, Alec had ignored him for months.

It took some time, and several apples, a good rubdown, and a promise to never ignore him again, but in the end, Alastor seemed happy enough. Happier still at the ride.

None of which sorted out his thoughts on the lovely, vivacious, and engaging Yara Conrad. Promising her things he could easily deliver was one thing. Horse races, seeing his stables in London—all easily deliverable, with no strings attached. No promises beyond the moment.

"You promised Miss Conrad you'd take her to the races. It's finally a beautiful day, and you're inside." He made a disgusted, guttural noise in the back of his throat. "Bah. Seeing to correspondence you haven't bothered with in weeks."

Godred snatched the letter Alec held but didn't bother focusing on. "It's upside down," he snapped.

Alec scowled at him and went back to ignoring both Godred and his pile of correspondence.

He wanted her. Wanted to taste the smile on her lips and feel her passion explode beneath his fingers. In his mind's eye, he all too easily envisioned her in his bed. Her tightly bound dark hair spilling over the pillows, her breasts flushed from his mouth, her body arching up for more—

Idiot.

That's what he was. A damned fool for wanting any of that. He had nothing to offer her beyond indulging their shared enjoyment of horses. No marriage, no future. Not even that night of passion he craved so badly he thought he could taste her. Anything less only insulted her, but he had no more on offer.

"Stop dawdling."

"These are important," Alec insisted, keeping tight rein on his temper.

To what extent? What happened next?

In the days since walking the beach with her, he'd thought about his reasons. This wasn't a courtship, yet escorting her to the races certainly made it seem that way. What did he want? Other than to forget his mistakes.

Alec snorted. He didn't deserve silence or Yara Conrad. She deserved better. Deserved a man who offered her everything.

"More important than escorting the lovely Miss Conrad?" Godred snorted. "You're mad."

Yes. Yes, he was. Mad for wanting her in the first place. "I don't want her thinking this is more than a simple trip to the races."

Alec stood, stretching well-used muscles that now ached

with his exercise. It didn't help. That same tension that crowded his mind had returned the moment he'd left Yara's presence. The screaming nightmares, the suffocating pressure of memory.

"What is it then?" Godred's tone softened, curious now rather than tetchy. "Why agree if you don't want more?"

"More?" Alec bit out a sharp sound that fell woefully short of a laugh. "What more can I offer her?"

"Alec." His friend—his only friend and confidant—sighed. "Do you know why I stayed?"

He jerked his head around and stared at Godred. Godred's eyes, a vibrant, crystal-clear blue, held his own with such concern, Alec wanted to punch something. His composure was hanging on by a thread.

"A lifelong desire to annoy and pester me?" The words came out harsher than Alec intended, scraping his throat, which closed around an emotion he'd rather not name.

"Besides that." Godred didn't grin, which didn't bode well for Alec's composure. "I stayed because you're destroying yourself. Whatever it is about Miss Conrad, she makes you smile." He held up a hand and scowled. "You're late for your engagement."

"It's not an engagement," Alec snarled, latching on to the easiest part of that sentence.

"Rendezvous? Assignation?" Godred winked. "Tryst?"

Before Alec realized it, he'd taken Godred—his only true friend—by the lapels of his coat and hauled him up against the wall. "*Do not* talk of Miss Conrad like that."

"I won't talk about her like that," Godred said seriously. "But perhaps you should think about why you're meeting with her. Are you stringing her along? A little diversion from all that's happened?"

"She is not a diversion," Alec ground out.

Alec dropped Godred and turned. The man brushed off his coat with an unconcerned flick of his fingers. A good two stone lighter than he, Godred couldn't best him in a fight. Not a fair one, anyway, but he was lean and fast. Mean, too. Alec had only managed the upper hand now because—well, hell. Because Godred proved his point.

Damn the man.

"Before it goes any farther, perhaps you should think about it. Miss Conrad is a lovely woman."

Confused, Alec frowned. "She is, but you don't even know her. What makes you say that?"

Godred shrugged, his gaze level. "Any woman who keeps you on your toes is lovely."

Alec didn't quite believe that was all Godred meant, but he let it slide. He stared at his friend for another moment. He had no further arguments, anyway.

Godred, calm and cool, held his gaze and waited. Annoyed, at a complete loss, Alec turned for the table and the pile of letters he really had no intention of sorting through. Before he did more than reach for the chair, Godred stopped him.

"*After* you keep your promise and take her to the races."

"I don't have a plan," Alec admitted. The admission hurt. "I don't know what I'm doing at all."

"Well, that's terrifying, Cap. But it's not surprising." Godred sighed, and his shoulders slumped. "It wasn't your fault." He scrubbed a hand over his face and head, ruffling his normally exemplary hair.

"We'll leave in the morning," Alec said, the words sharp against Godred's quiet admission. "Head back to London and—hell." He pressed the heels of his palms hard against his eyes. "I don't know."

"And Miss Conrad?"

"She deserves better, Godred. You know that as well as I." Alec ignored his friend's shrewd snort and watchful gaze.

"All women deserve better than us men. But when they choose you, it's the greatest joy imaginable."

Alec stared at his friend in confused wonder. In all the years they'd known each other, he'd never heard Godred speak like that. "Godred…"

"Have you asked her what she wants?" Godred scowled. "Have you asked *her*?"

Alec grabbed the jacket Godred held out and spun sharply on his heel. He stalked from the room, Godred's words swirling in his mind as if he'd had too much wine. He hadn't; Alec hadn't drunk a drop since meeting Yara. Half of him was afraid of what he might do with the wine swirling in his veins. Maybe something foolish, like knock on her door in the middle of the night.

The other half didn't want the vivid nightmares that plagued him, nightmares of that night—made worse by the alcohol.

Offering a curt nod to his butler as he accepted his greatcoat and riding gloves, he stalked out of the townhouse, a small, rented thing he hadn't bothered to investigate before he arrived. Alec slammed the front door closed. It didn't help his mood.

The day was bright, sunnier and warmer than it'd been since he arrived in mid-January. The wind didn't bite quite as much, and though clouds still dotted the sky, they moved quickly across the sun.

Alastor was ready and waiting. Alec chose not to think too much on why. (Godred, of course.)

"You're a good boy," he said, patting Alastor's side. "I've ignored you, and for that I'm sorry." Alastor looked over his shoulder and eyed Alec, sizing him up despite their ride yesterday. Then he snorted and shook his head. "Yes, I deserve that."

Climbing into the saddle, he turned for Whitehawk Hill and a day at the races. A simple outing that offered him a chance to enjoy something he appreciated, with a woman he—he what? His mind grasped for a word but couldn't find anything appropriate.

A woman he…admired. Yes. Admired.

"Then we'll return home, eh?" Alec nodded as if Alastor had agreed, though the horse merely snorted again in what definitely sounded like disagreement. And he hadn't even met Yara yet. "Figure out our next step."

ONLY UNA ACCOMPANIED Yara to the racecourse.

"Lady Conrad isn't joining us?" Una asked it innocently and sincerely, but Yara still eyed her.

"No," she said, not sure if her suspicion was warranted, if Una was somehow involved with her mother's sudden change in plans. "She's in an emergency meeting with the captain of *The Lady Olivia.*"

"Oh?" Una perked up, but she didn't sound suspicious, just expressing an interest in the family business. "My understanding was that the captains remained vigilant, keeping an eye out for anyone vandalizing the cargo."

Yara nodded, but her suspicion didn't abate. "Since Esme's investigation, no one seems to be using our ships for anything other than transportation."

"I'm happy to hear that." Una nodded. "Mary is still unhappy with the marchioness for leaving her behind."

Yara stifled a giggle. Esme's voyage from Portsmouth to Kingston, Upper Canada, four years ago had resulted in a series of adventures: the unveiling of a couple bent on damaging their cargo, one of whom was a French spy, and the man's attempt to rouse the Québécois to Napoleon's fight. Neither ploy had worked, and Esme returned triumphant.

And married to Landon, the Marquess of Strachan. They currently resided in the family seat and were expecting their second child. Yara was due to spend the summer with them, and she greatly anticipated it. She missed her young niece. All right, and her elder sister, and Landon. Landon, who had given her that first veterinary journal.

A pang of disappointment and regret flashed through her,

but Yara pushed it away. Today was not the day for such emotions, no matter how they hung over her like a cloud.

"Mary is a good friend." Esme hadn't taken her lady's maid on the voyage, not wanting her in any sort of danger. Mary had disagreed, and, four years later, apparently she still did.

As they neared the track, Yara looked out the window. It wasn't far from their townhouse, not more than a mile. But, given the uncertain weather, she hadn't wanted to walk. Nerves danced in her belly, making her heart race in a manner she'd only experienced the other day, when she and Alexander had walked along the beach.

Not even her mission for Hilton made her this nervous. As if every breath filled her with anticipation of seeing Alexander again.

Desire rushed through her, hot and demanding. Fingers curling in her skirts, she willed away that need. Yara freely admitted she hadn't much experience with men. Those few in the county who'd expressed interest in her had bored her. They also hadn't bothered listening to her, had only gone on and on about themselves.

Alexander listened, asked questions, commented, and made her feel seen. However, this was a simple trip to the horse races. Naught more. No matter how she enjoyed his company or how he made her laugh, the seriousness with which he listened to her—none of that mattered.

Simple trip to the racecourse.

Even if her nipples ached for his touch, and her breath came short at his mere presence.

"And their runs to Portugal?" Una's question startled her from her rather racy thoughts.

"Fancy a voyage yourself, Una?"

"No, miss." Una grimaced. "But the staff likes to keep abreast of the latest with the companies. Far as I know, none of us have heard a word about vandalism, theft, or cheating, but we do what we can."

Yara smiled and reached across the carriage, squeezing Una's hand. The staff were all loyal and vested in the family fortunes. It wasn't because their livelihood depended on that of the Conrads, though of course it did. But it was because they cared.

"In another world, Una, instead of my lady's maid, I do believe you'd be head of security."

Una laughed. "I'd like that."

Yara grinned in return, and they settled into silence for the remainder of the ride. She tried to shake off her melancholy as they went, but she suddenly missed her family with an ache.

When she'd agreed to this trip, she hadn't investigated all Brighton offered. The beaches were one thing, with their expansive shoreline and the interesting bathing houses she wanted to try. Though not in April, of course. She hadn't even known about the racecourse, which surprised her. Usually anything to do with animals caught her attention.

Had she truly fallen into such a deep sorrow that she'd missed it? What else had she missed? Yara prided herself on her observation skills. She needed the knowledge that went with keen scrutiny to protect the animals on her farm.

And the people.

Augusta wouldn't have asked for help, no matter how close she and Yara were. It simply wasn't done, disobeying one's father's plans for marriage. Yara had seen her friend's fear, the wide-eyed terror when Augusta had told her about it, and she'd intervened. Augusta had gratefully accepted her help. However, if Yara hadn't known all her friend tried hiding over the years, hadn't seen what was going on, Yara would've never known.

Yet here she was in Brighton as the carriage rolled to a stop at the track, and she hadn't bothered one bit of exploration. That's how mistakes were made.

Smiling at Bennett, she climbed from the carriage and nearly ran into Alexander's tall, strong frame. Cursing her carelessness, she blinked up at him.

"I didn't mean to startle you," he said quietly, a peculiar note in his tone. Rough, deep.

It intrigued her, racing over her skin like a caress. Yara couldn't place what it meant. Instead, she offered a grin and nodded toward the track, where people had already gathered. Startled? Yes, but in a most pleasant manner.

"Not at all," she lied. "I hope we didn't keep you waiting."

"We just arrived," he said, those eyes holding hers as if trying to convey a hidden conversation. All his look did was make her skin tingle with anticipation.

"We?" She looked around for a companion but saw only the other carriages and horses.

She tried not to stare at the animals, but that was like asking a fish not to swim.

"Alastor and I." He grinned, but it wasn't that free look he'd displayed during their walk along the beach. This smile, such as it was, held a darker tone. More reserved and just…darker. He offered his arm, and Yara accepted it, even as she puzzled out the change in him.

But then he led her a few paces to a magnificent stallion—fifteen hands high, at least—and she forgot all about his tone, his fake smile, and her concerns.

"Oh, hello, beautiful." She waited while Alastor sniffed her, eyeing her warily. She cooed at him, carefully reaching out and petting his neck.

Behind her, Una snorted. "*Cineálta*, you are."

Eyeing the horse, Yara ignored Una. She didn't know what that word meant. Una had taught her much in Irish, but clearly not everything.

"Alastair?" she asked, though she had a feeling she used the English pronunciation for the horse's name.

"Alastor was one of Hades's four horses."

"Ah, yes." She nodded, returning to the beautiful stallion, who had decided he liked her. "One of the horses who pulled Hades's chariot from the underworld when he brought Persephone down."

"You know your Greek mythology."

"I've named several of my own animals after Greek myths." She cooed at Alastor again. "A handsome name for a handsome boy. Well deserved."

"He seems fond of you," Alexander said, a curious new note in his voice.

She truly didn't understand him. He was the most peculiar man she'd ever met.

"I adore horses," she reminded him. "And they understand that."

Most men didn't appreciate her passion or knowledge about horses—nor anything else, for that matter. Alexander seemed different, and that, she'd run with. Pun intended.

"I thought you said your mother was accompanying you." He looked around, as if trying to catch her in a lie.

Giving Alastor one final pet, she concealed her frown. "She had an emergency meeting with one of our captains."

At least, that was what Kaya had told her. Not that her mother didn't have meetings, but apparently, she desperately and suddenly needed to attend this one. All of which led to Yara's suspicion that her mother had deliberately backed out of chaperoning her despite her instant agreement when Yara asked two days ago.

From the look on Alexander's face, he thought that as well.

Wonderful.

"You'll remember we're at war," she snapped. Annoyed with her reaction, her own suspicions, and his skepticism, she resorted to mockery. "We're contracted with the Crown to supply the Peninsula."

"I'm well aware of what supplying the Peninsula entails," he snapped.

She tiled her head. How curious. Not his words, but his tone. Once again, Yara had the feeling he hid something deep, an aching grief of some sort. She understood that, just as she understood she'd never ask outright.

"I'm sorry." Alexander sighed and offered his arm. "Let's walk toward the stands, shall we?"

Accepting his arm, Yara exhaled her anger and the sting of his recriminations. She knew what it looked like from his view —a young woman chaperoned by only her lady's maid. It looked suspicious. A scandal waiting to happen.

He didn't know her, of course, didn't know she wasn't in the market for a husband. Didn't know trapping anyone into anything didn't sit well with her at all. But, yes; it definitely looked exactly like that.

"Have you a favorite here?" She lightened her tone and gathered her illusion around her like a cloak, determined to make the most of today. "I confess, I know nothing about the horses racing today."

"I only bet with my life, never my money."

He said it seriously, but his lips tilted into a genuine smile. She returned that grin, and a small laugh escaped her.

The wind kicked up just then, carrying the sounds of the crowd. A beautiful day. She tilted her chin upward and was suddenly glad she'd taken extra time with her appearance. She hadn't much opportunity to show off her gowns, nor much desire to, but today she wanted to look and feel her best.

Not the most comfortable, mind. Her shoes were completely impractical, but looking this good made her happy.

"I know nothing about the horses who are racing," he admitted. "I haven't followed them in Brighton."

"I look forward to visiting your stables," she said, watching the horses being led around the track. Magnificent and beautiful, all of them. "Do you race?"

"I'm afraid I must rescind that invitation." He said it so matter-of-factly, she didn't understand his meaning at first. "I can't escort you anymore."

<h1 style="text-align:center">SEVEN</h1>

"Can't," Yara repeated.

Just then, the sun slipped from behind a cloud, illuminating her. The wind didn't abate over the field, but for one brilliant and terrible moment, the world stood perfectly still, and it cast Yara into a beautiful painting.

Alec sucked in a breath. What the hell was he even doing here? Accompanying a beautiful and captivating, but innocent, woman to the racecourse, spending time with her. Courting her —or giving off the impression of doing so. Madness, is what it was. Sheer madness. What the hell had he been thinking?

Her mother had conveniently begged off as chaperone, leaving only the pair of them here. Her driver disappeared, and her lady's maid had wandered off somewhere as well. It was all too…convenient. Yes, that was the word.

"I don't understand; you can't escort me to the stables anymore?" She frowned. In the next breath, understanding made her nod. Her frown didn't abate, only deepened, and damn it—why did that stab him through the heart?

"Oh. Oh, I see. Not you *can't*. You don't wish to." She turned from the track, her shoulders stiff and her head high. "I understand, Mr. von Stein." The way she said his name sounded like the grind of unoiled carriage wheels. "Don't feel you must stay; there's certainly no need."

With that, she stepped into the crowd.

Angry with himself, his entire handling of both this moment and the last few days, Alec stalked after her. He couldn't let her disappear, alone, into this crowd. He couldn't seem to let her leave, with her cool hurt simmering between them, justified though it might have been.

His longer gait ate up the surprising distance her far shorter gait had created in a remarkably short amount of time. He easily followed her through the crowd as she weaved around groups of laughing, smiling people. She didn't slow, didn't look around her. Simply kept walking.

Catching her by the arm, he forced her to a stop. "I didn't mean it like that."

Her eyes were clear and hard as they met his. "If you do not release me immediately, I'll break your fingers."

"What?" He dropped his hold. She meant it. He'd not only hurt her with his rough, bare words, but he'd angered her. Alec hadn't meant it, he'd—hell, he didn't know. "I didn't mean that," he repeated, voice lower. "Can we talk somewhere more private?"

"No." She turned again.

She truly meant to leave, no matter her single, unchaperoned state. He'd mucked up this entire day, and though he'd meant to create distance between them, he hadn't wanted her hurt. He only wanted to end whatever had started between them. He couldn't have it both ways. And yet now, as he stepped beside her and steered her toward the barriers surrounding the track, that's exactly what he tried for.

Yara sighed but didn't make a scene. "I know what you're doing, and believe me, there's no need." Her voice remained even, untouched, though he knew she felt otherwise. "You clearly have no wish to spend time with me, and no one is forcing you to."

She met his gaze, and behind the hard anger that burned through her, Alec swore he saw pain. The expected pain of rejection, given the way she stood, spoke...waited. Damn him. He scrubbed a hand over his face, floundering out of his depth.

"I'll save you the trouble of thrashing through your banal explanations." She held his gaze, fierce and unafraid, mouth set, hands curled into fists against the railing. *"As interesting as our conversations have been, Miss Conrad, I find myself needed elsewhere."* She waved a hand and didn't give him a chance to respond. "No? How about, *I'm sure we'll meet again in London; however, I find I must leave Brighton immediately for unspecified reasons."*

"No," he ground out, kicking himself, cursing her. "Who said that? What fool idiot said that?"

"Please, Mr. von Stein." She gave him a pitying look that made him want to punch something. Repeatedly. Preferably the damned fool who had spoken to her like that. "You are in no position to question me. I believe you're the one who, not ten minutes ago, said you couldn't keep the invitation you extended in showing me your stables."

Alec gripped the railing so tightly, it groaned under his hold. "What do you expect from me?"

"Nothing." The flat word dropped like a stone between them. "Absolutely nothing."

He'd meant before he uttered his stupid, careless words, but something in her tone stopped him. She meant that. "You didn't," he whispered as the crowd cheered and the first race started. "You don't. Why not?"

She didn't answer but looked at the horses, watching them thunder around the track. She ignored him, focusing on the animals, and Alec realized she always spoke of them rather than any friends. There was the Archibald woman she'd helped escape, but Yara hadn't ever spoken of anyone other than her family.

Only her animals.

"If you think I had made outlandish plans to run off with you toward Gretna Green, I'm afraid you have the wrong woman." She sneered the words "Gretna Green," and when she looked at him again, her dark eyes remained clear. She kept her face composed; no one watching them would know of her anger.

But Alec saw it. It burned deep within her, sparking in her brown gaze, curling her daintily gloved hands around the railing. What had happened in her life that not only kindled such fury, but forced her to keep it so tightly under wraps?

Rejection.

The moment he thought it, he knew it was true. Rejection. He didn't know why or who, but he knew. And on the heels of that realization came a new one—despite her status and wealth, rejection followed her like the hounds of hell.

"I'm not the right man for you."

She snorted in a most unladylike way and turned from the fence. "Good day, sir."

That was when all hell broke loose.

***

THE CROWD PANICKED.

Yara didn't know what was happening, what had set them off. One moment, she was pushing down the hurtful but not unexpected words of Alexander and trying to focus on the magnificent horses. She should've expected his reaction. After all, no one expressed interest in her; Augusta had been her only friend outside her family. Her vision blurred, and at first Yara thought it was from tears she adamantly refused to shed.

But the next moment, people were screaming and running.

Braced against the onslaught pushing toward her, she tried to make sense of the confusion.

Von Stein's strong arm banded around her waist and hauled her back against him. For one wild moment, Yara didn't think about the crowd nor the cause of the uproar.

All she felt was his strong, steady chest behind her, his arm holding her close and secure. His legs braced on the ground as if he stood on the deck of a ship. Nothing, not even the mass of terrified people, moved him.

In the next breath, she kicked his shins and elbowed his stomach. That small release of anger didn't soothe her, but she categorically could not tolerate being in his arms. He grunted and loosened his hold but didn't release her. Which she should've expected, she supposed, given his fight against three of the men sent to kidnap her—well, Augusta.

"Where's Bennett?" She raised her voice over the panicked din. The crowd pushed against them, and the poor horses shied from the mass of confusion. And still, von Stein held her as if he barely noticed them. "Can you see him? Or Una?"

Twisting her neck to see around his impressive chest, she willed herself not to overreact. She knew her staff. No matter where Bennett was before this chaos, he'd look for her and Una. Una, who truly had sneaked off, giving her privacy with von Stein.

"Your driver?" Von Stein looked incredulous. He frowned, his features sharp and angry.

Despite all that had happened in the last twenty minutes or so, she knew his anger wasn't directed at her but at the chaos surrounding them. He scanned the crowd, his gaze leaping over the throng. His hold didn't slacken, and his body didn't rock no matter who pushed past.

Of course she was attracted to a man who could take on the entire crowd without being winded. And of course he wanted nothing to do with her.

He stood much taller than she, so he had the better view. He shook his head, and suddenly he stilled, his hold tightening on her waist. Yara didn't fight him.

Then he nodded ahead of them. "Yes. Just across this crowd." A river of screaming, streaming people with no sense of direction. No matter her hurt and anger over his words, Yara was grateful for his hold, lest she be swept away.

"Did he see you?"

"Yes. He's with your maid; they're pushing through the throng."

"Let them know I'm with you." She held on to one of his arms as he raised the other to signal Bennett. "I doubt he—"

The ground shook. His arm tightened around her, and Yara held on as if the deck of a ship had suddenly dropped from beneath her. Shaking her head, slightly disoriented, she looked up at him. He looked furious.

"What was that?" But she already knew, and her heart thudded in reaction.

"Explosion by the barracks. In the munitions building, I suspect." He hauled her backward, away from the even more frantic crowd. People, terrified animals, horses, all of them pushed against them. But he parted them like a sea, walking through the frightened mass like an inexorable rock.

Hiking up her dress, she kept up with his long strides. She might've been furious with him, and so very hurt, but she was no fool. Staying by his side was wiser than pushing through this mob on her own.

"*Oomph!*"

In their mad dash away from the panic, someone slammed into her. Yara crashed to the muddy ground, cold rainwater seeping through her gown. A knee knocked into her head. Growling in pain and frustration and worry for Una and Bennett, she unsteadily pushed upright, shoving against the mass still spilling forth.

She had no idea there'd been this many people at the races.

In one smooth move that left her breathless, von Stein lifted her upright. His arm banded about her waist, and he shouted something over the ringing in her ears. In the next breath, he swung her into his arms.

Grateful for his solid presence, Yara allowed herself a moment. She closed her eyes and let him carry her as if she weighed no more than a bag of oats. Given the breadth of his shoulders, that might have been true. Lifting her head from his shoulder, she looked behind them but couldn't see anyone familiar as he carried her farther from the track and the carriage.

"Where are we going?" she asked, breathless. Her feet tangled in her skirts, but it didn't seem to bother him. Nothing seemed to bother him.

Well, nothing about this chaos, anyway. Apparently, her presence bothered him. But that didn't explain why he'd so effortlessly lifted her into his arms and carried her from the commotion. Some misguided sense of gallantry? Just her luck, being interested in a man who held gallantry in higher esteem than he did her.

"I'm getting you out of here. We'll meet your servants back at your townhouse."

Yara agreed with that plan. Solid, sound, reasonable—it was a good one. Until Sergeant Armstrong suddenly appeared in front of her.

"Miss," he gasped.

"Sergeant!" Yara pushed against von Stein's chest, the solid strength of him, and raced to the man. Her knees wobbled slightly, and her head pounded viciously, but she caught the sergeant just as his legs gave out beneath him. Together, they collapsed onto the ground. "What's happened? Who did this?"

Cold settled in her stomach, spreading dread through her veins. Armstrong was tall and heavy, and she struggled to lift his torso onto her legs. Blood coated his belly, but she didn't look. She already knew how bad his wound was. One pistol shot wouldn't have caused that much damage, but a stab wound would have.

She met his gaze and held it. "Who did this?" she repeated, anger freezing the words.

He clenched his belly, but Yara gently took his hand and held tight. She didn't know if he felt the gesture, but she held on to him anyway. She felt von Stein crouch beside her, his body shielding her from the still screaming crowd, protecting her.

That knowledge warmed her heart, even as cold anger settled over her like a shroud.

"It's Samuels," Armstrong gasped. "He's behind the information." He coughed, and Yara waited.

"What evidence have you?" She smoothed his hair from his forehead and kept her voice clear and even. She didn't know what else to do.

"Letter." He coughed. "Pocket. Hilton. He's after Hilton."

Von Stein bent over Armstrong and quickly searched his pockets. He produced a crushed letter stained with Armstrong's blood and tucked it into an inside pocket of his greatcoat without a word.

"I'll see he gets it," she promised.

"He knows, miss." His words came out weak and fractured on broken gasps of breath. "Saw us."

A litany of curses crowded her tongue. Careless. She'd been so eager to meet with von Stein. More the fool, her, that she'd been heedless of her surroundings. Perhaps Samuels meant yesterday, at their second meeting, but it didn't matter. Yara merely nodded. "I'll be safe. I promise."

Her heart roared in her ears, and she felt time tick away, as if a clock sounded out the vanishing seconds. Still, Yara didn't look away from Armstrong, holding his gaze as he struggled with each breath. She held his hand until the last. The crowd had thinned, and the now-trampled grassy area had quieted with the empty course.

Von Stein stood over her, as if protecting her from the mysterious Samuels. She sat on her heels, uncaring about her dress. It was ruined anyway; nothing could be done about that now. His strong legs braced her, and Yara let that power and comfort warm her in the suddenly cold day.

Taking one more moment, she whispered the prayer for the dead.

Yara stood on legs unsteady from staying in one position for so long. Once again, von Stein caught her, supporting her without a word. For one long heartbeat, she basked in that strength. She didn't understand him at all. She didn't understand her reaction to him, either.

"We need to leave," he said, voice more a growl than anything.

Yara tried to ignore the way that sound shivered over her arms. "Yes. And now."

Looking around the mostly deserted area, she didn't spot anyone who looked as if they wanted to harm her. Or kill her. Honestly, Yara wasn't entirely certain what her next step might be. Her mind raced with ideas, but only one made sense.

"Come on." Von Stein hauled her up and pulled her along the trampled grass. He didn't carry her again as they raced around the back of the track, perpendicular to those still pushing their way through whatever had initially caused all this pandemonium. "Alastor is nearby."

He wanted to take her back to the townhouse, but she couldn't go there. Not now. Not with this mysterious Samuels after her. But she needed to get word to her mother, so Kaya didn't send a quarter of England out to search for her.

"I can't return to the townhouse," she said as he hauled her onto Alastor. "Yes, good boy. Thank you." She absently patted him as von Stein settled in behind her.

"What was that all about?" he demanded, as if he hadn't heard her. Or maybe he chose not to. Typical. "What the hell are you involved in?"

"I can't tell you." She didn't look around as he wheeled Alastor away from the exit, far from the crowd.

"Can't?" Von Stein snorted. "Is this another of your schemes?"

"Schemes?" Yara shook her head and stared at her gloves, which were stained with mud and grass and Armstrong's blood. "No." She peeled them off and shoved them into her pockets. Her dagger lay securely hidden in the deep pocket, and she was grateful for its weight. "I was merely—"

She broke off. A courier. She was a simple courier between Hilton in London and Sergeant Armstrong here in Brighton. Information, that was all. Deliver a small packet of correspondence to Captain Blackwood at the barracks and meet with Hilton's man about a possible French spy, one neither Hilton nor Armstrong truly believed existed. Take a letter or two from Armstrong, return to London and Hilton with the information, and she was done.

It gave her something besides Nelda Hall and her disappointment. Let her do something worthwhile so she could forget those silly dreams of becoming the county's first female veterinarian.

"No," she whispered. "*No.*" She straightened and turned around as much as her position allowed. He glared down at her but stopped Alastor. "I'm not returning to the townhouse. It's too dangerous."

The enormity of her situation settled over her, a weight that made her nauseous. She'd placed her mother in danger, all their staff, and Micki, because she'd—she'd what? Wanted to help the war effort, yes. But she also wanted adventure. Anything away from The Hall and the farm and the memories of not being enough because she was female.

"Ride out of town," she said. Or pleaded. Yara didn't know. "Anywhere."

He stared at her, those blue eyes as stormy as the sea. For a moment, Yara knew a refusal lay on the tip of his tongue, and he was about to turn around and head back despite her plea. One scenario after another raced through her mind—jumping off the horse, struggling with a man who was no stranger to a good fight.

Von Stein sighed. "I'm going to regret this."

EIGHT

lec didn't know what possessed him, but he'd turned Alastor from the main street and the Conrad townhouse. Perhaps it was the thread of fear in her voice. Or the knowledge that if he didn't, she'd find her own way. Stubborn woman that she was.

Stubborn and capable and beautiful.

Keep his distance? He could hear Godred laughing at him.

He didn't know where they headed, but he urged Alastor farther inland, away from the wharves and the beach and the racecourse.

It wasn't the feel of her body in his arms, nor the way she leaned against him, as if drawing strength while the sergeant had lain dying in the grass. Nor the memory of her smiling at him right before he'd opened his mouth because his heart had pounded in his chest, terrifying him. Yet here he was, all but whisking her away from respectability and home, into the middle of nowhere.

They rode in silence beyond Brighton proper and into the countryside. The sun hid behind a slow-moving cloud, and the wind picked up. She sat straight, staring ahead, as if searching for something or someone. Or perhaps thinking. Alec decided that was the most dangerous thing she could do.

She was scarily good at planning, with an eye for the more outrageous details. However, from the single plan he'd encountered, she was also excellent at carrying out her plans.

"Miss Conrad," he began, shoving the feel of her body against his far from his mind. The warmth of her pressed against him, the way she settled so comfortably in his arms.

"I suppose you can call me Yara." She offered a bitter chuckle. The woman who rode with him was nothing like the vivacious one he first met. Nor even the cold, angry one of earlier. "After all, we've ridden from the racecourse together, very much without a chaperone, and we are now heading anywhere but back to Brighton."

"Alec, then." He pressed his fingers against his eyes, wondering if he could even guess what came next. "As we're being so informal."

Her head tilted. Though he couldn't see her, he knew those luscious lips of hers quirked upward. Those lips he desperately wanted to taste. Though, given his earlier words, he had no hope of doing so now.

"I would've said practical, but 'informal' works as well." She offered another brief breath of sound, less bitter now. "I'm afraid this isn't how I envisioned the end of our day at the races."

He wanted very much to know what she had envisioned. What she'd fantasized about. His cock stirred, and he shifted awkwardly in the saddle. Yara tilted her head again but didn't comment.

What she'd thought about before he broke off whatever lay between them.

Jaw clenched, hands so tight about the reins he wondered he didn't snap them, Alec swallowed his questions and tried to think of something appropriate. At the very least, something relevant to their current situation.

"Are we brigands now?" he only half joked. "Or should I not ask? Now that I've most definitely kidnapped you."

The slightest of giggles escaped her, and she relaxed. "It doesn't look good, does it?" She sighed, a long, drawn-out breath of resignation. "And I promised I wouldn't cause trouble."

"I'd say that promise is nothing more than ashes in the wind." He shook his head. "Which doesn't answer my question. Am I about to be called out, pistols at dawn?"

"After very plainly telling me you want nothing more to do with me?" She snorted again. "No."

"We aren't courting," he insisted. The harsh words tasted like sludge "What did you expect from me?"

"Before?" Her voice cooled, but retained something—bitterness? Hostility? Yes, but it was a deeper tone he couldn't identify. His stomach twisted. "Conversation. Companionship." She waved a hand backward, toward Brighton, but she didn't turn around. "Nothing more, I assure you. Do that many women throw themselves at you that you assumed I would?"

Well, now he was a cad as well as a rogue. Perfect. His jaw clenched so hard he thought it might break. "I'm not a man you should be seen with. I should have never offered to accompany you today." He sighed. "Though I suppose at this point it's far too late. Pistols at dawn it is, then."

"There's no need for that." She stopped and shook her head. "Let's stop. I don't know how Alastor puts up with you, but I prefer the walk."

Muttering beneath his breath, he did as she bade. He helped her from Alastor, though, given her love of horses, he knew she could dismount on her own. Alec wanted her in his arms again, if only to prove she didn't fit there as well as he'd first imagined. But she did. Her gaze held his, hands tightening on his arms as if she feared he'd drop her—or not, given the way her deep brown eyes darkened and her breath hitched.

"Would you really have broken my fingers?"

"Probably not." She released him, and he let her slide onto the ground. Turning away, chin tilted once again, she looked out at the vast field surrounding them. "The screaming in pain from such a thing is hard on the ears, you understand."

Snorting, Alec took Alastor's reins and gestured ahead. "You're a very violent woman."

She shook out her skirts, once more ignoring him. Alec cursed himself for missing her body against his. Damned fool. Her eyes now watched him, serious and tired, but she remained as determined as anyone he'd ever met.

He admired that about her far more than was probably wise.

"I'm not," she said softly. "Now then." She sniffed and straightened, untying her bonnet, which hung askew. "You wanted to know about Sergeant Armstrong."

"I'd prefer the entire story," he said, temper bubbling beneath the surface.

She'd nearly died in that damned crowd. They'd escaped not to the safety of her home, but into the middle of a nameless field. His control was gone, that thread snapped, and he wanted to hit something, but there was a dearth of hittable objects.

He was the violent one.

Now she stood before him, calm and collected except for that one moment of broken pain he'd glimpsed in her gaze. He'd been right in wanting distance between them. As much as her pain scraped over him, she deserved someone better. Kinder. With fewer demons haunting him. She drew him in like no other, promising things he had no right to want, let alone promise in return.

Fear. It burst from him in a harsh breath that scraped his insides.

He'd been terrified when that crowd turned on her. His first and only thought was to protect Yara from the panicked mob. The explosion hadn't helped, but he had a feeling all of it was tied to that bleeding man who'd collapsed at her feet.

Flexing his hands, Alec rolled his shoulders. It didn't help to control the fear that made his temper spark dangerously close to eruption.

"Let's start from the top, shall we?" He kept his voice even, though he doubted a raised tone might scare her.

Yara looked around the field, but nothing moved save what looked like a random pheasant in the far distance. He might've only known her a week, but he had a feeling whatever was about to leave her mouth was not the truth. Folding his arms over his chest, Alec glowered.

"The truth."

She looked skyward and shrugged. "Let's walk." She took Alastor's reins and petted his neck. Whatever she whispered made him nudge her, a gentle push against her own neck. "Yes." She smiled, and Alec was suddenly unreasonably jealous of his horse. "Yes, you're a good boy."

"You're stalling." And he was still jealous, damn it.

"I'm thanking Alastor for taking us to safety," she snapped.

Wonderful. They were miles from Brighton, her reputation most certainly ruined, her mother no doubt sending half the household staff after her. And all they'd managed was to snap at each other.

"I owe you the truth," she started in a calmer tone. "But when I think about it, it's a bit fantastical." She met his gaze around Alastor's head. "Do you know where we are?"

"About two miles northeast of Brighton." He eyed her. "We can still return; claim we got turned around."

No one who knew him would believe that. Given what he knew of Yara, he doubted anyone would believe that of her, either. It was an option, however, and one she could embrace without further damage to her reputation.

"I've already placed my family in danger." Her tone brooked no argument. "Sergeant Armstrong died trying to warn me and I will not allow that sacrifice to be in vain." She shook her head. "London it is." She paused again but stared straight ahead. "The short answer is, I was given a simple courier task of bringing a packet of letters from the Duke of York and Albany and Lieutenant Colonel Hilton to the commander of the Preston Barracks."

"Hilton?" Damn that man, and damn Alec, too. He knew Hilton, had run blockades for him. Scavenged information from Napoleon's navy and delivered it back to the man.

"It was meant to be a simple assignment," she continued, as if she hadn't heard him. "I needed to get away; we've known Hilton for several years, and he needed a messenger."

"I won't ask whether there were a hundred—a thousand—others who could've done this." No, he just wanted to know why she needed to get away. Why that bitter note crept back into her voice just now as her smile fell.

Secrets. They all carried them, like Atlas and the weight of the world.

"Trust," she snipped. He heard the truth in that, but the mystery remained. She'd left London, or wherever she lived, taken her mother and her dog, and decamped to Brighton. There was a reason for that, and Alec had a feeling it wasn't a pleasant one. Not for King and Country, not for Hilton, and not because she wished it.

She sighed and stared down at her gown. Bloodstains mixed with dirt and grass. She looked a right mess, but merely brushed her bare hands over her hips and nodded. A right mess, perhaps —but also the most beautiful woman he'd ever seen.

"He supposedly had information. That's who I met the other day, before we walked the beach. I traveled to Preston and my meeting with Sergeant Armstrong."

Now that she mentioned it, he remembered his burning

curiosity about her meeting. But then he'd tried talking himself out of his fascination with her and hadn't given it much thought. She'd had a previous engagement but had seemed eager enough for a later meeting. And there were worse things than walking the cold spring beach at sunset with a woman he wanted to taste.

"I hadn't expected your return, and I didn't want you thinking I wasn't interested in spending time with you." She muttered something else he didn't catch and sighed, a tired sound that punched him in the gut. "I suppose I was wrong in that."

That tone told him she wasn't used to men wanting to spend time with her. Alec curled his hands into fists. He wanted to thrash every man within a twenty-mile radius who had ever treated her poorly. Including himself.

He rolled his neck and looked skyward. On the other hand, he wanted to thank them for being fools and letting a beautiful, vibrant woman such as Yara Conrad step into his life. An opportunity he had subsequently botched.

Pushing aside his curiosity at her interest in him, Alec circled back around. "We'll come back to that," he promised. "So you were meeting this man in Preston? A bit obvious, I'd think, for so clandestine a meeting."

"He was only supposed to offer information. Maybe a letter for Hilton. I'd stop there, meet him, take whatever information he offered, and leave." She sighed again. "It was simple. Until it wasn't. You're right; this is more complicated than I thought."

"You weren't supposed to meet with him again?"

"Sergeant Armstrong gave me the letter that day. We met yesterday but he had nothing further. He agreed that I'd deliver his letter to Hilton, and he'd await further instructions. Mama and I were staying only through the beginning of next week on shipping business, and I was headed straight back to London and Hilton with my letters." She shook her head and stopped. "We never do anything the simple way."

Alec thought he might be developing a headache, and he wondered if there was a tavern nearby. A quick glance reassured him of the vast field and nothing more. Not for miles.

"Dare I ask what Armstrong discovered that cost him his life?" He reached into his pocket and handed her the rumpled packet. He asked, but he knew Hilton. Knew the intrigue the man uncovered.

"Spies."

"Spies," he repeated. Alec didn't even sigh. Of course that's what it was. "He sent you here with letters for the barracks commander and a meeting with someone who had information about French spies."

"If you say it's unlikely he'd do such a thing because I'm a woman, I may have to punch you." Yara growled the words. She looked so righteously infuriated, he swallowed a smile. God, she was beautiful.

Rubbing a hand down his face, Alec shook his head. "It's—in this climate? The fact he sent any one person when he suspected French spies doesn't make sense."

"Would you have preferred a battalion?" Yara snorted and resumed walking. "These aren't the right shoes for such a trip."

Alec peered down at her footwear and agreed with a silent shake of his head. "No, but we're committed now. Too much time has passed for any sort of respectable return."

Even if they returned now, he doubted anyone would believe their story about getting turned around. He didn't mention it again, mostly because her fear for her mother, indeed her entire household, vibrated between them.

"Hilton wasn't even certain what Sergeant Armstrong had was relevant. The sergeant wasn't either." She stopped, and her shoulders drooped. "Apparently it was. Whoever this Samuels is, he killed Armstrong to stop that information from reaching Horse Guards."

"Have you read the letter?" The contents of both letters placed Yara in danger. "The one he gave you the other day?"

"No. It wasn't for me." She didn't look at him but didn't move from his side, either. "It's at the townhouse now. I'm sure Mama will pack it up and take it with her to London."

"You're certain she'll head there?" he asked, incredulous. "How do you know? Did your mother know why you were here?"

"She knew I was on an errand for Hilton. Not the specifics. And when Bennett and Una return and tell her you were with me, she'll figure out we most likely headed for London."

"With a murdering spy on our trail."

"Better ours than hers," she snapped. "This isn't my best plan, I grant you that, but I will not place her in danger. Samuels is after me and when he realizes I'm no longer in Brighton, he'll leave Mama alone."

Alec held up a hand. "I'm not saying I'd prefer your mother in danger. I'm simply stating facts."

Yara nodded, looking exhausted. She rubbed at her temples, lips pinched. "It's likely in code. The letter I mean. Hilton has a reputation of ferreting out the truth from the most unlikely clues. And no matter what the military might need or suspect, spying is a very nasty business, one they don't support as they probably should."

True. Spying was frowned upon, not a gentlemanly pursuit. Certainly not a lady's pursuit, either. A dirty method no respectable person, army, or country admitted to. Everyone did it, of course, yet no one mentioned it. And they certainly didn't invest in it.

"I'm familiar with Hilton," he grudgingly admitted. He kept his gaze straight ahead when her head whipped around, and she stared at him incredulously from across Alastor.

"You are?" Yara laughed, a low, soft sound. "For a spymaster, he does have a reputation. Has he tried to recruit you as well?"

She asked it so simply, with a short sort of interest in her voice. He met her gaze and said simply, "Yes." Alec left it at that.

The screams returned then. A cacophony of recriminations and accusations. Jaw clenched, knuckles white, Alec shook his head. The memories remained, breaking through the barriers he'd erected, had hoped might stay in place.

"Alec?" Yara stood before him with her hand on his cheek. He blinked her into focus, confused. "What happened?" Her voice soothed him, soft and understanding. "It's all right." Her fingers were warm on his cheek despite the rapidly cooling day. "I'm here. Breathe; that's it. I'm here."

He blinked again, focusing on Yara's beautiful dark gaze, so sincere and concerned. On the feel of her fingertips against his cheek. Their rhythmic stroking grounded him, as did the calmness of her voice as she repeated herself.

It's all right. I'm here. You're not alone.

He caught her hand and held it in his. Only then did he realize he was still wearing his riding gloves. Damn it, he wanted the feel of her skin against his. Curling his hand around hers, he offered a quick nod.

"We should find shelter." The words sounded as curt as the jerky nod of his head. "It'll be dark soon, and I doubt the weather will hold."

It wasn't at all what he wanted to say, but *those* words caught in his throat like a thousand daggers.

"Was—" She nodded. "All right." She stepped back, but Alec couldn't release her hand. His fingers simply wouldn't obey him. "Have you a direction we should travel in? I'm unfamiliar with the area."

"Aye." He swallowed against those daggers of memory and looked around. Yara's hand settled comfortably in his, and she didn't seem in a rush to pull back. Considering how he'd treated her, he wouldn't blame her if she were, but he was grateful for the contact. Looking around the area, he shrugged. "We can't go back, and we don't know if what Armstrong said about that spy knowing about you is true."

"We have no description, nothing more than a name." She turned in a semicircle, looking out at the wide-open space. "I'd never know who he is."

"I won't let anything happen to you." The promise came straight from his soul. Alec didn't bother being surprised by himself. Instead, he lifted their joined hands and kissed the back of hers. "I promise."

She blinked, clearly surprised. "Thank you," she said on a rush of breath.

They walked in silence, heading onward despite the nothingness of the area. Not even a plume of chimney smoke.

He was absolutely the last person any woman should trust to return her home safe and sound. The ghosts of his past haunted him, and Alec deserved that. He deserved the nightmares and the accusations.

Yet here they were, he and Yara Conrad, walking hand in hand through a vast field of grass, Alastor at his side. Spies chasing them, her mother no doubt out of her mind with worry and about to send half the county after him.

Oh, yes. A perfect day.

NINE

"There's a fence."

It was the first thing she'd said since Alec had disappeared into his own head. She didn't know what visions haunted him, and she hadn't asked. Was it something he'd done for Hilton? A mission the man had sent him on?

She knew so little about him, and yet she trusted him more than was probably wise. Than was *definitely* wise, given the way her heart had skipped several beats when his lips caressed the back of her bare knuckles. He hadn't even remarked about the calluses on her hands.

The damned man confused her. One minute he was pulling back, telling her he was leaving and couldn't see her again. The next, he was saving her from the crowd and literally spiriting her to safety. Her head pounded, and Yara was only half certain it was from the knee that had slammed into her.

"A boundary marker, but I still don't see a dwelling."

He turned this way and that, but all Yara saw beyond the fence was openness, grass, and more openness. She wanted to run through the field, laughing with Micki or riding Masika, her mare. Wanted to scream into the openness and let the wind whisk her anger away.

"There." He pointed off to their right, where the faintest lines of smoke could be seen in the distance. If the sun hadn't come out from behind the cloud when it did, she doubted she'd have seen it at all.

"Let's go then." She turned in that direction, but Alec pulled her to a stop with a swift tug of his hand. He looked incredulously furious.

Again.

He somehow managed that look at least once every time they saw each other. Why was she the fool who enjoyed his company so much? Perhaps she should stay away from him. Even if he was the only man who'd ever made her feel alive. Made her feel worth more than her money or her knowledge of animal husbandry, or anything.

Made her feel like herself.

"You're going to knock on that door, looking as if you were involved in a deadly brawl, a spy who may or may not know who you are tracking you down to kill you for that letter in your pocket, and ask for shelter for the night?"

"When you put it like that," she muttered. "I've no better idea." She frowned and tried to stretch her toes, but they cramped. This was what happened when she chose impractical footwear for a day out. "My feet hurt, my head is pounding, and I'm cold, hungry, and thirsty."

And she desperately needed a chamber pot, but privacy was nowhere to be found in all this open space. She worried for herself, but also for her mother. Oh, Kaya Conrad knew how to take care of herself. After all, she'd been the one to teach all her children how to fight with the Egyptian khanjar. But she was still Yara's mother, and her actions here put her in danger.

Yara wasn't certain heading to London with Alec was the right thing. All she wanted was to keep her mother and the household safe. Was heading for London with Alec the right plan? She had no idea, despite her insistence.

"All right. Let's go." He sounded resigned, and Yara presumed he hadn't a better idea, either.

"Something simple, I think," she said into the sudden stillness. The sun still shone, much lower in the sky now, but the breeze had stopped. "Carriage accident? And we decided to seek out shelter."

"And we didn't make our way back to Brighton or Hove or Preston because…?"

She shrugged. "Turned around? Or we were on our way, perhaps. Yes, we were heading toward Brighton, and our carriage hit a rock and—"

"I thought you said simple." He chuckled, and it was such a welcome sound from the odd silence they'd walked in, Yara didn't know what to make of it.

She hadn't minded the silence, hadn't felt the need to break it with inane chatter because it scraped over her skin. Perhaps it was the way Alec held her hand. As if he always had and always would and it was as simple as that. But perhaps she was reading far too much into that gesture.

He was definitely a man of contradictions—not that she helped much. She liked the feeling of his strong fingers around hers.

"You don't think they'll ask what we're doing, walking with a single horse, my gown and pelisse in tatters, looking as if a band of highwaymen attacked us?"

Attacked her, at least. The knees of his trousers were stained, and his gloves had seen better days, but overall, she definitely looked the worse for wear.

"We could say that." He slanted her a sideways glance, his lips quirking upward. "I'm sure the roads are littered with highwaymen waiting to pounce upon unsuspecting people. But we aren't coming from the road."

"True," she conceded. "All right, what's your story then?"

"Stoic silence?" She snorted, and he laughed. "You're right; that might not get us far. The carriage accident isn't a bad story, but we are definitely coming from the wrong direction for that."

"I'm not going to faint," she warned. Poking a finger at his chest, the solid mass of it, she wondered if he even felt it. "I refuse to play the simpering woman."

"Simpering?" His laugh was loud and long, full-bodied and rich with warmth and humor. It washed over her, sending shivers down her spine and over the more private parts of her body.

Oh, she was in so much trouble.

"I can't see you simpering at all. No, that's the last word I'd ever use to describe you."

Yara opened her mouth only to snap it closed. What words would he use? The question begged asking, but part of her feared the answer. What did it matter? He'd already wanted distance, but now they were stuck together.

She had no idea what to think about him. Or them, if there even was a them.

"I can," she said instead as the house came inexorably closer. "If there's a need. But, as I don't see one, no."

"Another one of your schemes?" His smile hadn't abated, and those beautiful eyes of his watched her, his laughter crinkling them at the corners.

"If the role calls for it," she said haughtily. But her smile ruined the tone. "I should clarify that I've never simpered; however, I'm certain I can. I merely refuse to under normal circumstances."

"Noted. No simpering." He squeezed her hand and stopped suddenly. "Your gown is a right mess; that'll cause more gossip and speculation than our arrival."

She couldn't argue with that. Without another word, he shrugged off his jacket and draped it around her shoulders. His hands were gentle as they straightened the coat, his fingertips brushing the side of her neck.

"You are the most confounding man," she whispered around a tight throat.

Yara desperately wanted to feel his bare skin against hers. Just for a moment, one single moment. Whatever she thought might develop between them, it had only been a foolish hope. Men didn't like her. She'd learned that the hard way. Her fortune, her way with horses, yes. But they always scoffed at her independence, her desire for more than the traditional role of a woman.

She'd accepted that. Mostly. Rather, she had learned she could live with it, could make her own way and not worry about what society thought. She was lucky in that respect; she had the money to indulge in her dreams and the backing of her loyal and understanding family.

Alec von Stein had gone and upended all that. Now she hoped for something more, and here they were, walking through someone's field, escaping a man who wanted her dead, causing scandal with every step away from Brighton.

And Alec didn't even want her.

"Thank you," she whispered, throat closed. She cleared it and swallowed the emotion she'd rather not name. "This has been a most unusual day."

He snorted, and his grin widened. His hands cupped her cheeks, and he pressed a kiss to her forehead. She felt his smile against her skin, warm and promising. Then he laughed again, that rich sound that shivered through her.

"I'd say that's the understatement of the year." He stripped off his gloves, shoved them into Alastor's saddlebags, and retook her hand. "But it's only April."

"Don't say it!" She grinned up at him, hoping her smile hid the way his skin against hers made her feel. Illusion—she pulled it around her like a cloak. But it faltered, and Yara heard a note of longing in her voice. That inescapable need for more. "You'll curse us."

Not that she believed in curses, but, given the way her day had gone, no sense taking a chance.

"Yara, I'm afraid we're already well past that." He shook his head, and they walked in silence for several more moments. "I have no better idea," he finally admitted as they neared the house.

"Who knows when or if they'll hear about what happened at the racecourse. The house is quite isolated."

"We can tell them, spread a bit of gossip, but the question remains—why didn't we go home from there?"

"I have no answer for that." She had no answers for many things at the moment. Instead, she huffed out a breath, trying not to inhale Alec's scent. It was no use. The warmth of his coat surrounded her, and the dark scent of him enticed her. How she didn't drown in it, Yara had no idea.

"Spies are out, and the truth is out, which leaves us with my original story—or a new one you've yet to share."

"Carriage accident it is, then." He nodded and looked at Alastor. "That all right with you?"

The horse eyed him and snorted. Yara took that as a yes. "As we're all in agreement, there's one final detail."

"Only one?" His lips did that upward tilt again, his eyes shining with suppressed humor.

She wondered if he'd ever release the tight grip he kept on himself and let humor shine through. She wondered what made him keep such careful control.

"We'll have to be married."

He blinked, face blank as he no doubt fought to understand what she meant. Yara nodded. *Men.* Alec had been so concerned about her reputation earlier, as they fled the racecourse, the mayhem, the death of Sergeant Armstrong. But faced with a situation that required discretion, he froze.

"This is true," he said slowly. "Or you could be my sister."

Another stab at her pride. He'd already told her he wanted nothing to do with her, and here she was, still hoping. Yara curled her hands into fists, hidden beneath the length of his jacket sleeves. She could accept his distance. She could.

She could even accept the blow to her pride. Lifting her chin, she met his gaze and kept her own cool and steady.

"Marriage protects both of us and causes fewer questions."

"All right, Mrs. von Stein."

She snapped her jaw shut. No. No, she'd not be tempted by such a phrase. Clearing her throat, she offered in a light tone she didn't feel, "Something not connected to either of us."

"All right. My mother was Prussian, too. Your mother's maiden name?"

Oh, not that, either. Aunt Hannah's? No, von Almey worked as well as von Stein. Aunt Nadia's? A Russian name in the country? No matter how she tried to think of something simple, her mind had already latched on to Mrs. von Stein.

Stupid, stupid, stupid! She was a fool.

"Shaw. Mr. and Mrs. Shaw."

He eyed her shrewdly. "You know any Shaws?"

"Yes. My aunt's closest friend is Shaw. We grew up with their children." She waved a hand. "They live in London, and I'm certain there are thousands with that last name. It won't be connected to me."

"Mrs. Shaw." He bowed slightly as the house came clearly into view. "We've been spotted."

The Hobsons—Roland, Beth, and their three sons and two daughters—greeted them with open arms, smiles, and, most importantly, hot water. Yara didn't ask about its source, nor did she ask about the wool blankets they'd warmed by the fire. She just gratefully accepted their hospitality, their offer of a clean gown, and their fussing.

"I don't know if the blood will come out of this." Beth frowned at the once-beautiful gown, now stained and torn.

Yara quickly tied the ribbons of her new bodice. She didn't want to look at the reminder of her day. She'd already transferred her dagger into her pocket, and she kept her bag of coins secreted there as well.

"I'm afraid it's set," Yara agreed, her voice even.

She wouldn't cry. Would *not*. Not over the beautiful gown she'd taken great pleasure in wearing. The way it brightened her mood, the joy she felt by simply putting it on. And she certainly wouldn't cry over what her ruining it said about her.

"Have you any salt?" She swallowed around her closed throat. "It may be too late, but soaking the silk in salt might help."

"I'll fetch it." Elsbeth, the youngest girl, who was no more than ten, disappeared from the room.

"Such a tragedy about your coach." Beth tutted in sympathy. "Have you family close by, Mrs. Shaw?"

"Yara, please. And I do appreciate your hospitality." She smiled and deflected the question. The less she said, the more believable their story—such as their story was, given the absolute fabrication of it all. "We're so turned around, I'm afraid I'm a bit lost."

As Yara listened to Beth go on about the area, Elsbeth returned with the salt, and they set about trying to salvage her gown. She didn't have high hopes for that. She admired the embroidered yellow narcissus creeping up the right side. So lovely. It'd made her so happy—

Stupid.

There was a small commotion outside, and Beth looked out the window. "I believe your husband has returned. So lucky he was riding separately."

"Yes," she whispered, swallowing hard at the word 'husband.' "I'll just see what's..." She waved vaguely in his direction and disappeared. Yara ignored Elsbeth's giggles and Beth's knowing smile.

The Hobson household was clearly well-off. The small library tempted her; however, the impressive stables beckoned her outside. Yara had no trouble spotting Alec. He stood more than a head taller than Roland Hobson and his three sons. He'd washed, his wet hair slicked back and curling at the tips by his neck. Someone had offered him a fresh shirt, too, which was entirely too small and stretched over his chest in a most pleasant way.

She did not stare. Absolutely not. One too-fast move and the fabric would tear, and Yara most definitely did not wonder what his bare chest looked like beneath that shirt. Nor what it'd feel like beneath her fingertips. Solid, unyielding. She curled her fingers into fists in a vain attempt to ward off temptation.

Alec was one giant, walking temptation she desperately wanted to taste.

Taste? No, not—Yara sighed. She'd never been so attracted to a man, and he didn't want her. On top of all that, she'd forced him on a scandalous ride across southern England. He'd never speak with her again.

At least her mother and the household would be safe. That was the entire point and what she needed to focus on.

He was the most handsome man she'd ever met. Not in the traditional sense, she supposed as she confidently walked across the muddy yard. His angular features and sharp blue eyes drew her in. But it was the way he watched her. As if she and she alone was all that mattered.

It sent her pulse skittering. No one had ever studied her with such attention.

He smiled as she stopped beside him and reached for her hand. Yara froze. His thumb rubbed just once over her knuckles, a gentle, reassuring touch. It had been one thing to hold hands in the field with no one around as they figured out their next step. Quite another for him to reach for her now, in front of people.

Oh. But of course. They were married, at least as far as the Hobsons were concerned. Then Alec remembered their ruse as well, and he dropped her fingers as if her touch scalded him. Pushing aside her hurt—her foolish, unreasonable hurt—she nodded to the Hobson men.

"I was just telling Roland here that we'll be riding back to Brighton." His hand brushed her hip, though Yara couldn't tell if his touch was deliberate. An accident or a warning.

Schooling her voice to fit the mirage she'd shrouded herself in for far too long, she nodded. Curse those stupid, stupid shivers racing over her skin.

"Yes, I believe that's for the best," she agreed despite Roland's dubious look.

"Mrs. Shaw, at least let us see to your carriage."

Alec's hand found hers again and squeezed. Hard. She merely shook her head—at both the offer and Alec's unnecessary warning. "Oh, that's very kind," she began. "Darling?" She tilted her head toward Alec, whose eyes widened at the endearment. She nearly choked on a laugh.

"I told them it's not necessary, generous as the offer is. I'm sure our driver has seen to the repairs by now." He nodded cordially toward the men. "If it's not too much trouble, we'd be grateful if you'd put us up for the night. Come dawn, we'll be off."

"Aye," Roland said dubiously. "On your horse, then?"

Mind racing, Yara stepped into the stables as she fleshed out their plan. She was the planner of the family, examining her final goal from all angles and thinking through the necessary steps to get there. Of course, usually she did so over the course of days. Not a half hour while walking in a field with few other options.

One of the horses peeked out of her stall. Distracted, Yara veered toward the magnificent creature. "Hello there, what's your name?" The horse watched her, a mare with a gleaming brown coat. "Oh, about ready, are you?"

Yara reached out and let the mare sniff her hand, whispering in Egyptian as the horse decided whether she liked her or not. Apparently she did, for the mare nuzzled Yara's hand and allowed her light touch.

"Yes, you are a beautiful, sweet girl."

"She hasn't been that calm in a fortnight." The eldest boy—Guy, she thought—eyed her suspiciously. But Yara was used to that. "The local vet said it's because she's about to foal."

"Hmm," she agreed. "What's her name?"

"Cosima."

"Let's have a look, shall we?" She opened the gate and entered the stables, letting Cosima decide whether she wanted her in the stall or not. Yara stayed still, listening for any change in the mare's gait, but she offered no objection. Guy, she noted, stayed outside the stall.

"What do you know of horses?"

"I love horses," she said absently as Cosima wandered her stall. "If you ride horses, you ought to know how to care for them, don't you think?"

Guy snorted but didn't move and didn't speak again. She felt the shift in his stance as it went from scoffing to curious. Cosima paced the stall, and Yara watched her, keeping out of her way.

"She's nervous. Horses are prey animals," she whispered, leaving the mare to her space and settling on a short bale of hay opposite her. "No matter how they feel about us, whether we take excellent care of them or not, giving birth puts her in a vulnerable position for attacks."

"So you're saying she needs a protector?" Guy huffed, but it wasn't in ridicule.

"Doesn't everyone?" Yara turned and met his gaze. He nodded, and they sat in silence while Cosima paced.

"Making friends, are we?" Alec's voice startled her. She blinked at him and met his amused, patient gaze. With a nod, she took his proffered hand and stood.

"I was planning," she muttered. Guy still stood at the gate, but he'd stepped back, offering them privacy. "Cosima side-tracked me."

He snorted. He did that a lot, she noted. Or perhaps it was only around her. "And what have you planned?"

"I was trying to figure out a decent story, but…" She waved a hand at the barn. "Animals distract me, so I didn't come up with much beyond what we already had. What did you and Roland discuss?"

"His insistence on finding the carriage and that we couldn't possibly continue onto Brighton on a single horse and maintain any sort of respectability."

"That was his concern?" Yara shook her head. Alec reached out and plucked a piece of straw from her hair. He stood far closer than she thought necessary, making her heart pound and her lungs forget how to work.

"Honeymoon."

"I beg your pardon?" He looked confused. She didn't blame him; she'd blurted the word so fast, she was surprised he understood it.

"Honeymoon. Have you said anything about why we're traveling?" He shook his head, still looking bemused. Yara nodded. That decisiveness didn't help her breathlessness. "We're on our honeymoon, and rather than spend time fussing with a broken carriage, we've decided it'll be far lovelier to explore the countryside. Just the two of us."

"Honeymoon," he repeated. "We're on our honeymoon in Brighton in April."

She dismissed that with a flick of her wrist. "We were on our way for the summer; they don't know whether we were coming or going, do they?"

Again he shook his head, and she wondered if his bemused look was solely for her, or if anyone else had confused him the way she had.

"You are the most interesting woman I've ever met," he muttered as he ushered her from the stable.

She couldn't decide if that was a compliment or not.

TEN

Then, of course, there was the matter of the single bed.

Alec didn't sigh; he had nothing left in him. He'd used every ounce of willpower he possessed not to touch Yara. He spent the afternoon and evening playing nice with the Hobsons and doing his best not to think *Yara* and *wife* in the same sentence. It didn't even matter that they called her Mrs. Shaw.

He knew.

Every time one of the Hobsons asked after her, every time they asked him what he thought about whatever the hell they discussed, he didn't hear "Mrs. Shaw." He heard "Mrs. von Stein." Which was ridiculous. He'd already decided they'd part ways. He couldn't lead her on any more than he already had.

And now here they were, standing on opposite sides of the bed in a room lit by a single candle, and he had no idea what came next. Alec ran a hand down his face. No, he had nothing. Not one idea, not one hint of what happened now.

Could he easily envision them in this bed, wrapped around each other? Oh, yes. Far, far too easily. He was not letting that happen. He wasn't going to ruin Yara.

"If you think I'll somehow forget myself—"

"No," he snapped.

No, he'd hurt her enough with his words, and he doubted Yara saw this situation as anything more than it was. A simple sleeping arrangement. He, on the other hand, was the one who had trouble remembering his own reasons for wanting distance.

"Are you worried for my reputation, then? The Hobsons believe us married." She ticked off her reasons on her fingers—long, lovely fingers Alec wanted on his skin. Idiot. "No one else need ever know what happened." She ticked off a second finger. "If you prefer, I can easily sleep in the chair."

"The chair?" Startled, he looked around the room he hadn't bothered to investigate before. Sure enough, a heavy chair, covered in green fabric, sat between the window and the fireplace. "Why would you sleep in the chair?"

She shrugged. "I've slept in worse. I've slept sitting upright in the barn during spring storms when I couldn't leave the mothers."

"You are not sleeping in the chair," he growled. One more piece of Yara Conrad's puzzle. He knew she loved animals; they'd spent considerable time speaking of them. He hadn't realized how closely she tended to the farm, going so far as to sleep there during birthing season.

"I doubt you'll fit." She lifted a pillow from the bed. "If not the chair, then the floor."

"You are sleeping in the bed," he snapped.

"Lower your voice," she hissed back. "You want the entire household to know we aren't sharing a bed?"

He didn't care. This was a mess far more complicated than he'd first envisioned when he agreed not to turn around in that field. But he should've turned around, and he knew it then as he did now. But her tangible fear of putting her mother and the household in danger spoke to him more deeply than Alec thought she realized.

She wanted the danger to follow her. Which terrified him, but he understood. It also sparked a need to protect her. At all costs.

"Tomorrow," he started, grabbing his own pillow, "we're heading directly for London. I don't care if I have to hire a coach; we're going there. You will be safe and unharmed, your reputation intact."

Face blank in the dancing shadows, she offered a curt nod. "The sooner I see Hilton and reassure my family and staff I'm alive, the better." She paused and added softly, "With any luck, Samuels is already searching for me. That was the entire purpose of this." She waved a hand, encompassing their situation.

"You terrify me," he muttered. "Just because Samuels knows what you look like doesn't mean he'll follow you. He might go after your mother."

Even in the darkness, he knew her gaze held cold steel. "He'll be lucky if she and the staff dispatch him instead. No one harms my family."

Her conviction settled over him. "The more I learn of you, the less I know."

"I'm not hard to know, Alec," she said in that quiet voice. "It's just that no one's ever bothered to try."

"I'm sorry about that." Her hurt slashed through him. He hated that he'd heaped more upon what she already carried. He yanked the top blanket off the bed and dropped both it and the pillow onto the floor. "But we're still heading directly for London—with or without Samuels following you."

The sooner he left her, the better. The sooner he put distance between them, the better. The sooner he forgot about her, the better.

He doubted he'd ever forget her.

Not even bothering with his shoes, Alec lay on the floor beside the bed and closed his eyes. He listened as she climbed into bed, snuffed the candle, and shifted into what he presumed was a comfortable position.

Sleep did not come.

"This is strange." Her voice drifted over the side of the bed, warm and soft in the darkness.

She moved, and when Alec blinked open his eyes, all he saw was her face peering at him over the side of the bed. "I can't imagine that's a comfortable sleeping position."

Her soft hum of laughter washed over him. "Are you at all comfortable down there?"

No. He slept parallel to the bed, which ran crosswise to the floorboards. One particularly vicious board had warped and now gouged him in the back. All he could think of was her, on the bed. Alone.

"For a floor, it's not bad," he lied. Not that he had extensive experience sleeping on floors. "There is a slight draft," he admitted. "Hence the greatcoat."

"Thank you for thinking of my reputation." Her voice barely drifted down, but he heard the sincerity in it. "I oftentimes forget."

She shifted, disappearing back onto the bed. Alec thought she'd gone to sleep, leaving him with his thoughts, his imagination about what she'd taste like, and a very stiff cock. Not the way to find a good night's sleep. Or a bad one, either.

"How do you know Hilton?"

Not the question he expected. Alec folded his hands behind his head and stared up at the ceiling. He'd shifted away from the poking floorboard, but the chill still seeped through the greatcoat he used as a barrier.

"You don't know what it is I do?"

"Do?" She sounded confused. "I heard you own boxing and fencing clubs. Horses." She paused. "Something about ships, too, I think."

His lips quirked. "The bit about the horses distracted you," he guessed with a fondness he should've nipped but let escape anyway.

Yara huffed. "Always."

"It's not as extensive as Conrad Shipping," he admitted. "But it's profitable. It's allowed me the opportunities I need."

He left it at that, wondering if she'd ask. He honestly didn't know if he wanted her to or not.

"For investing?" She hummed again. "They're good investments," she admitted. "Solid for the future. What about your crew?"

"My crew?" He frowned. She poked her head over the side of the bed again, her long braid dropping over the edge. "What about them?"

"Do they also invest in the future?"

They had, once. They'd all invested in their future. The unwanted sons, the bastards, the slower men whose parents hadn't wanted them. They'd gambled with their lives, taken all the spoils they could and ensured their future was brighter than their past.

Until the accident. Until Alec dismissed everyone who'd stayed and walked away from those who blamed him.

"Yes." His throat closed on the word, and he swallowed hard. Nothing more came out.

"Is that how you met Hilton?" She skirted the obvious chasm, as if she knew. Her voice gave nothing away, and in the darkness he couldn't see her clearly enough to discern whether she understood or not.

"Yes." Alec forced the word out, his chest tight with memories. Clearing his throat, he tried again. "He found me at a gaming hall one evening. No idea how."

"He has a way." She sighed and settled in. "He knows all kinds of things. But he listens, I'll grant him that."

"Possibly," Alec admitted, curious as to how she'd fallen in with a spymaster. A question for another time. He didn't think she'd let him deflect, not tonight. And he wouldn't. Not after the many hurtful things he'd spat today.

"So he found you," she prompted.

"Aye, wanted to know if I was interested in running French blockades. Engaging the French and their allies. Slipping through to the Continent with missives."

"Running blockades is risky enough, but for a civilian ship? What made you agree?"

Money. The payment Hilton offered and the promise of French spoils. Not only for him and his crew, but for his future. The more he made, the more he had, the less he needed to worry about falling into poverty. Again.

"The future."

She waited, but Alec had nothing more. "I don't understand. You mean your future?"

"Yes," he said again.

His future. To show his father he wasn't a good-for-nothing. Not that it mattered anymore—the old bastard had gone and died three years ago. When his eldest brother returned home for his inheritance, he'd reached out, offered an olive branch. Alec hadn't responded. He'd been so full of anger. Then time passed, and he realized he wasn't angry with Christian. But it was too late. By then, Alec hadn't known how to reach out again.

So he hadn't.

"Good night, Alec," she whispered.

"Good night, Yara."

Alec closed his eyes, but instead of the wreck or his father, he saw her. The vivacious smile she often graced him with. The sparkle in her eyes, the way her entire face lit with passion about her chosen topic.

He was not sleeping tonight.

ALEC ROSE LONG before the sun did. Moving quietly so as not to disturb Yara, he peered over the side of the bed—and nearly laughed out aloud. She lay sprawled over the entire surface, pillow bunched beneath her head, blankets folded double atop her.

Placing his own blanket over her, he set the pillow beside her. Temptation beckoned him, and he traced a finger down her cheek. She didn't move, didn't even sigh. Snatching his hand back, he curled it into a fist and spun from the bed.

What in God's name was he thinking?

He washed quickly, and he didn't look at Yara again before he slipped from the room. The household barely stirred; the sun certainly hadn't. The morning lay cool and misty over the farm as he stretched muscles that ached from yesterday's journey and a poor night's sleep on the floor.

As he stalked toward the stables, he debated waking Yara and leaving now. It made sense. The earlier they started out, the faster he could deliver her to her family and Hilton and end this disastrous meeting.

Courtship. Not courtship—no, that definitely wasn't the word. But "meeting" sounded so dull and not at all like the last few days.

"Good morning," he whispered as Alastor greeted him at the stable's gate. Alec rubbed a hand down his neck, but Alastor wasn't having it. The traitorous horse peered around Alec, looking up and down the barn.

Narrowing his eyes at his horse, Alec scowled. "She's not here."

Alastor pulled back, watched him for a long, seemingly disbelieving moment, then looked again. Alec sighed. "You're still mad at me, eh?"

He opened the gate and set about readying the horse for the day's ride. Alastor allowed it. He stood still, though he snorted whenever Alec tried to pet him.

"I don't blame you." He sighed and leaned his head against Alastor's side. "I shouldn't have ignored you for so long. It's not your fault."

He apologized to Alastor until the youngest of the Hobson boys, Eddie, appeared. He looked far more awake than Alec felt, and he whistled one of the popular army songs about beating Napoleon.

"You're leaving, then?" Eddie eyed him, then Alastor.

"As soon as Y—Mrs. Shaw is ready." He nodded and took Alastor by the reins. "After our adventures yesterday, it's best we get an early start."

Eddie shrugged and stood by the pregnant mare's stall. He cooed to her, and Alec left him to his chores. Walking around the yard, he watched the sun rise over the field. He hadn't realized he'd spent that much time in the barn.

"It's a beautiful morning." Yara's voice startled him, and he cursed.

"I didn't know you were awake." Even Alastor snickered at the inane greeting.

She smiled as she approached. "I'm not normally fond of mornings. I'm trying to understand their appeal. My eldest brother, Grayson, he loves mornings."

Her tone took on a wistful note, and Alec couldn't pinpoint if she missed her brother, or if it was something else. The puzzle pieces he tried to fit together never quite made a complete picture of Yara.

"Claims they're peaceful and quiet. The perfect way to start a day." She rested her head against Alastor's neck. "I'm not sure I agree, but I promised him I'd try to enjoy them. What about you, handsome?"

She spoke to Alastor, and Alec rolled his eyes at his traitorous horse, who accepted Yara's praise as if Alec wasn't standing right there. He was definitely *not* jealous of the quiet, fond tone her voice took on when speaking to the horse. Absolutely not.

"I don't normally watch the sunrise," he admitted. Frowning, he thought back, but he couldn't recall watching a sunset, either. "Not even on deck. I don't specifically watch it, I mean. I am awake at that hour quite often."

"Life is like that," she agreed, still cooing at the horse. "Every day is full, busy with things. It doesn't matter what those things are. Tending to animals or crews or meetings."

"You've given this a lot of thought?" He grinned, stepping around Alastor and watching the sunrise with Yara. "You always watch the sunrise?"

She gave him a slow, quiet smile that made his heart pound double time. Traitorous thing. He was surrounded by traitorous things. "I'd rather lie in my warm bed, Micki by my side, a fire in the grate, and a fresh cup of coffee."

She paused, and he waited quietly as she gathered her thoughts. He didn't like the greed with which he gathered these pieces of information about her. Distance, he told himself. Again. Distance. But it was no use, and he knew it. She drew him with every smile, every silence.

"When Grayson returned from his own mission for Hilton, mornings were the only times we had to share together. Life is busy enough, with our various businesses, the farm, the ever-growing number of people we employ." She shrugged and sighed, a slight, wistful sound. Alec didn't dare breathe. Just waited.

"Esme, my sister, she'd already married Landon—the Marquess of Strachan—and moved away. I adore Grayson's wife and their children, but I missed him. So I forced myself awake at ungodly hours so we could spend time together."

He peered around Alastor's strong, still neck and met her gaze.

"Now I like this time of day, when the potential is laid out before you," she whispered. "The beauty of possibilities."

A frown crossed her face, there and gone in a flash. Without thinking, Alec reached for her hand. He had no words of comfort, nothing that might erase the darkness that took hold of her every once in a while. He did, however, have understanding.

So they stood there in silence, just the three of them. The sun cast startling, vivid yellows and oranges over the land, silhouetting the distant trees. The birds swooped across the beams, and he watched them soar on the wind.

"Are you ready?" he eventually asked, feeling more settled than he had in years. He tried to thank her, but the words sounded trite. Too brash in the peace and quiet of their shared morning.

"Yes." She turned that slow, quiet smile on him again. "Let's go."

They said their goodbyes, accepted the small bag of food the Hobsons offered, and turned for the road. Alec left a bag of coins for the family, much to Yara's accepting grin. The bright morning had turned overcast with the threat of yet more rain. However, the wind had calmed.

"Roland said there was a coaching inn a couple miles east." Alec nodded in that direction as he walked beside Yara, who sat atop Alastor.

"I'm not convinced hiring a coach, or even paying for a public one, is the best idea." She looked straight ahead, sitting in the saddle as naturally as if she'd been born there. "However, I agree. Arriving in London as soon as possible is for the best."

The silence stretched between them. He watched her as she stretched her wrists and arms, chewing her lip in thought.

"What will you do after our return?"

The question startled him. "After?" he repeated and shook

his head. "I don't know," he admitted. "I hadn't thought that far ahead."

"Oh." She nodded. "Not one to plan?" she teased.

Alec shrugged. "I am, yes. I always had to know what step came next." He stared ahead at the village growing nearer. "I cared about my crew," he said, the words more defensive than he'd intended. "Their safety." He paused. "Our futures."

"Cared?"

Of course she'd latched on to that word. He couldn't even be angry; the ache in his chest eclipsed all else. He didn't answer her. Didn't know how without delving into a story he didn't want to repeat.

"I no longer have a crew," he admitted as they entered the coaching inn's courtyard. He helped her from the saddle and met her gaze. "I fired them all."

Her face registered her surprise, but she didn't ask. Her hands gripped his arms for a moment, tightly, as if reassuring him. "I'm sorry." She licked her lips, her eyes serious. "We all have reasons. Just as we all have choices."

Alec set her on the ground and stepped back. He didn't know what she meant by that. "Go inside," he said gruffly. "See about buying food. I'll ask about a coach."

She didn't look at him, just nodded and disappeared inside. Alastor eyed him but didn't roll his eyes or snort. Perhaps he'd forgiven him the months of neglect. Leading him toward the stables, Alec paused just outside. He couldn't have said why he hesitated; thousands of people used coaching inns across Britain. The public coaches left at all times of the day, including this early hour. Despite the heaviness of their conversation and the memories it had stirred, he retained just enough awareness of his surroundings.

Planning, Yara had called it. And he was a planner, each step meticulous. That meticulousness ensured everyone survived, ensured they achieved their end goal and went home all the richer.

Which was why he listened to the instinct that made him pause at the low murmur of voices. A reasonable part of his brain scoffed. What were the chances Samuels was in this particular coaching inn at this particular time and Alec had happened upon him?

"There's no one fitting her description," the man said. Alec couldn't see him clearly in the dim barn, nor could he see the companion. "I asked last night," he said, sounding as if he repeated himself.

Cold slithered down Alec's spine, spreading through his veins like the giant glaciers of the north. She was in danger, and he'd spent the last day worrying about her reputation. Her life mattered. *She* mattered. And he'd do anything to keep her safe.

"This is the first coaching inn between Brighton and the London road," another man snapped. "Where else could she have gone?"

Who else could they be speaking about? Fury colored Alec's vision, and he used every bit of his willpower to not step into the barn and beat up the men. Tie them up and interrogate them. Temptation had him stepping forward, but reason prevailed. Clearly, there were others involved in Samuels's scheme.

He could waste time with these two—neither of whom might be Samuels—or he could find Yara and leave. Now.

It didn't matter if they were speaking about Yara. Even if they were after another lady, he didn't like their attitude or tone one damn bit. But deep in his bones, despite the lack of information, he knew they wanted Yara.

Spinning on his heel, he urged Alastor back into the courtyard and frantically plotted their next step. He didn't look around; he already knew where everyone stood. The men hadn't left the stables, and only a few lads lounged at the edges of the courtyard, clearly bored as they awaited the next coach.

Terror warred with impatience as he waited for Yara by the inn's door. She stepped out, a relaxed smile playing around her lips. As he watched her, it hit him hard, right in the solar plexus.

He'd protect her with his life.

"What's wrong?" Yara asked the moment she spotted him. Her smile dropped, and Alec hated that it had. "What's happened?"

"We're leaving." He hauled her onto Alastor and climbed up after her. "Two men in the stables talking about following a woman."

She didn't look around but slouched in front of him, using his body as a shield. Impressed, he wondered just what she got up to on that farm of hers.

"We'll ride to London ourselves." Not his best plan. But, at the moment, his only one.

Given her current situation, the last thing on Yara's mind should've been the way Alec's arms felt around her waist. Or the solidness of his chest against her back. Or the way his warmth seeped into her and warmed her bones.

Her skin felt on fire from his nearness, aching with anticipation. She wanted his hands on her skin, fanning those flames until she combusted.

She pressed a finger against her forehead and focused her thoughts. Alec shifted behind her, and those thoughts scattered to the four winds. Annoyed, she kept her head straight; she definitely did not lean against him. No matter the temptation to do just that.

"Did they see you?" She clutched the bag of food as if it were their last meal.

Focus—someone was out to kill her. She should not think about Alec at all, let alone the strength of his arms, the solidness of his chest. The need that clawed through her with his every touch.

"No." The word rumbled from his chest, once more scattering her thoughts. "I'm not even certain they were talking about you."

"I hope they were; I don't want any other woman subjected to that sort of threat." She couldn't control her hot anger at the very thought. It warred with her burning need for Alec.

She had half a mind to turn around and confront the men herself. Which was utterly foolish, given the reasons she and Alec were currently on the run—that sounded far more melodramatic than necessary. But Yara couldn't think of another term just then.

"We have two choices," she decided. Her head leaned back against his chest, and she cursed her weakness. However, the simple act made her feel safe. Only she felt safe with a man who'd told her quite clearly he wanted nothing more to do with her. "We can keep ahead of them and hope they head toward London and Horse Guards."

"Thinking they'll intercept you?" He rumbled an agreement, arms tightening around her. She'd do better at keeping her distance if he wasn't constantly holding her so tightly. "That's the most likely scenario. They underestimate you already."

She didn't sigh but grimaced at the truth of his statement. Being underestimated was the main plot in her life story.

"Why didn't you ask them?" She paused. "Were there only the two?"

"I'm not sure either one was Samuels, and, given there is at least one other man involved, that we know of, it's likely he's employed others." He paused, and she nodded into his expectant silence. "If we keep ahead of them and reach Hilton first, that doesn't necessarily mean you're safe."

"No," she agreed slowly. She forced herself upright, away from the temptation of Alec. "But I have more resources in London."

"I won't let anything happen to you." His promise shot up

her spine, tingling along her nerves. His arms tightened around her, as if protecting her from those men.

"Thank you," she said around a dry throat. This man confused her beyond reason. "Alec—thank you."

"What's choice number two?"

She cleared her throat and frantically organized her thoughts. Choice two? Oh. Right. "We fall back, hide in the wood, wait for them, then follow them."

He was silent for so long, Yara craned her neck around and looked at him. He frowned—still not an unusual sight on his handsome face. He frowned a lot in her presence. Shame, too. He had a gorgeous smile. He tore his gaze from the empty road ahead and met hers. Finally, he nodded.

"We could," he agreed, though he didn't sound convinced. "But they're looking for you." He cursed and lifted his arm. She didn't look at him again but had a feeling he rubbed at a headache. "Should've stayed longer and listened. I don't know if they're following your mother."

Cold spread through her veins. The entire reason she chose running rather than returning to Brighton was to keep her mother out of danger. Now, she had no idea if that had worked or placed Kaya in greater peril. Before fear could dig its claws too deep, Yara scrambled for the logic that had served her well all these years.

"Mama is no doubt already halfway to London." She exhaled at the truth in those words. "She'd have headed there first, looking for me." She paused, mentally following the carriage route from Brighton. Nodding, she pressed a finger against her temple. It did nothing to alleviate the sudden pounding there.

"You're certain?"

Yara wasn't certain of anything at the moment, but she nodded. Too many thoughts raced around her head. Worry for the household in Brighton, for Micki. For Mama's safety, though she knew her mother could defend herself. It didn't matter; she'd placed her mother in danger and that sickened her.

"I am." She paused. "She didn't know why I was in Brighton, but she knows I met with Hilton before the trip."

"And she was all right with that?" His voice rose with incredulity.

"I'm my own woman," she snapped. "My parents raised all of us to be our own people." Breathing deeply to stop the fear from bubbling over, Yara tried to hold back her next words. But, broken with anger and fear and sickening worry, they tumbled out anyway. "I make my own choices, just as you do."

"I still don't understand why Hilton asked you."

"Because I had nothing else," she snapped again, that anger overriding her logic. "I was at wit's end, unable to follow my dreams and furious at the world."

Hands curled into fists around the sack of food, she clenched her jaw so tight it ached. Blast the tears swirling her vision! She would not cry. Not anymore, and certainly not in front of Alec. The only creatures who had ever seen her cry were Micki and Masika, her mare.

"I'm sorry." His words were stilted, but his arm curled around her waist once more. He drew her against his back, as if protecting her from her shattered dreams.

Yara fought for control, pushing her disappointment and impotent rage down, deep down, as far as she could push emotions she spent years fighting against. And losing.

"What happened?"

She didn't want to talk about it. Not now, not ever again. Yara had planned to sit in stoic silence for the next two days as they crossed southern England. But her story had other ideas.

"I knew it was a foolish idea." Her throat ached saying the words, and her eyes burned from unshed tears. "I know the world we live in, but I wanted it so badly."

Alec didn't push, and for several long moments they rode in

silence, Alastor moving along at a slow, even pace. Yara wanted to race along the road, to run from her past and the failures that littered the path. It hadn't worked in Brighton. She couldn't run from herself.

"The Royal Veterinary College does not accept women."

He didn't laugh. Yara had braced for that, for the laughter she was certain would erupt from him when she confessed her crushing disappointment. It didn't come. He continued to hold her tightly, his chest a solid warmth behind her.

"I'm sorry." His simple words didn't sound trite but sincere. Heartfelt. That understanding battered her control. "We don't live in a just world."

"No." She swallowed hard, but the word came out husky with sorrow and frustration and pain. "I shouldn't complain; I have options so many women don't. So many *people* don't. I don't live with the threat of war knocking on my door, threatening my loved ones. I'm a free woman with money and options."

"It doesn't matter." Again his words sounded sincere, soft and genuine in the morning light. "And I'm still sorry you won't be able to see your vision through."

Yara nodded, not trusting herself with words. She squeezed her eyes closed and focused on her breathing. "Thank you," she finally managed.

"What do you plan now?"

"Plan?"

She couldn't see him, given their positions, but she felt his patience as he awaited her answer. Even after so brief an acquaintance, she knew he understood her need for a plan. "One step at a time. My mother always says that."

"Good advice."

"I have options. And a good inheritance." She swallowed around the disappointment and heartache closing her throat. "I don't know. But I don't have to decide today."

THEY DISMOUNTED JUST past midday in a small copse off the main road. The clouds, thick and gray, had moved inland again. Alec eyed them, but he already knew it'd rain before sunset. Too many years relying on the weather had taught him more than he'd have liked about rain and wind.

Not enough, however, and the memory sickened him.

"We should move off the main road." He reached for Yara, her body warm and soft in his arms.

She nodded, still not speaking. They'd ridden in silence since her confession. What had it taken for her admission? The pain of rejection had been all too clear in her words, and Alec had no response in return.

"For the best," she agreed, her voice tired. Still, she offered that smile of hers, bright and laughing. Her own mask. It broke his heart that she hid her pain, that she had pain she needed to hide. That she felt she had to hide from him. "After all this, no sense letting one sloppy mistake ruin our chances."

"Chances?" He shook his head. "Of making it to London alive?"

She made a face, wrinkling her nose at him. But her eyes lightened, a faint spark behind the anger and grief. "Alive? Not the word I'd have used."

"In one piece?" He grinned, letting her have her mask. He understood all too well. "Same meaning."

"You don't have much faith in us, do you." She sighed and stretched, petting Alastor. "What about you, hmm? Have you any faith in us?"

Alastor, besotted with Yara, nudged her shoulder, making her laugh. Alec smiled at the sound and unpacked their meager belongings: a single blanket, the small bag of food she'd purchased at the coaching inn, and a compass his grandfather had given him when he turned five.

"I didn't pack for a trip," he admitted, spreading the blanket over a boulder. "If we can't find shelter, we'll have to keep walking."

"I'm used to long stretches of sleepless nights." She moved through a series of exercises, slow and precise. "We should keep on. Even in the rain." She made a face at such a notion. "The sooner we reach London, the better."

He couldn't argue. Yes, her reasoning was sound; that wasn't the point. Her body. Oh, good lord, her body. He watched, fascinated by the way her nimble body stretched and shifted. Her eyes closed, and she glided through what were no doubt long-practiced movements.

Her torso shifted in one smooth motion, sweeping low only to arch high.

Mouth dry, Alec knew there were reasons—many reasons. A thousand, million reasons he was absolutely not going to cross the distance between them and kiss her. But he couldn't think of one.

His feet moved before he realized his intent.

"Yara."

Her eyes shot open, deep and beautiful. He could drown in them. Her lips parted, and he thought she might've whispered his name, but all Alec heard was the roaring in his ears. It sounded suspiciously like her name, over and over.

He cupped her cheeks, cool and soft beneath his rough hands. She deserved softness, not the calloused hands of a sailor, a fighter, a rogue. His fingers tangled in her hair, thumbs brushing her cheeks, and all he saw was her.

"Are you going to kiss me?" The words floated on a quiet breath between them.

"Do you want me to?" *Please say yes.*

"Desperately."

As much as he wanted a soft kiss, a gentle one, something indulgent and new, that didn't happen. The moment his lips touched hers, Alec drowned in her taste. She sighed against his lips, her fingers wrapping around his wrists.

She tentatively opened to his mouth, and the desire that simmered far too close to the surface burst forward. Her touch jolted him, desire burning through his veins like wildfire. Out of control and utterly unrestrained. He deepened the kiss, taking all she offered, his body aching for more.

He walked her backward, toward the boulder. One hand slipped down her waist, drawing her closer. She weighed barely anything, and he easily lifted her against him, carrying her those final few steps.

He set her atop the rock and stared. Simply stared. Her breathing came hard and fast and her cheeks flushed a lovely shade, her eyes dark as they met his. She licked her lips, and he kissed her again, pressing her onto the blanket, her body shifting until it fit against his.

"Alec." She pushed against his chest.

He pulled back, leaning against his elbows. All at once, all those thoughts about why this was a terrible idea, everything he'd tried to grasp moments ago, flooded back. As if a wave of ice water doused him, he scrambled upright. Alec swore he heard Alastor snicker.

"I'm sorry."

Yara snapped her mouth closed, frowning. "You're sorry? For kissing me?"

No. Not one damn bit. He couldn't ever be sorry about that. "For taking advantage."

"Of me?" Her eyebrows shot upward. "I don't understand. You're sorry for kissing me, or for taking advantage of...something else?"

"Of you," he ground out. His cock ached, and no matter what he told himself about mistakes, he wanted her. Wanted her mouth on his, wanted to kiss down her neck and discover all her hidden secrets.

"You're apologizing for kissing me?" Her voice was flat.

"You're angry?" He shook his head. One kiss shouldn't have addled his brain, but here he was. Or perhaps it was the way he once more spectacularly messed something up between them. "At my apology?"

He had no idea what was happening with this conversation. Nothing ever went as planned with Yara. She pushed off from the rock and stood, quite obviously angry. Shaking out her skirts with sharp, jerky movements, she tilted her chin and coolly met his gaze.

"You kissed me." She jabbed a finger at him. She didn't step closer, for which he was grateful. Clearly, his control lacked… well, control. "If you're apologizing for taking liberties, that's one thing. But I don't believe that is your intent. It's the kiss itself, isn't it?"

"Yes. No." Alec sighed and rubbed his forehead. "Damn it, don't twist this around!"

"I'm not twisting anything," she said, words heated but quiet.

Oh, he'd hurt her. Badly. He hadn't meant to. Rather, the opposite. Stay away. That's all he had to do, stay away from her. But he couldn't even manage that. Yara Conrad drew him in, and he was helpless to stay away.

"I'm not apologizing for the kiss," he said, jaw clenched. "I'm apologizing for kissing you in the first place. I shouldn't have."

If he hadn't watched her so intently, he'd have missed the flash of hurt that crossed her face. There and gone in the space of a heartbeat. Her chin tilted again, and that cool, blank expression fell into place.

"I see."

"Damn it," he growled. He excelled at hurting her. "You don't."

"Enlighten me, then." The mocking words fell hard from her lips, which twisted into an equally mocking smile.

"I'm not taking advantage of you, Yara. I'm not going to ruin you." Frustrated, he gestured around them and nearly laughed. "As much as it looks the exact opposite, I'm not the sort of man bent on ruining innocent women."

For a long, painful moment, she said nothing. Then her chin fell, and she nodded. Alec didn't think she'd forgiven him, which made him wonder if that kiss had wound through her as wildly and fiercely as it had him.

"Apology accepted." She took a deep breath. "I'm sorry for jumping to conclusions."

She turned away after that, and it took him a moment, but her meaning rang clear. "You—have you been kissed before?"

"I'd rather not talk about it." She looked over her shoulder, then back at the food bag she'd dropped when he kissed her.

She had. He wasn't certain if that kiss, or kisses, was by choice. Either way, she'd clearly enjoyed their kiss, which made Alec wonder all sorts of things. The first of which was what conclusions she'd jumped to. The second was what her skin tasted like.

Well, the first was actually that he'd kiss her again. But, given the way he'd made a mess of everything after *this* kiss, he doubted that would happen. He could still taste her, the sweet, slightly dark taste that burned through him.

He was in so much trouble.

The wind picked up just then, a sharp breeze through their small sanctuary. He eyed the sky and the clouds that had darkened while he'd been otherwise, and most pleasurably, occupied.

"It's going to rain." Alec scooped up the blanket and turned for Alastor. He ignored the way his horse eyed him and swore he heard another knowing snicker. "We'll need shelter; no sense catching a chill."

"I left my umbrella in my other gown."

The small quip, along with her faint smile, shifted the mood. Alec accepted that change of subject, but he didn't like it.

Another piece of the Yara Conrad puzzle slotted into place. Deflection. She was good at that, using humor and witticism as part of her mask against the world.

Damn it, Alec didn't want another thing they shared in common. But he understood that impulse all too well, and he empathized with her.

Without a word, he helped her onto Alastor and picked up his reins.

"You're not riding?" She peered down at him, the blanket folded in her arms, her lips lifted in a curious tilt. She cocked her head and shook out the blanket, settling it around her head and shoulders.

With her in his arms again? The temptation he thought about constantly? After that kiss? No. Besides, the moment he settled behind her, she'd know exactly how aroused she made him.

"Thought I'd give Alastor a rest." He nodded ahead, as if that would deter his thoughts. It did not. "If we can't find a barn or house or something in the next half hour, we'll make do with a rocky outcropping."

A barn or house where they'd pretend to be married again. Which was worse: their fake marriage, or spending the storm in close proximity? Alec had no idea. He trudged ahead, most definitely not thinking about that kiss, her taste, the feel of her in his arms.

TWELVE

The rain held off for another half hour or so. By then, Yara had regained her equilibrium. At least, she'd convinced herself she had. She'd pushed the feel of Alec's lips from her mind—or tried to. Now, she worried for her mother.

She also lied to herself.

Not about the worry for her mother—that was very true. She still wasn't convinced leaving with Alec without telling anyone was for the best. She'd been so concerned about keeping her loved ones safe, she could admit to not thinking this plan all the way through. But she was committed now. Committed, all right. She slanted a look beside her, where Alec walked as if no kiss had ever occurred.

The feel of his hands on her cheeks branded her. His mouth on hers made her feel things she'd never imagined. And Yara prided herself on her imagination. She knew what happened between a man and a woman. Her parents could barely keep their hands off each other. Esme and Landon were just as bad; she'd often caught her oldest brother, Grayson, and his wife, Adelaida, in compromising positions around the house and yard, both flushed and laughing and so happy.

She had never felt such things herself.

Even now, sitting atop Alastor as the skies opened up and the rain poured in buckets, her body flushed. She wanted more. Wanted his hands lower, on the most intimate parts of her, his mouth there. Wanted to taste him, feel the solidness of his chest beneath her fingertips.

"There's a barn." She nodded toward the clearly abandoned structure in the distance. It was partially collapsed, a good mile from the nearest house.

Without a word, Alec swung into the saddle and urged Alastor faster. His arms wrapped around her, but Yara sat stiffly in front of him. She made that mistake once, leaning against his chest. How many rejections could she handle before reality sank in?

He did not want her.

That kiss said otherwise, but his reaction afterward... The blasted man confused her to no end.

"Not sure about a fire, but it'll be dry enough for shelter." He paused, and she knew he eyed the structure with the same dubiousness she felt. "Probably."

It didn't take long to cover the field. Of course, it was too late to keep dry, but Alec had once more covered her with his greatcoat, the warmth of which sparked a myriad of ideas in her mind that had everything to do with physical warmth of a different sort.

She was truly a fool.

By the time Alastor stepped inside the barn, she'd tamped down those ideas, but her body had other designs. Once more flushed, aroused, and annoyed that she wanted a man who did not want her, Yara kept her focus on the horse. Not the man.

She petted Alastor while Alec scouted the area, such as it was. She didn't immediately see any brush, but there was a pile of hay in the corner he might enjoy. It didn't look moldy, which made her wonder just how long the barn had been abandoned.

She leaned her forehead against Alastor's neck. "I'm such a fool, aren't I? Maybe it's better I retire into the country with my animals, far from society." She leaned back and met Alastor's impassive gaze. "And men."

"Who are you talking to?"

His voice startled her, and she stepped back. "Alastor, of course. Who else?"

"There's no one else in here," he confirmed, and she nodded. "Though I don't think resting beneath the loft is a good idea. Those beams are rotted nearly clear through."

She turned in a tight circle, her neck craned to better see the openness of the roof. Part of it had collapsed, creating a sort of lean-to against the loft. Neither of which looked steady.

"Come on." He took Alastor's reins and walked both Yara and the horse toward the corner, beside the doors, which were hanging from their hinges. "This is about as good as we're going to get today."

"We can't stay until the rain stops." She took off his coat and shook it out, instantly missing its warmth. "That could be days."

"We'll rest a few hours," he agreed. "We all need it. It's still a day and a half or so until London, and we'll need to be on guard. More so there."

"We'll head straight for Cavendish Square." She spread the blanket on the ground as he tended to Alastor. Gingerly leaning against the wall, she relaxed in increments, but the wall didn't give way as she feared.

"Is that where your townhouse is?" He looked over his shoulder, barely meeting her gaze.

Yara closed her own eyes and hummed. "My aunt lives there. Mama will head there first. No doubt she's already waiting for me."

"And Hilton?"

"Oh." She waved a hand. "I'm certain he'll be waiting as well. It's only another day." She opened her eyes, but the light in the barn didn't offer much illumination. She'd never be able to read the letter in this gloom.

"I would like to read Armstrong's findings." She closed her eyes again and wished for another blanket. The day had turned cold, and the barn was drafty despite the cover of their corner. "Hopefully in the morning, with the light. Then we'll know better what we're dealing with."

"You're confident in all this." He settled beside her, spreading his greatcoat over them both. "Why?" he asked, almost in accusation.

Her eyes shot open. At his warmth, his closeness, his accusation. "Why what, exactly?"

He scrubbed a hand down his face, and even in the dim light she noticed his tiredness. Her eyes narrowed—had he slept at all last night? He didn't look as if he had.

"I'm not used to going along with others' plans," he admitted.

She frowned. That wasn't what she'd expected to hear. He didn't look at her. Rather, he leaned his head against the wall and studied the open sky as if it offered all the answers he'd ever sought. His long legs stretched before him, crossed at the ankle, and he looked relaxed beneath the coat.

Beside him, Yara knew otherwise. Tension vibrated from him like ripples in a pond.

"You're a ship's captain," she offered, uncertain where this conversation headed. "You're used to being in charge."

"Aye." His lips tilted upward. "Set the plan, see it through. I was good at that."

Something in his tone told her otherwise. Not that he wasn't good at planning. What had he said about running blockades and gathering information for Hilton? Only that, she thought now. Something else coated his words with regret.

"What happened?" she whispered. Slowly, so as not to stop him or scare him off, she reached for his hand and held it gently in hers. He didn't seem to notice.

"Running blockades was profitable. People don't like to do without, no matter what it is. They're willing to pay whatever you ask just so they have their goods again. Wine, silks, lace, it doesn't matter."

"I agree," she said, keeping her voice soft and even. This wasn't the time to talk about Napoleon's Continental System and its many failures. Alec didn't look at her, but he didn't pull away either. His fingers tightened around hers, and she didn't pull back, no matter the slight uncomfortableness.

"There was an accident." The pain in his words chilled her, squeezed her heart far more agonizingly than his hand squeezed her fingers. "Rough seas, a rocky shoreline." He shook his head. "It all happened in a blink. We sailed off the coast of Denmark, a voyage we'd made a hundred times. The storm came suddenly, the waves—"

He broke off, but she didn't speak. She knew all about rough seas and rocky shorelines. Oh, she'd been fortunate enough to never run aground, but that was one of her first lessons about sailing: keep an eye on the weather, and never trust it. Know the seas, but also know they're a fickle creature no one can truly understand.

"How many?" She finally asked into the grieved silence.

Alec turned toward her sharply. She couldn't see him in the fading light, but she knew he'd forgotten she sat beside him. "Eight." He swallowed hard. "Eight crew, all friends."

She remembered what he'd said about the future, how they did what they did for that future. Heart breaking, she stroked his hand, hoping it eased him. Knowing it would not.

"I'm sorry."

He nodded and swallowed hard. "I forgot you're Conrad Shipping." He breathed a partial breath of a laugh, and she smiled at his attempt. A reminder of their first day together, when he realized who her family was. "You've sailed much?"

"Yes." She swallowed the lump in her throat caused by his

grief. "From the time I could walk, I learned." She allowed the memories of that time to wash over her, and she smiled at the comfort they offered. "My mother, she suffers from horrible seasickness. So my father took us all on a ship as soon as he could, to see if we suffered the same."

Alec's hand had loosened around hers, but he didn't release his hold. Instead, his thumb brushed along her hand so softly, Yara didn't think he realized it.

"I take it you did not?"

"No, none of us do. Lucky for a shipping family," she added with a levity she didn't quite feel. "With the wars, and the blockades, I never had the chance to travel as I wished."

"So you looked after your farm animals?" He relaxed. Not much, but bit by bit, as if talking helped alleviate his pain. She allowed him this change in subject. Yara understood that talking too much about one's own problems usually led to annoyance, not relief.

She sighed dramatically and smiled up at him. "It's a problem, I admit. I want to travel, see the world. Feel the ocean wind on my face and see the unending skyline. Set foot on new lands and meet new people. But I also love my animals, and I don't want to leave them."

He chuckled and relaxed a bit more. "I see your problem. How does Lady Michaela feel about ship travel?"

"She's not fond of it," Yara admitted.

She reached for her dog, but of course Micki wasn't beside her. Sighing, she closed her eyes, alternately pleased Micki wasn't in danger and wanting her company.

They settled into silence, the rain an unending patter overhead. Alastor rested on the opposite end of the barn, in his own corner.

"What are their names?"

"What?" His voice jerked hard and sharp, but she knew he understood. "Why?"

"We honor the dead," she continued quietly. Yara didn't open her eyes, but she didn't pull from his touch, either. "They are still a part of us."

"Go to sleep, Yara," he said gruffly. But he urged her head onto his chest. Cold, tired, hungry, worried, she didn't resist. "I'll keep watch, though I doubt anyone's followed us here."

She agreed on that, at least. However, she doubted she'd ever understand this man.

PETER. Johnnie. Elis. Jasper. Davey. Noah. Rickey. Giles.

Alec mentally repeated their names over and over, like a mantra. He pictured each man in turn as he said their names. Though he wasn't a religious man (Alec couldn't remember the last time he'd set foot in a church), he hoped they passed into a good afterlife.

His mind drifted as he repeated their names, but one thing remained clear: he'd hidden long enough. Four months was four months too long.

As he sat in the barn, Alastor ignoring him and Yara sleeping against his chest, he knew exactly that. After he returned Yara to London, he'd see his crew. Or what remained of them. Then he'd plan for the future. Wasn't that what he always did?

He'd visit the families of his dead men; they deserved that much, even if they hadn't wished to see him after the funerals.

Peter. Johnnie. Elis. Jasper. Davey. Noah. Rickey. Giles.

He knew Godred thought he was wrong to leave, and he wondered how his friend hadn't physically dragged him back. Alec felt terrible, disappearing without a trace, but hopefully Godred heard about what happened at Whitehawk.

He must have slept, because when he opened his eyes, Yara had disappeared from his side.

"Yara?" Panicked, he stood and looked around the barn—empty save for him and Alastor. "Yara?" he called again, louder.

The rain hadn't stopped, but night had fallen. They slept longer than either had anticipated. He couldn't see clearly in the barn. Had something happened? He would've heard if a beam crashed, would have felt her struggle if Samuels had tried to take her.

Cold froze his veins at the thought, and he shrugged on his greatcoat and stepped into the constant drizzle. "Yara?" he called, voice echoing over the field.

"I'm not dead." Her voice came from around the corner.

Spinning in that direction, heart racing, he jogged the length of the barn. He turned the corner just as she stood, looking wet, bedraggled, and annoyed.

"I needed a bit of privacy," she said primly.

Even in the darkness of night, he saw her cheeks flush. Alec opened his mouth, but nothing emerged. Instead, he felt his own cheeks flush in embarrassment. "Oh."

He stepped back around the corner, leaving her to her privacy, and shook himself awake. Not that it helped his embarrassment. He walked back to the opening, packed their meager belongings, and readied Alastor.

"Ready?" she asked, sounding as if nothing happened.

Alec narrowed his eyes. As he led Alastor to the barn doors, he watched her, but she gave nothing away. "Are you certain you want to continue in this rain?"

Just as he asked, a rumble of thunder echoed in the distance. Alastor shied, and Alec petted him in reassurance.

"Suddenly not so much," she said. "Beth Hobson's cloak is nice, but not nearly large enough to shield the rain." She rubbed her eyes and stretched her neck from side to side. "We'll have to spend the night."

"And hope the storm abates by dawn," he agreed. He eyed the sky. "I'm not certain it will."

"No, and we're low on food."

She flicked her hood up and exited the barn, stepping around the corner. Within a moment, she reappeared, her too-small cloak already wet despite her short walk. "The farmhouse is about a mile away, but we'll be soaked through—again—by the time we reach it."

"No sense bringing on a chill." He rubbed his hands down Alastor's legs, then grabbed a handful of hay.

Yara shook out her cloak before joining him in rubbing down Alastor. Alec worked silently, but she hummed a tune he'd never heard before. He wanted to ask what the song was, but he kept his distance.

He had tried to keep his distance since meeting her, but that hadn't worked out at all. The more he promised himself he'd stay away, the more time he spent with her. Not that he minded. She made him laugh, and he enjoyed her company. But she carried her own pain, which hurt him.

Though he'd honestly never thought a woman might be interested in joining any school, he had seen Yara's compassion for animals, as well as her extensive knowledge.

Distance.

No matter how he reminded himself, it didn't work.

"What's that tune?"

Her humming abruptly stopped. In the darkness, the rain falling harder through the hole in the roof, only the occasional streaks of lightning illuminating their shelter, he couldn't see her. He didn't have to; he knew she didn't want to tell him.

Looking heavenward, as if divine intervention might help, which he knew it wouldn't, Alec suppressed a sigh.

"It's a lullaby my mother used to sing." Yara cleared her throat and resumed Alastor's rubdown. "Her mother died in childbirth, but Derya, her mother's lady's maid and her governess, I guess you could say, she raised my mother. She used to sing this to her."

Another small piece of the puzzle that was Yara Conrad hovered in front of him, but Alec couldn't figure out where it slotted into place. "It's beautiful. I've never heard such a tune before. What does it mean?"

Yara didn't answer at first. That in itself intrigued him, and he wondered why she'd hold back such simple information.

"It's Turkish," she admitted quietly.

Her voice barely carried over Alastor, who stood perfectly still between them. Alec frowned. Turkish? He had a feeling his earlier thought about simple information had been wildly mistaken.

"It's about the rain falling softly outside the baby's room." She cleared her throat, and even in the darkness he saw her shake her head. "I thought it appropriate, given the storm. Thought it might help Alastor relax."

Speechless, and with far more questions than answers, Alec returned to his horse. But with both he and Yara tending to Alastor, they finished quickly. Alec stepped back, keeping beneath what cover the partially destroyed roof offered.

"I always seem to have more questions about you than answers," he admitted, spreading the blanket back on the ground.

Alastor, much to Alec's surprise, lay down with them. Alec blinked at his horse, then moved closer to the corner of the barn. Alastor shifted slightly, and Alec realized he didn't want the rain falling on him. Not that he blamed the horse—even with the corner shelter, the cold seeped in, and the rain angled toward them with every gust of wind.

"Yes," Yara crooned to Alastor, petting his neck in long, slow strokes. "Yes, you're safe here. We won't let anything happen to you."

She stepped around him and sat on the blanket, accepting the greatcoat as cover. As she watched him in the darkness, he felt the weight of her gaze. "Now you know how I feel about you. You're a contradiction I might never understand."

He snorted and closed his eyes. "I don't understand myself, either," he muttered.

Perhaps he'd understand himself if he managed to keep his distance from her. Or if he figured out why he couldn't keep his distance. Talk about contradictions. Kissing her and then pushing her away weren't the gestures he wanted to show her.

Not that he knew what gestures he did want to show her. A contradiction. He snorted and folded his arms over his chest. Yes, "contradiction" was a good word.

THIRTEEN

The rain didn't let up until midmorning the next day. Which meant Yara spent most of the morning trapped between a rock and a hard place. In this case, the barn wall and Alec.

Alastor had lain next to them for a little while, which she found endearing. That level of trust after he'd only known her a few days warmed her almost as much as his body did during the cold, damp night.

She and Alec had shared his greatcoat, which had also warmed her. Or perhaps his body had, though he'd maintained a respectable distance, all things considered. Which meant Yara hadn't even leaned her head against his shoulder, despite the temptation.

And oh, was she tempted.

Instead, she spent a most uncomfortable night leaning against the barn wall, by far the most uncomfortable position she'd ever slept in. Uncomfortable and alarming. She'd never actually felt attraction toward a man, and Alec's nearness made her body ache for his touch. It also caused her unsettling dreams about throwing whatever caution she retained straight into the wind and climbing onto his lap.

Luckily, she had not. Though even now, she thought about it —far too much for her own sanity.

Stretching sore muscles, she rolled her head from side to side, but it did little to alleviate the stiffness in her neck. She debated her usual morning exercises, but she was far too tired and grumpy.

"Thank you for keeping me warm," she whispered, running a hand down Alastor's nose. "And for your trust in me." He nuzzled her hand, and she smiled, accepting his affection. "At least someone doesn't mind my presence."

She didn't look at the barn opening Alec had disappeared through some time ago. Scouting out the area, apparently, though the open field showed nothing suspicious. Unless he thought a French spy lurked in the tall grass?

Sighing, she rubbed her hands together. She was definitely not dressed for the weather.

"It's another long day of walking; are you ready?" She ran a hand over Alastor's back before hefting the saddle. "I'm sorry. You deserve more rest, but we have to keep moving." She glanced at the roof and shuddered. "Even in this miserable weather."

"Talking to Alastor again?" Alec asked as he entered the barn.

"He listens," she said, securing the buckles. "And he's a good boy."

She'd actually wondered if her mare, Masika, might be a good match for him. But that meant spending more time around Alec, even if only through his stewards. Which she had no intention of doing, thank you.

Even if she did want to kiss him again.

"Are we in the clear?"

"Yes." He rubbed his hands together despite his gloves.

Frowning, he looked at her. "We can head toward the farm-house, see if they have more suitable clothing."

Damn the man, how did he know? Yara bit her tongue and resisted asking. It was rainy, cold, and miserable, and her dress was thin despite her wool undergarments. The cloak, while lined, did little to ward off the elements. Of course he knew.

"We'd only have to reiterate our lies and explain why we don't have a carriage." She checked the saddle again and faced Alec in the uncertain light. "I admit, it wasn't my best idea. But it was our only option." She bit her lip then pressed her chapped lips together. "If Samuels followed the main road, he never found the Hobsons; even if he did, chances are slim he'll connect Mr. and Mrs. Shaw with Yara Conrad."

She hoped. During an uncomfortable night spent dozing more than sleeping, she'd worried about that. About Samuels following them off the beaten path in his quest to stop her. She doubted it; why would he?

Heading directly to London, to Hilton, would be her best choice. Samuels would have followed that logic and that route. He was likely already a day ahead of her.

"Whether or not the man you overheard at the coaching inn was Samuels or one of his acquaintances, it's best we keep moving." She paused, looked at the problem from as many angles as she could figure, and nodded again. "Even if he saw me speaking with Armstrong, we only met twice."

Too bad she hadn't thought to wear that blond wig when she was sneaking about Preston—a mistake she normally wouldn't have made, but until this moment, she honestly hadn't thought about it.

"You think he won't remember what you look like?" Alec shrugged and nodded, setting his hat more firmly on his head. "That's possible. How many dark-haired women were in Brighton? Many, and with time and distance, whatever idea he had about you would fade."

"Agreed." She paused but knew the answer. If Samuels had followed Armstrong to the races, he'd have no doubt tried to kill her there. Meaning he hadn't been there but had stabbed Armstrong elsewhere. Samuels hadn't counted on Armstrong's stubbornness to find her and warn her.

"We'll need to keep to the main road," he said, taking Alastor's reins and leading him toward the barn's doors. "I agree with your plan, and your reasoning. But we'll need food. If you don't want any of the farms involved, we'll need a town or a village or another inn where we can buy something."

"I'm hesitant to stop at any of them." She ticked off her reason. "A couple on a single horse, no carriage, no luggage, no servants?"

"I know." He sighed and glared up at the persistent rain. "In a village, even a larger town, we're still noticeable. A coaching inn, too. Someone might remember us, and there's very little people won't do for a coin or two."

"You're very pessimistic," she grumbled.

Flexing her fingers in his warm, lined gloves, she flicked up her hood and followed him out of whatever sketchy shelter their barn offered. The weather had not improved. The rain remained a constant, misty drizzle, and oh, look—now a brisk breeze cut across the open field. No matter. She couldn't wait any longer.

"I'd have said practical." He paused. "Yes, practical. Realistic, even. Or sensible."

"Hardheaded," she muttered from the other side of Alastor. Then, louder, she begrudgingly admitted, "I have no other plan. The farmhouse is tempting, but the explanations are not."

He chuckled. "We'll find something, even if we have to hold up a carriage."

Yara tried to swallow her chuckle, she really did. He had the strangest sense of humor, one she liked, one which complemented her own. "It won't come to that."

She hoped. Except now that he spoke it, she had a sinking feeling this day would not go as smoothly as she hoped.

"Do you want to ride Alastor?" He peered around the horse's nose.

"No. He needs the rest."

"Considering he spent a goodly portion of the night lying next to us, I'd say he slept just fine." Alec grumbled something else she didn't catch. Something about being a traitor.

"Horses trust me," she admitted. "And he obviously felt safe lying against us, even for a little while."

They walked in silence then, the rain turning into a fine mist. Yara decided that was even more annoying than the constant drizzle. The wind snatched her hood and cut through her while the rain sneaked its way beneath her gown, chilling her to the bone. Finally, they reached a road.

"Which way?"

Alec pulled out his compass and studied it, though they only had north and south as options. She shifted closer to Alastor, and his warmth, though the walk at least, kept her blood moving.

"This way." Alec nodded and headed off.

Sighing, Yara looked at Alastor. "I'll never understand him."

She swore the horse snorted in agreement as they followed the contrary, annoying, and far too attractive for his own good man. They walked in silence for a bit, but Yara was tired of that. Tired of the uncertainty and the strain.

"Have you any siblings?" she asked for want of any conversation. The silence gave her too much time to think about things she'd rather not.

Like her attraction. It persisted, no matter how he annoyed her. No matter how many times she told herself he didn't want her. He'd shown her he didn't want her, even after kissing her. Contrary man. No one else had ever set her skin on fire like he could. With a simple touch, a look from those beautiful blue eyes.

He didn't want her, plain and simple. Despite that kiss. Damn him for that.

Yara rubbed her nose, which was cold from the rain and wind, and stared at the road before her—"road" being generous, of course. A muddy trail, more like. The rain had caused deep puddles in the carriage grooves, not that she saw any carriages in either direction. Definitely not weather for travel, but they had no other choice. Stepping over the carriage ruts, she stood in the center of the road and waited for Alec.

"Yes," he finally said. That was it; that was all.

Yes? She stared at him, her mind racing. She had no idea what he was talking about—oh. Siblings. It'd been so long, she'd forgotten she'd even asked the question.

It was clearly a sore subject, which Yara understood. In the stilted silence she once again had no idea how to breach, she debated climbing onto Alastor. Her feet were wet and cold—these still weren't walking shoes—and she desperately needed a cup of coffee. And a fire. Oh, what she wouldn't give for a fire.

"Let's ride for a while." He stopped and rounded Alastor. "I'll cover us both with the blanket; it's right miserable out."

Once she was atop Alastor, the wool blanket settled around her, Alec's heavy greatcoat shielding her arms, Yara once more wondered about him. His solid presence behind her warmed her back. How was he always warm despite this miserable weather? She envied that.

She bit back that retort. Because he was also kind and considerate. Thoughtful, even. He ensured she remained as warm and dry as possible, given the weather. Perhaps he was merely polite and naught more. Courteous. Well-mannered.

"Christian."

His voice startled her awake. Yara hadn't realized she'd closed her eyes as they plodded along the road. "Yes?"

She had no idea what he meant.

"My elder brother, Christian."

She hadn't expected his answer, and she blinked herself awake, trying not to otherwise indicate her rapt attention. "Hmm?" she hummed, hoping that sound conveyed enough interest for him to continue, but not so much so she appeared nosy.

She was definitely nosy. Interested, perhaps—yes, that sounded the better word.

"And a younger sister, Sabine." He paused again, then coughed. Not the sound of an impending cold, thankfully, but as if clearing his throat. "I haven't spoken to either in years."

Questions burned on the tip of her tongue. Grasping a moderation she had never truly learned, Yara said softly, "Families can be difficult."

Hers was supportive, even in the face of her somewhat outlandish dreams. They didn't stop her, though even Yara knew the unlikeliness of her Royal Veterinary College application. And when the inevitable rejection had returned, thankfully in a curt letter and not in a mocking, jeering, face-to-face interview, they'd rallied around her.

They still had their secrets. Secrets they'd all promised they'd never reveal until they found the right person. For one hopeless moment on the beach in Brighton, Yara had thought maybe. Maybe with Alec. Maybe they could grow close enough she could share those secrets with him.

Now, despite their ride from danger and Samuels and whoever else he had in his employ, despite the time they'd spent together that had definitely ruined her reputation, she doubted she'd ever share that part of her.

"My mother died of fever when we were young. I think Sabine was only six or so." He continued as if he hadn't heard her, and Yara let him. "My father wasn't a kind man. He was hard on both Christian and me, demanding better and more and..."

Alec trailed off, but she remained quiet. "He barely acknowledged Sabine. I'm not sure if that was better or not. She had governesses and tutors, but other than the two of us, no one in her life."

Yara licked her lips, her fingers resting for just a moment on the outline of her dagger. Not for protection or defense. Because she had a family who stuck together. Who argued and laughed and supported and loved each other. Always.

She didn't know what to say, but she tilted her head around just enough that she briefly met his gaze. It reminded her of the truly terrible sleeping position last night. Her neck ached. Yara didn't move, however, until his gaze flicked down, meeting hers for the barest of breaths.

"Christian joined the army." He looked back at the road, keeping his gaze straight ahead, unblinking even as his arms tightened around her. "The moment he was old enough to buy a commission, he did so."

"And Sabine?"

"Married some minor baron during her first season." He snorted, but it sounded choked. "Neither Christian nor I attended the wedding, though I'm certain he saw she kept both her dowry and inheritance in the marriage contract. He was always practical like that."

"And you?" She quietly cleared her throat and wiped at her nose. "What about you?"

"The old bastard disinherited me. Couldn't do the same for Christian—he's the heir." Alec offered a bitter chuckle that left a sour taste in her own mouth. "Or maybe he could, I don't know. But then he'd have been forced to let me inherit, and he'd never have done that. Or some cousin, I suppose; I'm not entirely certain of the family tree. But I had already left. Took what little money my mother left me and bought my first ship."

He paused again, and she wondered what memories he saw. Slipping her hand around his, she squeezed and hoped he understood her silent support.

"That's how I found Godred."

"Godred?" she repeated.

"My first mate, my closest friend." He chuckled again, this time less bitterly. "Current valet and pain in my—uh, neck."

She swallowed a laugh. She'd heard worse around the farm—had uttered worse herself. However, Yara appreciated his restraint.

"He's been with me since the first. We recruited those who needed work, the men with families in need of support. Or whose families had abandoned them for whatever reason—too slow, or crippled, or didn't bring in enough money begging on the streets."

Her heart swelled. Curse it, she hadn't wanted to admire him any more than she had before that disastrous meeting at White-hawk. Alec didn't make this up to impress her.

Impressing her clearly wasn't on his agenda.

He had taken in men who needed work, money, food. Support and friendship.

"That's very noble of you," she offered.

He snorted, then paused and cleared his throat. "They needed work, and I needed a crew. Couldn't pay them at first—spent all my inheritance on the ship." He sighed. "I miss that ship."

Biting her lip so as not to ask about that, she waited. His arms didn't relax from around her, and his hand had turned, gripping hers as if he held a lifeline.

"Most of them stayed with me. Us. When the old bastard died and Christian inherited, he reached out."

He hadn't responded. Alec didn't have to say that; she knew.

"I ignored the letter—*letters*—from Christian and Sabine. I'd found a family who wanted me, who cared for the man I was and didn't treat me like the second son, the spare, the disappointment."

He was titled? Rather, his father—or she supposed his elder brother now. It certainly sounded like it. She hadn't picked up on it before, and she wondered how she could've missed such a thing. Yara rubbed her nose again. It didn't matter, but he offered so few pieces of information about himself, she couldn't put everything together.

That bitter chuckle returned, harsh and raw. "Until they left me, too."

Yara squeezed his hand, winding his arms more securely around her. He wasn't alone, and if all she could offer was comfort and understanding and support, as a friend, she would. "I'm sorry. Do you want to talk about it?"

"No." The word bit off, angry and final.

"Even Godred?" He'd said Godred was his current valet, so Yara didn't think he'd abandoned Alec, too. "He left, too?"

"I'm quite certain he'll never speak to me again after this." The chuckle came out forced, but it was lighter than the bitter anger that coated his story. "He's no idea what happened at the racecourse. I left without a word, so I'm certain he will be in a fine Irish temper."

She let it go with a single nod. That, she understood. Her mother was no doubt frantic with worry and anger, no matter the logic of Yara leaving immediately after Sergeant Armstrong found her. Una and Bennett were also going to be furious at her, each with their own fine Irish tempers.

"There's a carriage up ahead."

Startled, Yara looked ahead of them. She was half certain he'd made up that carriage so as not to speak about his family. But, sure enough, in the middle of the mud and rain, a carriage blocked the road, maybe a mile from their current position.

"Something's wrong with it." She frowned but couldn't see anything clearly through the mist and rain.

"It's stopped. The doors are open, but no one's fixing anything," Alec growled.

His tone sent shivers down her spine. Yara involuntarily tightened her grip around his, cursing her attraction. And the heat pooling low in her belly. He distracted her to the point she initially missed his meaning.

Not fixing anything could only mean—

"Highwaymen."

"Of course."

FOURTEEN

"This is your fault," she muttered as he slid from the saddle. She quickly followed, landing ankle-deep in a muddy puddle. Wonderful. She wrinkled her nose down at the ground, but there was no help for it now.

Riding Alastor allowed a better view, but it lacked the maneuverability of being on the ground. They had stopped well away from the carriage and the robbery. Even the keenest sharpshooter couldn't hit them from this distance. Though from here Yara couldn't see anyone; they must all have been around the front of the carriage.

"I don't see how," he muttered, slipping a dagger from his saddlebag. "I didn't conjure them."

"You very specifically stated, and I quote, *'I'm sure the roads are littered with highwaymen waiting to pounce upon unsuspecting people.'*" She sighed dramatically and slipped her khanjar from her pocket. "That makes this your fault."

She placed the dagger's sheath in the saddlebag and took a bare moment to stretch muscles sore from little sleep, uncomfortable positions against barn walls, and her ever-growing confusion over Alec. It would really help if she didn't want him, didn't sympathize with him, and most definitely didn't want to kiss him right now.

He watched her silently, his face set. "You're going in?"

"You don't know how many are there, what they carry, or who they've already hurt." She flicked him a glance. She was mad at him.

At herself, too, for wanting him still.

"Unless you believe I can't handle myself?"

He snorted and patted Alastor. "I've seen you with that knife of yours." To Alastor he said, "If anyone comes by, bite them."

She bit her tongue, half annoyed at his casual use of "knife" and highly amused at his orders for Alastor. Knife, indeed. An Egyptian khanjar was no knife, but a sleek, precise dagger, curved for deadly accuracy. Meeting his gaze, she waited for something more. About women and daggers and whatever else he might think.

When nothing more came but a single nod, she looked ahead. She'd never understand this man.

"Let's see what sort of welcome we receive."

"Are you always this straightforward?" he asked from beside her as they made their slow way down the muddy road.

"Would you rather I prevaricate?"

He snorted again but didn't look at her and didn't slow down. She envied his boots; her feet were never going to dry out. "I'd rather you stay with Alastor. Safe."

"No one is truly safe."

He grunted wordlessly, but she felt it was in agreement. No, she'd never understand him.

Frowning, she watched him as they neared the carriage. Other than its open doors and stationary location in the center of the road, nothing appeared wrong with it. Well, the lack of humans, maybe. And she didn't hear a sound, not even from the horses.

She supposed the carriage could be deserted. Perhaps the

wheels had caught in the mud and all the inhabitants walked toward the nearest village for help. She didn't believe that, but she supposed it could be possible.

Alec stilled her several lengths from the carriage. He cocked his head, but she heard only the nervous pawing of the horses. Which meant the carriage wasn't abandoned—no one would leave their horses. Rotating her wrist and listening over the wind and rain, Yara heard nothing more. A quick glance at Alec showed he hadn't either.

After a moment, he gestured left and motioned for her to proceed right. She nodded, easing through the mud and rain. Yara glanced at him as he moved with a stealth she definitely should not have found as attractive as she did. Even from the other side of the carriage, she felt his anger, that vibrating rage he carried with him like a shield.

The puddles lay deep in the wheel grooves, and she wondered how the carriage had made it this far. Huffing a silent breath, she mentally said goodbye to her shoes and wiggled out of them. Her feet pulled free of the mud with a muted squelch. Ah, well. The shoes were useless anyway in this weather. The cold mud sank between her toes, and she grimaced but remained silent.

"Another step and I'll slit her throat."

Yara stopped, though she didn't think the voice spoke to her. She hadn't moved beyond the rear carriage wheel. A quick look around the wooded area showed no one else. She looked up and confirmed no one hid atop the carriage, either.

"Ah." Alec's clear voice made its way through the eerie silence. Yara slid her feet through the mud, making no sound at all as she rounded the right side of the carriage. "I thought the carriage had a broken axle. I was offering my help."

"Where's your woman?" another voice demanded.

Her heart definitely did not flip in her chest at that question. *Your woman.*

"By my horse." His tone indicated the obviousness of that even as Yara inched closer. "Where else would she be?"

Stifling a snicker, she peered around the carriage for a quick glance. Five people: three bandits wearing masks that sloppily covered their lower faces and two others, a man and woman, each with a knife to their throats. It made no sense. A carriage like this? A driver, at least a single footman for a guard, and at least one passenger. Daring another look, she swept the area and only then spotted the others.

Two more passengers had been forced onto their knees, behind the leader of the highwaymen and two of his compatriots. Four passengers in total, five bandits. The man, the driver or footman, looked dazed but resigned, as if he'd fought and lost and now understood his fate. The lady of the carriage looked outraged. Terrified but angry, with bright splotches of color on her pale cheeks and mud coating what was once a nice, expensive, and highly impractical dress for traveling in this horrid weather.

The leader jerked his head and sneered. "I'll enjoy your woman after I take care of you."

Cold shivered down Yara's spine. If the bandits planned to violate her, they'd do the same to the two women here. She took another look even as she felt Alec's anger in the distance between them.

"No. You will not." His words, each one bitten off, stilled the highwaymen. "You won't touch her."

Despite the weather, the situation, the fear of the passengers, and her own confusion over his actions, Alec's threat settled deep inside her and blossomed there. *Stupid, stupid Yara*—she knew better. His actions had told her how he felt, and yet here they were. Here she was, aching to kiss him again.

"Release these people, and I might let you live." The threat chilled the already cold air around the carriage.

The leader gave off a snarling laugh. "I don't think so."

Yara stood even with the horses now, one hand on the closest so as not to frighten him. With her khanjar held firmly in her other, she inched another step closer. "I doubt you think much at all," she said.

It took a good long heartbeat for the group to register her presence. The woman, despite the knife against her throat, watched in wide-eyed surprise. A companion or lady's maid, Yara thought. She met the poor woman's gaze and flicked her eyes to the ground.

Unfortunately, the terrified woman didn't understand Yara's admittedly vague signal. Instead of dropping onto the muddy road, she looked down, as if a clue might be hiding there.

"Drop," Yara hissed, and she moved just as Alec leaped into the fray.

Yara grabbed the woman's arm, yanked her from her confused captor, and shoved her out of the way. She'd apologize later for that roughness, but at least the woman's startled squeak showed she remained uninjured.

"I don't condone threatening innocent women." She met the bandit's gaze, arms wide as an invitation for him to attack. They always did, believing her open and vulnerable. "Or women at all, for that matter."

He moved, sloppy in the mud and from whatever drink he'd imbibed before setting out. Yara easily slipped aside, her feet sliding through the mud, and slashed her dagger along his hand. He immediately dropped his own knife, yelping in startled pain. She didn't hesitate but moved again.

"Or innocent men," she added, hitting him with a solid punch to the jaw. He stumbled backward, feet slipping in the mud, and collapsed onto the ground.

A second man decided running was the better part of valor, but his friend vacillated. Yara stepped forward, dagger at the fore. This man, too, fled. Satisfied, she glanced at the third man on the ground, but he was already scrambling to his feet. Without a glance in her direction, he ran after his friends.

Spinning around, she immediately found Alec, who unleashed his pent-up fury on the final two men. Yara watched for a moment, once more admiring his form and skill. A tall man, built for the sea and all the trouble one found there. He fought the two men easily.

Satisfied that Alec had that well in hand—and desperately trying not to fantasize too much about his magnificent body—Yara turned toward the passengers. She could handle them. The hot need spearing through her? She had no idea what to do about that.

"Are you hurt badly?" She knelt beside the driver, who was gingerly poking at the nasty gash along his forehead.

"I'm fine, miss." He grunted but didn't pull away. Then he gasped, favoring his right side. "'Tis nothing."

She frowned, but wounds around the face often bled profusely. "Your ribs?" She rested her hand along his side, and he gasped again. "I can wrap them, if you have a length of—"

"He'll be fine," the woman snapped. Her voice shook, but her words came out sharp and commanding.

Eyebrows shooting upward, Yara slowly turned toward the woman. The splotches on her face hadn't abated. Yara didn't miss the near-quiet grunt from the driver.

She tilted her head. "And you know this how?"

Oh, she had a lot of practice dealing with women like this. Not everyone in the county appreciated the way the Conrads ran their businesses. Helping the less fortunate with a few coins in the local poor box or a meal around Christmas might be all well and good, but socializing with them? Speaking with them as equals?

Scandalous.

When Esme married Landon, many of the *ton* looked down upon them. Merchant class? Not even gentlemen farmers? The gossip had spread far and wide, dragging all of them through whatever mud the so-called upper class could find.

"I demand you help me." The woman's voice cracked as she tilted her head and held out her hand, as if expecting Yara's assistance.

Yara didn't move toward the woman. Instead, she stood, ignoring the mud on her dress and still freezing through her toes. From the corner of her eye, she saw Alec dispatch the final highwayman. She stepped toward him, more concerned with his well-being.

She reached out, hand resting on his chest. "Are you all right?"

"I'm going to scout through the woods." He met her gaze, frowned at the scene beside her, and raised an eyebrow.

"I have this handled," she assured him.

He gathered her against him for a short, hard hug. Then, leaning back, he wiped along her cheek and pressed a kiss against her forehead. "I'd expect nothing else."

She watched him turn toward the wood, his long strides eating the distance, his greatcoat flapping around him like an omen. Her cheek tingled where he'd touched her, and her forehead burned from his kiss. Yara admired his form, his strength, his way of fighting. She admired his compassion.

And, oh, did she admire his mouth.

He disappeared into the wood just as the woman squeaked in indignation, "Do you know who I am?"

"I'm afraid I cannot help you with that. If you don't know, how should I?" Oh, but she loved that line. Her Aunt Hannah had taught her that when she was a child. It'd been her first trip to London, and also the first time someone had tried to use their so-called superiority against her.

The woman's mouth dropped open, and the color in her cheeks heightened dramatically. The companion, who had stood from where Yara had unceremoniously pushed her, rushed to the woman's side.

"Are you all right?" Yara asked the maid.

"I'm fine," the woman mumbled, eyes cast downward as she furtively brushed the mud from the woman's dress.

Yara was not satisfied with that obvious lie, but she nonetheless turned back to the woman. "Your driver is injured, your footman looks as if he received a blow to his head, and your companion has had quite the scare." Yara nodded to the poor woman, who looked resigned as she crouched beside her mistress. "I am sorry for pushing you, but I wanted the bandit's attention—and that poor excuse for a knife—on me."

Surprised, the companion nodded. Her mistress pushed her off, and once again the poor companion stumbled into the mud. Yara grimaced and took a step toward her just as the woman turned her furious blue eyes on her.

"I'll ruin you for this insult!" she screamed.

"Oh, do keep your voice down; I don't yet know if more bandits are in the woods."

"Who is your employer?" Somehow, the poor companion helped her mistress stand. "I'll have you sacked!"

Swallowing a laugh as she helped the driver up, Yara ignored the woman and prodded his ribs. "I don't think they're broken, merely bruised. You'll be laid up for a few weeks. Two, three, I think."

"What is your name? I demand your name!"

"What's yours?" Yara asked.

"I am Mrs. Antony Highsmith of…"

Yara ignored her after that. She honestly didn't care. Watching the wood for any sign of Alec, she let the woman harp on about her name, her husband, her…something else Yara missed. Fortune and connections no doubt, but Yara had other concerns. She turned toward the horses.

"Is she always like this?" she asked the pair, who of course didn't answer.

Alastor, who had apparently grown tired of being left behind, trotted beside Yara and nudged her shoulder. She stroked his nose, and only then remembered she still held her khanjar. Finding its sheath, she replaced the dagger in her pocket.

"He'll be back," she promised. And though a small shiver of worry settled in her stomach, she believed that.

"—how to treat your betters—"

"Enough!" Yara whirled on the woman, who looked startled enough she quieted. "I don't care if you're the Duke of York and Albany himself! You don't treat people this way. I'm certain you were frightened, terrified, even, and for that I don't blame you. However, you have other people in your charge. Others who are injured, and whom you've ignored."

"Miss, don't," the driver hissed.

Tired of being talked down to, of being ignored and dismissed, she stalked a step forward. A spark of fear once more flickered in Mrs. Highsmith's gaze. Words, a litany of them, crowded Yara's tongue. Her own lineage, her family, the wealth she never flaunted but always appreciated.

"Yara?"

Alec's timely arrival stopped those words. Just as well. They were, after all, trying for discretion. She spun on her heel and met him halfway along the road.

"What happened to your shoes?" He held her arms tight, pulled her against him for a fierce but all too brief hug, then frowned down at her feet.

"Shoes?" She shrugged, anger and indignation still burning through her. "They're stuck in the mud."

"Is that a euphemism?" He huffed a laugh and brushed her hair from her cheeks, then cupped her face. "You're unharmed?"

"Yes." His eyebrow lifted again, and she sighed. "Annoyed

with Mrs. Pretentious, but unharmed. Any sign of other highwaymen?"

"No, but I didn't venture far. Just the immediate area." He eyed the silent but clearly annoyed woman. "I take it she's unharmed, too?"

"Except for her pride when I didn't bow down." Yara eyed the driver, who hovered between her and Mrs. Highsmith as if he might protect her from his employer. She gave him a small smile and nodded, including the footman and companion in that gesture "If you're in search of new employment, any of you, speak to Mrs. St. James, either at the Bear and Wolf Tavern in London or at their Cavendish Square house."

His eyes widened, but he nodded. "I'll let them know."

"Good." Still indignant, Yara met Alec's gaze. She frowned harder at his obvious attempt to hide his grin.

"Making friends, I see."

"My toes are cold and wet. I'm annoyed and irritable."

He laughed and easily lifted her into his arms. "You'll see these two are taken to the local magistrate?" He frowned. "Where are their friends?"

"Run off." Yara waved distractedly in the direction of the wood.

The footman nodded, a slow, obviously painful movement. He still looked stunned, and one hand held his head. "Aye, we'll see to them."

"Good." He carried Yara toward Alastor. "I'd ask that lovely woman for a fresh pair of shoes, but, given the litany I over-heard, I doubt she'd be so accommodating."

"I wouldn't waste your breath."

"Come on." He helped her mount Alastor, then he followed suit. "We'll find shelter." He sighed as they slowly made their way around the carriage. "At this rate, we'll never reach London."

"This was your fault," she reminded him. "Though I suppose my missing shoes are not."

"If you catch your death before London, I'll be furious."

"I promise I won't; however, I won't say no to a warm fire and a hot cup of coffee." She sighed and leaned her head against his chest. No matter how many times she told herself not to, each time they rode she found herself doing just that. "And food. I'm starved."

His arms wrapped tightly around her, holding her close. "We'll find somewhere." She swore she felt his lips press against the top of her head. "After this, no one will recognize us no matter what alias we use."

She giggled, then laughed outright. Curling her cold, wet, muddy hands around his, she closed her eyes. "And a bath. A hot bath."

"I'll see to it," he promised quietly and held her tighter.

Yara relaxed against him, already imagining the bath. She imagined him in the tub with her. His long, hard body pressed against hers. Jerking upright, she blinked, but the image didn't dissipate.

"Relax, I'll hold you." His voice rumbled through her, a soft promise.

That was exactly the problem.

FIFTEEN

By the time they reached an inn he deemed suitable, another mile or so up the road and far from the closest one they'd passed, the rain had begun again in earnest. Yara shivered in his arms, and Alec urged Alastor faster despite the miserable weather and even worse roads.

"Yara." He bit back the litany of curses on the tip of his tongue. Gently shaking her, he ignored the stable lad waiting impatiently at his side. "Yara, we're at the inn."

"Good." She shivered again. "I'm freezing." She spoke clearly enough, but he heard the heavy exhaustion in her voice.

Worry settled in Alec's stomach like a stone, and he quickly dismounted first. He all but caught Yara in his arms when she fell out of the saddle. Cursing, he left Alastor to the lad and carried her into the inn.

"What in heaven's name!" A short woman frowned at him as he entered. "What happened to her? Here, get her to the fire."

Alec, already headed that way, tried to smile, but his lips froze in fear. Yara knew horses. The fact that she nearly fell out of the saddle, and that she hadn't even bothered with a quip about anything in the last half hour, made him fear the worst.

163

There was a reason not many traveled in such weather. The threat of a sudden chill loomed strong and dangerous.

"A bowl of soup and some wine," he said to the hovering woman.

"Aye, aye," the woman said. "Betty, dear, bring a pair of blankets!"

"No wine." Yara half turned toward the woman's voice. "Just soup."

"Yara, you need to warm up." He frowned down at her, his heart thundering in his chest.

"I need soup for that." She snuggled back into his arms. "And a bath," she added, her voice trailing off.

"A room, if you have one?" he asked the hovering woman. "And a hot bath."

"Aye, aye." The woman bustled off, and the noise of the room resumed.

Alec ignored it, though now that he sat before the fire, he couldn't ignore his own cold, wet state. Turning so Yara's feet lay closer to the fire, he glanced around the room but saw nothing suspicious.

No Samuels, no one who looked like they were overly curious about the newly arrived couple. A group of four men who looked ready for a fight, but he ignored them as well. Good. For the moment, Yara remained safe.

"This way." The woman returned, carrying a stack of blankets. There was a younger, smaller woman behind her carrying a tray loaded with food.

"What happened to the dear?" the woman asked, directing the servants as they arranged the tub and some buckets of water.

Alec admired her efficiency. "Carriage accident." He sighed. At least this time he had truthful details—well, partially truthful. "Highwaymen ambushed us. Our driver and footman are seeing to them now. We rode for the nearest inn."

Yara giggled in his arms. She wasn't as far gone as he thought, and relief spread through him. He held her tighter, her slight body warming against his.

The woman tutted as another set of servants entered with two more buckets of water. "No one is safe these days. But you say you subdued them?" She looked Alec up and down and nodded decisively. "Aye, aye."

"My wife." He swallowed around the words, but they flowed easily from his lips. Too easily. He didn't look down at Yara. "She'll need a new gown. And shoes."

"We'll take care of it." She eyed him again. "You need help with her?"

"No." The word shot out of him, sharp and resolute. Only then did Alec realize she meant undressing and bathing Yara. Oh. He swallowed hard, but it was too late.

"If you say." She turned and left the room just as another servant arrived with a pile of linens. "I'll be back with another tray of food."

The woman eyed him again, and Alec had the feeling she also meant she'd be back to ensure he hadn't drowned both of them. Or flooded the room. He merely waited until she left before setting Yara on the low stool beside the tub.

"Can you sit up?" he asked softly, brushing knotted strands of hair from her cheek.

"I'm tired and cold." She opened her eyes, her exhaustion so clear he wondered how she remained upright. "Hungry. Not half dead." She frowned but didn't move. "My feet are freezing."

"Let me undress you and set you in the tub."

He should've asked for help.

After all, most men wouldn't undress their wives; that was what a lady's maid was for. However, Una was in London with Lady Conrad, and Alec hadn't thought his answer through when he told the proprietress he didn't need help. He hadn't wanted anyone else in the room, hadn't wanted to relinquish her from his arms.

Yara stared at him another moment before blinking slowly. "I don't understand. Undress me?" Her voice rose just slightly.

Alec cleared his throat. "Una isn't here, and I sent away the proprietress and her staff."

He stood, waited to ensure she didn't fall over, and shed his greatcoat. Hanging it by the fire, he stripped off his boots and shirt. So much for propriety.

"Turn around." The words came out gruff and low. He watched Yara's eyes widen as she shifted on the stool, toes curling on the rough floor.

It'd been a while, a long while, since he undressed a woman. The ties on the gown Yara borrowed from Beth Hobson had tightened with the rain, but he managed. It probably didn't matter; he'd already requested another gown, but ripping the garment seemed crass somehow, given her state.

"Another gown ruined," she lamented with a mournful sigh. "My winning streak continues."

Swallowing around a dry mouth, he tried to follow her line of thought, but with every inch of skin he revealed, he forgot how to form words. "Winning streak?"

"I don't wear nice gowns. Some days, especially during birthing season, I wear trousers beneath my skirts." She was shivering again, curling within herself.

Cursing his slowness, Alec tugged harder on the ties and reached for his dagger. Damn it, he'd left it in Alastor's saddlebags. Urging Yara upright, he slipped a hand into her pocket and pulled out her dagger.

"Makes sense, what with the mud and rain." He sliced through the ties in one smooth cut. "I love this dagger."

"You can't have it," she said hotly. Turning, she wobbled as her gown pooled around her feet. She smiled as he steadied her. "But I'm glad you like it."

He tried to form words, but even her chemise was wet, clinging along her curves and leaving nothing to his imagination. He turned her back around and tugged the material over her head, tossing it aside with a wet plop.

Alec did not look. He absolutely did not look at her long back, the curve of her hips and arse. The strong shape of her thighs and calves. Closing his eyes, he lifted her into the tub, stopping only when she hissed at the heat of the water.

"Thank you," she sighed as she sank up to her chin. "This is divine."

"Don't drown," he ordered, eyes on hers. "I'm just fetching the soup."

"What kind is it?" she asked, her voice stronger now.

Kind? He had no idea. He also didn't see the bottle of wine he'd requested, but he didn't argue. Yara had said no, and clearly the woman had responded to that. Now that he thought about it, she hadn't offered any wine, nor any other spirits, at their first meeting.

Shrugging it off, he carried the tray to the tub and sat on the stool. "Looks like barley broth. And bread, still warm."

"Perfect." She met his gaze, looking stronger now, and smiled. "I think I can finally feel my toes."

The heat from the water had put color back in her cheeks. Alec had half a mind to set the tray over the tub and run as far and as fast from this room as he could.

Instead, he broke off a chunk of bread and offered it to her. His heart was in so much trouble.

WRAPPED IN A WARM DRESSING GOWN, a fresh pair of wool stockings covering her feet and a steaming pot of tea beside her, Yara kept her back firmly turned to Alec. She devoured the second bowl of broth, as well as a fresh loaf of bread and a selection of cheeses and chicken.

"Do you know where we are?" she asked, searching for any topic that didn't remotely touch on the fact he'd undressed her.

"Farther up the London road. I didn't stop at the first coaching inn, despite what I told the proprietress. I'm certain our loud missus would have, and I didn't want the hassle." He grunted, and Yara smiled. "This is the second one I spotted. Not sure what the name of this inn is, but they had a room and a fire."

"Can't ask for more." She sipped the tea. Not her favorite beverage, but it was hot and strong, and she needed that. "What's the name of the woman who oversaw everything?"

He paused, and she glanced over her shoulder before she caught herself. Snapping back around, she glared at her broth. The image of Alec's strong shoulders and impressive muscles burned in her mind. Oh, his muscles were quite impressive.

"I didn't ask," he admitted. "I was too busy worrying about you. How are your feet?"

"Warm." She stretched them toward the fire, rotating her ankles. "And dry." Tilting her head, she finished the broth and chewed a small bit of bread. "Did I hear you ask the proprietress about a new gown?"

Given hers lay in wet, muddy tatters on the floor, she sincerely hoped so. Yara tore her gaze from it and focused her mind. Not on the way he'd undressed her, nor the fact she'd barely been awake enough to enjoy it. On—anything else.

"Yes. And shoes."

She curled her toes again and stretched her legs once more toward the fire. Oh! Her gown! Yara stumbled to her feet, startling Alec, who scrubbed his hair. Not that she'd looked. Peeked, perhaps. But not outright looked.

"What's wrong?" His voice sharpened, and from the sounds of it, he half rose.

"Armstrong's letter." She searched her pockets but couldn't find it. "Did you take it?" She half turned. "Yes, last night. Where's your greatcoat?"

He didn't have a chance to answer before she spotted it and hurried across the room. In a deep inside pocket, the letter lay safe and dry.

"What does it say?"

She didn't turn, though she heard his every movement. He'd stood, and she imagined water dripping down that chest she very much wanted to run her lips across. And her hands. And—Yara stilled.

Clearing her throat, she slowed her movements and turned back around. *No looking*, she warned herself. Instead, she poured another cup of tea. It in no way stopped her imagination from running wild.

"Would you like a cup?" Her voice sounded low and husky, but there was no help for that.

"I'd prefer wine or whiskey." He sighed, and she heard the rustle of linen. "But you didn't want any."

"I don't drink." She tried for dismissive, but she'd managed a look at his naked body, and that was all she could focus on.

"So you said." His voice had quieted, but she still didn't turn.

Temptation ran hot over her skin, and for a moment Yara wondered if she hadn't caught a fever.

"What does it say?" he repeated.

She skimmed the letter and frowned. "It's not even in code. Or it's a very light code." She looked at the bottom, the list of names, but they were clearly laid out for anyone to read. "No." She shook her head. "No, nothing. Looks like he wrote it in a hurry."

Returning to her seat by the fire, she kept her gaze on the letter. The writing slanted sloppily over the page, the corners creased with dried blood.

"He lists a few others by name, along with the reason he

suspects them. Gambling debts, mostly." She cleared her throat and broke off another chunk of cheese. "Blackwood spends most of his time writing correspondence, with a number of couriers arriving daily. Hmm." She shook her head. "Armstrong and I discussed that. Blackwood, the commander of the barracks, his fingers were so stained with ink I wondered if he hadn't dipped his hands in the pot."

Alec laughed from beside her, and Yara chanced a glance. He hadn't dressed, not completely, but had wrapped his own borrowed dressing gown around him. They'd pay the proprietress handsomely for her thoughtfulness. She certainly knew how to run an inn.

"That only means he had a lot of paperwork." Alec sighed and shook his head. "Running a business requires a ridiculous amount of paperwork."

"Agreed. Tea?" She held up the pot again, and he nodded. "However, from what Hilton asked of me, I don't think Blackwood is sending that many missives to Horse Guards." She frowned and picked up the letter again.

"Lieutenant Robert Samuels…oh, you do have an interesting number of gambling debts. And a demotion, too."

"How in hell wasn't he drummed out?" Alec shook his head and cursed again. "The army can't be that desperate."

She snickered and finished her tea. "According to Armstrong, Samuels was paid enough by the French—or some other country hostile to England, I suppose—that he did what he could to stay in the army. And in Preston." She hummed again. "How does one stay in the barracks and not be shipped overseas?"

"He knew someone. Perhaps he and Blackwood were working together." Alec shrugged. "Once we reach Hilton, that's something he'll have to discover."

"Yes," she murmured, trying to decipher the scribbles at the bottom. Another name? It was smudged, and the journey from the racecourse hadn't helped that. "I can't make out this last line." She sat up straighter. "Oh."

Be wary, Miss Conrad. Stay safe.

Emotion closed her throat, and she wordlessly handed the letter to Alec. Armstrong, despite his initial reticence to her appearance, had warned her, even as Samuels hunted him. Closing her eyes, she murmured a prayer of thanks and remembrance.

"What does that mean?"

Startled, she met Alec's gaze. "It's a prayer for the dead." She paused, uncertain what to say, how much she wanted to admit. With a small, dismissive wave of her hands, she jumped in. "I told you; we remember and honor the dead. No matter what Sergeant Armstrong did in his life, he met death with honor and courage. And one of his final thoughts was for my safety." Her throat closed again, and she took the letter back, folding it carefully. "If he has family, I'll find them and express my condolences in person."

"Is that why you don't drink?" His question startled her, but Yara supposed it shouldn't have. He was far too observant for his own good. "You're Muslim?"

How had he come to that conclusion from a simple prayer for the dead and her refusal of alcohol? This wasn't something they talked about. Outside of her immediate family, only Esme's husband and Grayson's wife knew of their heritage.

"The words you just said, they're Arabic, yes? And at the Hobsons' you didn't eat any dinner; it was sausage. I didn't make the connection until now."

Yara didn't know what to say, and she silently met his gaze.

"I won't spread any gossip." He said it simply, but something deeper weighed on the words. He knew about gossip and wouldn't spread it against anyone. "I promise, Yara." He reached for her hand and held it. "Your secrets are safe with me."

She believed him. Trusted him. For all her confusion over

his actions—kissing her and pushing her back, courting her and telling her he could never see her again—she trusted him.

"It's our secret," she admitted. "My mother is Egyptian. Well, Turkish and Egyptian. And no, she does not drink. We were raised with this knowledge, but our choices were always ours. I honor her beliefs." She licked her lips and turned her hand over in his. "But my father. He's the real reason. He had the addiction. Long before they met."

She stopped again. She'd sworn to Esme and Grayson that she'd share this only with the man she'd marry. Yara pushed down her disappointment, her sorrow. No matter her feelings for him, she'd not be marrying Alec.

Still, she did trust him. As he'd trusted her when he told her about both the accident that tore him from his crew and the disinheritance that tore him from his siblings. Perhaps nothing more would come from this acquaintance but friendship and trust, and Yara would cherish that always.

"Before they met, he'd been trapped in the opium dens. His friends dragged him out, forced him sober."

Alec watched her with an understanding gaze. "I've seen the dens. They're nasty, dirty places. People wasting away, unable to move, lying in their own waste. The only thing they care about is their next puff of the drug."

She'd imagined that often, though she had never witnessed an opium den herself. "My great-grandfather contracted him to marry my mother—quite against her knowledge or will." A story for another time. "However, my father, he promised her he'd stay sober."

"I can't imagine that's easy." Alec kept his gaze on her. "I've seen people trapped in the drink, unable to climb out. He must be a strong man."

"He's committed," she agreed. "And we're committed to ensuring he stays that way. Trust, it's not always easy, but it's necessary for keeping us all from falling into that particular pit.

When we were old enough, he was honest with us about his past. It wasn't difficult to abstain after hearing what he went through."

"Thank you for trusting me." He lifted her hand and brushed his lips over the back of her fingers.

"Alec—"

The knock at the door cut off whatever else she had to say—"thank you" or "kiss me again." Given the way her body burned for his touch, probably something more like the latter.

He rose and answered the door, talking quietly to the woman. Yara didn't listen but thought about her family, her promise.

Her trust in Alec von Stein.

"Yara, Mrs. Bagshaw has a gown for you." He stepped back and closed the door, holding his own clothing. "I'll dress and check on Alastor while you're fitted."

She nodded and turned to give him privacy, all her words dried up. When he stood before the door again, she stopped him.

"Thank you." She kissed his cheek. "For listening and keeping my secrets."

He nodded, traced a finger along her jaw, and disappeared. Yara turned for Mrs. Bagshaw with a bright smile and wrapped the illusion of a happily married woman around her like a warm blanket.

SIXTEEN

The weather had not improved.

Alec trudged through the muddy courtyard and toward the stables, where he checked on Alastor. Given the warm, dry interior, he needn't have bothered. Alastor looked well-fed, his coat gleaming, and happy he stood completely out of the rain.

"I don't blame you," he said, offering his horse an apple.

Alastor took it without a single judgmental look. Alec considered that a win.

With one final pat and a promise he'd return in the morning, Alec left the cozy warmth of the stables and trudged back through the mud and rain. He entered the taproom, where he spent more time than necessary by the fire. Thinking.

Rather, letting all the emotions he'd ignored, suppressed, and badgered into nonexistence crowd through him. Some were about the guilt he carried over his dead crew. Godred and Yara were correct—the accident was just that, an accident.

It didn't ease his responsibility or his guilt.

No matter how he'd studied the weather, how well he knew the sea, his ship, or that harbor, everything was unpredictable.

The storm came up so fast, sweeping them along the rocks. As if the hand of Poseidon had reached out of the water and batted them like a fly.

That wasn't his fault. Alec didn't control the weather.

The aftermath, in which he'd fired everyone in a fit of anger and shame and culpability, that was.

"More wine?" Mrs. Bagshaw peered down at him, watching him steadily.

Alec shook his head. He hadn't even taken a sip of the mug she'd poured a half hour ago. After Yara's confession about her family, it hadn't seemed right. She'd trusted him with that secret, one that could have far-reaching consequences for the entire Conrad family.

"I'll take that tray now," he said, standing. "My wife has a new gown and shoes?" His lips tilted, something in him softened, and once again the anger that sat so heavily in his heart eased. He tried not to dwell on "wife" but found it difficult. Impossible. And utterly confusing. "Warm ones?"

The old woman's eyes twinkled. "Aye, aye. She did mention that. Not fond of the cold, eh?" She shook her head. "I don't blame her. We'll have them for her first thing."

"Good." He slipped Mrs. Bagshaw a pouch of coins. Between him and Yara, they carried enough to buy this inn. He hadn't asked why she carried so much money when they'd only planned on seeing the races.

Then again, he hadn't offered his own reasons, either. Always best to be prepared.

"Thank you."

The pouch smoothly disappeared into Mrs. Bagshaw's apron, and she nodded. Without another word, she cleared the table and called back for the tray.

He waited for it. No sense returning to the room only for the staff to interrupt them. Not that Alec had any idea what he'd find upstairs. A sleeping Yara? His gut clenched. Even days later, he could picture her so clearly as she slept in the Hobsons' bed. The soft turn of her mouth, the way she curled beneath several layers of blankets, one hand disappearing beneath the pillows—no doubt holding her dagger.

Despite his better judgment, his insistence upon the contrary, he cared for her more than he ought. More than he thought possible. She was strong-willed, capable, smart—so very smart. Witty. They most definitely shared a like-minded sense of humor.

Kind, compassionate. Understanding.

Even when he contradicted himself—kissing her then pushing her away—she listened as he shared secrets not even Godred knew. For all their closeness over the years, Alec had never told his friend about his family. Not about Christian or Sabine, not about his father disinheriting him. None of it.

Only he and Yara knew that.

"Thank you." He smiled at the girl and took the tray.

The steps squeaked beneath his boots as he climbed to the rooms. He didn't know what he expected, nor did he understand his own expectations. All he knew was he wanted to see Yara, and that guided his steps down the hall.

"Yara?" he yelled through the door, unable to juggle the tray so he could knock, and unwilling to kick the door in disrespect.

"How's Alastor?" she asked as she opened the door.

"Warm and dry." He set the tray on the table and looked around the room. Anywhere but at her.

A losing battle.

"I'm glad." She latched the door and faced him, as if they shared a room every day. He supposed, for the last week, they had in one way or another. She'd braided her hair and wore a heavy dressing gown that barely reached her ankles. "As much as I know we need to arrive in London sooner rather than later, I think we all needed this rest. At least, the warmth of a fire and good food." She poked around on the tray and nodded in satisfaction. "I'm not too hungry, not after the soup and bread, but the chicken looks fresh."

"Eat up." He suppressed a shudder at the memory of her limp in his arms. The feel of her shivering and quiet had terrified him. He doubted he'd ever forget those agonizingly long moments. "And no more walking barefoot in the mud."

"That wasn't my choice." She settled in the chair facing him. Her mischievous grin returned, and he breathed a little easier. "My shoes simply refused to stay on my feet. Here." She handed him a plate. "You didn't eat much earlier."

He'd been more concerned with her health than his—still was, but she looked like her usual self. Her cheeks might've flushed more than usual, but the room stayed warm, and the hot bath had done her wonders.

No thinking about that, either. But the image of her long, muscled back teased his mind's eye.

He sat beside her. The only other choice was the bed, and he absolutely did not want that temptation. "We'll leave first thing in the morning." He didn't bother to look outside. "It'll be a wet ride. Again."

She wrinkled her nose. "I'm not made for English weather. My sister-in-law, Adelaida, she's from Portugal. Says it's warm and beautiful there."

"I imagine, with your mother's heritage, you prefer the warm weather. Has she ever thought of returning?"

"Oh." Yara chuckled and shook her head, pouring a fresh cup of tea. "She suffers from terrible seasickness."

"Right." He managed a lopsided smile. "You did tell me that."

At a loss for any other conversation, Alec finished his plate in silence. Oh, he had questions. About her Portuguese sister-in-law, and hadn't Yara also said her sister married the new Marquess of Strachan? Her family fascinated him. Yara entranced him. Her need to help animals that burned so deeply within her that she'd applied for the Royal Veterinary College despite knowing she'd be rejected.

All he wanted to do was kiss her again.

"YOU SAID you planned for your future." She paused, and he met her gaze, his confusion clear. Yara wasn't sure herself where this conversation headed, but she had always been decisive.

Plan things out, execute said plan. Adapt as necessary, but a good plan always accounted for the unexpected. The only thing she hadn't ever planned for was not attending the Royal Veterinary College. Which was foolish on her part, but she'd wanted it so very badly.

Not as much as she wanted Alec.

"Monetarily, yes, as much as possible. I can't captain a ship forever; it's hard work." He leaned back in his chair, stretching his legs before him. She did not stare at his thighs. Really, she didn't. "Investing in other things diversified the risk."

"A good plan." She nodded, quite at a loss as to how to bridge her wants. This need for more about him and their next step. "And now?"

"Now?" he repeated.

"Buy a new ship, start again?" She shifted in the chair, curling her legs beneath her and leaning her arms against the back for a better view of him. His face—not his thighs. "Or stay in London, see about your other investments?"

He frowned into his tea, silent for long minutes. She wondered if he planned to answer her question. If he'd even thought that far into the future.

"I thought about it. Starting fresh, new crew." He grimaced and met her gaze. "Don't much care for that. They were my family, and whoever I find now, we'll never be that close. Stay in London?"

He shrugged and leaned forward, elbows on his knees. He studied the floor for a bit, and she desperately wanted to know what he thought. She didn't ask; rather, she allowed him these moments. Given all they'd shared these last few days, she had a good idea what he needed. After a moment, he raised his gaze again.

"Not sure about that. Brighton was the first time since I left home that I stayed still for longer than a month or two. Well, since I was kicked out." He shrugged in dismissal. "I wasn't planning on anything." With another shrug, he offered a rueful chuckle. "That's changed."

"Good." She tilted her head. "Even if you sail with others, talking about what happened will ease you."

That's what she wanted. For the anger she saw in him to lessen, for the guilt that choked him to alleviate, at least somewhat. And if he never spoke to his siblings again, that was his choice.

"What about you?"

He seemed closer now, more intense, though neither one had moved their chairs. Yara knew if she reached out and touched him, he wouldn't pull back. Except he might eventually. And that was what scared her.

That was also what tempted her. A night of passion with no promise of an afterward? Yara wouldn't have ever thought of it before meeting Alec. But no man of her acquaintance had ever set her senses on fire like he did. Made her want so badly she could taste it. Taste him and his kiss.

"What about me?" She sighed and closed her eyes, but that didn't stop the disappointment from choking her. "I don't have the options you have."

"I know." Alec took her hand. The warm strength of his touch wound through and settled in her. "I'm sorry for that. You have money, an inheritance?"

"Oh, yes." She swallowed the bitter words she wanted to say

and held on to his hand as if he were her only lifeline. "Have you heard of Conrad Creams?" He shook his head, but she'd expected that. "We diversified, too."

He met her half smile with a patient look, calm and understanding. Damn him—they really did have more in common than they ought.

"Conrad Creams is something Mama and my Aunt Hannah started once they moved into Nelda Hall. They employ as many local women as want the work. Some, their husbands don't want them working outside the home." She grimaced and wrinkled her nose. "Those are the men who don't like all we do for the village."

"I'm afraid there will always be those sorts of people."

"Yes, but it's still frustrating." She leaned her head against her arm, still holding his hand. Her skin tingled from her fingertips to her toes. "For others, it's their sole source of income, though we ensure everyone has enough food, clothing, and medicine."

"And this business is yours?"

"It will be. Esme, my elder sister," she reminded him, but she wasn't sure he needed that reminder. "We were set to inherit together, should neither of us marry. When she married Landon, the Marquess of Strachan, the business went to me." Even if she married, the business would still be hers, part of her own dowry.

"Is that what you want, then? To run Conrad Creams, tend to the animals?"

"I don't know," she whispered. And why did he feel so much closer? "I thought so. I'd hoped Brighton might offer answers—insights, at the very least." She sighed. "It didn't."

It had offered something far better. Alec.

"What do you want, then?" he repeated.

You. The word leaped onto her tongue, but she didn't speak it. Swallowing around a dry mouth, she tried to lie, but those words stuck in her throat, too.

"Yara?"

"I want to feel what it's like between us," she admitted. "I want your mouth on mine, and I want this need that burns through me—" *Sated*. She had a feeling it'd never be that, and she'd want it more than once. Always more than once. "Just once," she said, as if she hadn't paused. "I want to feel you just once."

His eyes darkened, and the hand that had wrapped around hers tightened. "You don't know what you're saying."

"I always know what I'm saying," she whispered. "Except once again I'm faced with the fact you don't want me."

She'd thought, after the kiss they shared, after the tender way he'd carried and cared for her, after all that, maybe. How wrong she was. How stupid.

"I do."

Yara blinked. "What?"

"I do want you. But I have nothing to offer you. My life isn't in any order." He frowned and stood, still holding her hand. "I've alienated myself from the only family I wanted, even from that family I left. I have nothing."

"I'm not asking for a commitment." She stood as well, holding his gaze in the warm room. His hand tightened around hers again. "No one knows us here. We aren't leaving until daybreak, and I haven't a deck of cards."

His laugh surprised them both, and in one swift tug, he pulled her against him. "I don't want you regretting anything."

"I have a couple regrets," she admitted. Her free hand rested on his chest. "I regret thinking I could change the minds of the Royal Veterinary College. I regret thinking Brighton might help me heal from that disappointment, which only followed me. But I don't regret kissing you."

Yara wanted that burning heat through her veins, the caress of Alec's hands on her bare skin. Breathing heavily, she pulled back just enough to look at him. Then she leaned onto her toes and pressed her lips to his.

He pulled away and said, "Yara, if we do this, there's no turning back." Her chest tightened with anticipation and that other emotion she refused to name. She ignored that and focused on the passion beating in time with her heart. In the warm room, with the faint but constant drone of rain beyond the tightly shuttered windows, that passion curled through her.

She wanted to lean up and kiss him again, taste that passion on his lips and let it explode between them. Throw whatever caution remained into the wind. Instead, she waited. If he truly didn't want her, so be it. But the dark look in his blue gaze, the way his hands tightened around her shoulders, the rough breath he couldn't quite control, told her otherwise.

"If you're worried my family will force us to marry—"

"They should." His voice was rough and low. "Even if nothing happens tonight, we were alone for nearly a week; they should insist." He leaned just a breath closer. "I should..."

He should offer. Ask now, before they took that final step. He wouldn't, but suddenly Yara knew it wasn't because he didn't want her. Or didn't care about her. He did on both counts.

Suddenly, everything they'd discussed since rushing from Whitehawk made sense. His crew, his family, leaving one voluntarily, running from the guilt of the other. Alec cared deeply, so deeply, but he hadn't the words to express it.

"I'm not going to reject you." She hadn't realized how alike they were until now. Foolish, it'd been laid out in front of her. He pulled back just like she did, closed himself off from prying eyes like she did.

That didn't necessarily mean they shared any particular suffering. But Yara knew that now, knew him more deeply. Knew he truly believed he had nothing to offer anyone. That marriage—a true marriage, not one for monetary gain or in order to save her reputation—was impossible.

She had no answers.

Instead, she thought the next moments, the next night, through.

Her parents might insist, of course. However, she refused to marry a man who didn't want a future with her. And if she didn't demand they force him, they wouldn't.

"I made my choice."

She'd wait, allow *him* the choice. And if he didn't choose her, well, at least she tried. She'd regret never trying.

Those large hands she'd admired since their first meeting framed her face. He watched her, silent for a painfully long heartbeat. Yara had a feeling he read her soul, and she wondered what he discovered.

"Yara."

Her name came out a strangled groan of need that made her whimper. She wasn't even a little embarrassed by the sound she made, her moaning hunger of agreement. It shot through her, hot and fast, curling her toes and pooling between her legs.

His hands slid down her shoulders, along her arms, spanning her waist. In the next breath, he easily lifted her, as he had several times this past week.

Only now, as he carried her to the bed, did she admit how much she enjoyed that. How needed it made her feel, being held in his arms. How cherished.

"I don't want you regretting this," he repeated. His mouth brushed hers, hesitant and soft.

Yara tasted the restrained passion in that touch and fought for her own control. "I know. Will you?"

"I could never regret making love to you." He kissed her jaw, his hands tightening around her hips. "I've wanted you since the first time we met."

Her breath came short, but she managed an amused sound. "In that alleyway? With me in the blond wig?"

"You moved so surely, so confidently." Soft kisses down her

neck. "That's what caught my attention at first. Not necessarily your predicament, though I'd have helped nonetheless. The way you taunted those would-be kidnappers."

"I wanted you then, too," she admitted, the words tumbling from her lips. He untied her sash and spread her dressing gown open. "I very much admired the way you tackled those two men."

He paused, pressed a firm kiss on her shoulder, and pulled back. Squinting at her, he grinned sharply. "Did you now?"

Yara walked her fingers over his chest and down to his waist, where she untucked his shirt. "Very much so."

Tugging the material off his shoulders, she tossed it toward the chairs but didn't watch to see if it landed on one. He quickly pulled off his boots and trousers, and she watched each movement with unbridled interest. Oh, but he stood before her a magnificent specimen of a man, one she very much wanted to taste.

"Enough talk." The words came out strangled. Licking her lips, she forced her gaze from his impressive cock back to his own.

"Yes."

SEVENTEEN

$\mathcal{Y}$ara decided that next time, she'd undress Alec. Slowly peel off his clothes and reveal each part of his body. She'd kiss every newly exposed inch of skin and feel the hard muscles of his chest, that glorious chest, beneath her fingertips.

And his thighs. Definitely his thighs.

Right now, however, was for touch. For his naked body pressed against hers. His mouth on her skin. Her gaze made its slow way up his bare chest, and she licked her lips. Dark passion burned in his stormy gaze. Hunger.

She ached for his touch. All her breath left her at once.

"Oh." Yara didn't know if she'd said that aloud or not.

Her fingers trembled as she reached for him, skimming the warmth of his chest. Her nipples were already hard and aching for his touch. She wanted to discover everything. Explore all the passion that burned inside her at his smile, his kiss. Definitely his kiss.

Yara hesitated for a heartbeat. Once. One time. Well…maybe one night. No one would know.

Alec didn't move but waited for her. A rush of that same

emotion she refused to name spread through her. He wanted her, she knew that clearly enough. More than the lust she'd often seen in the eyes of the county men. The emotion she refused to name burned in his gaze, too.

She tossed off her chemise and leaped that final step. She wanted him more than she wanted her next breath. And she refused to dwell on any thoughts about how improper this might be. So was riding across England alone, on a single horse.

So was sharing a room and pretending they were married.

He growled her name, and the low, sexy sound raced through her. In a single smooth move, he gathered her into his strong arms. All the breath rushed out of her at the feel of his naked body pressed so close against hers, and Yara wrapped her arms around his broad shoulders.

She adored those shoulders.

He leaned over and put his mouth on hers, a hard, brutal kiss that stole her breath. Her fingers dug into his shoulders, keeping him close, wanting more. One large hand skimmed up her waist and traced over her breasts. Just the slightest touch, the barest stroke.

He broke the kiss, eyes dark.

"Alec," she gasped, frantically gathering her scattered wits. It was no use.

He tasted down her belly, over her hip, his fingers just grazing her sex. She arched into his touch, but he continued his light, teasing caress. His mouth skimmed over her hips again, his fingers finding her heat. She hovered on the edge, clawing the bed, gasping for breath.

She moved her hips, arching, seeking his touch, but Alec held her still. Yara whimpered. Her heart pounded in her ears, blocking out any other sound. But her body ached for every teasing touch. Every tantalizing kiss as he explored her.

All she felt were Alec's hands. His fingers as they slipped through her heat, circling her nub but never fully touching her.

She needed more. Suddenly, before she found the words, his mouth pressed against her.

Finally, finally, his fingers pressed hard against her nub, rubbing in short, firm bursts. Then his mouth pressed to her sex. "Come for me, Yara."

She flew over the edge. Her orgasm crashed through her hard and fast, and she ground her hips into Alec's touch. His fingers slid into her in short, shallow movements as he tasted her pleasure. She rocked against him, desperate for his touch, that addictive feel of ecstasy rushing through her.

His fingers curled within her, and that wonderful pleasure built again. Breathing hard, body trembling, Yara forced open her eyes and watched him. The room was too dark to see him fully, but the image of him between her thighs, one hand on her belly, the other still moving inside her, set her afire.

Her orgasm rushed through her again, stealing her breath. Oh, but she might never get enough of his touch. More than once, indeed.

Somehow, she uncurled her fingers from the bedding and moved her limbs, which were limp with satisfaction. She wanted to taste him, explore his body as he had hers. Take her time and learn everything he liked, watch him come undone as she had. He met her gaze, breathing hard himself.

Later.

He moved with that same deadly smoothness she'd admired when he fought. Pinning her onto the bed, he watched her. She couldn't tell what he was thinking. Desperate for his body against hers, for the promise of more, she shoved all that aside.

"Alec," she whispered, framing his face with her hands and kissing him softly.

He adjusted her on the bed, lifting one leg over his hip as he settled between her legs. Oh, the feel of his hardness against her sent another bolt of arousal skimming over her skin. He entered her slowly, jaw clenched with restraint. Shifting her hips against his, he slid deeper.

"Yes," she breathed. Nails digging into his back, she wrapped her legs around his waist.

He shuddered, against her. "Yara," he whispered, and her name sounded like a fallen prayer on his lips.

Despite its fierce pounding, her heart flipped. That passion built again, urging her faster, but she paused. Kissing his neck with a tenderness she didn't understand, Yara moved her hips. She might not have been able to see his expression, but she felt him in other ways. The gentleness with which he moved. The tenderness in his touch.

He planted his hands on either side of her head and held her gaze.

She grasped for words, but they caught in her throat. Moving her hips against his, she wordlessly opened herself. He slid in deeper, and her breath stopped. All that mattered was this moment, and her blood sang in her veins.

She tightened her thighs about his waist.

"Yara." He sounded as if he wanted to say more but cut himself off.

She knew. She couldn't admit it, either.

"Are you all right?" His rough voice moved along her arms, sending shivers of pleasure over her.

"Yes," she breathed.

"Too sensitive?"

Wordless, she shook her head.

Then he moved, slow, even thrusts that built that fire once more. The fire carried her orgasm higher, and she let herself go, let herself simply feel and hoped that was enough. For now, it was.

She leaned up, found his mouth, and kissed him. It was sloppy and rushed and everything she desired—she wanted more. One of his hands cupped the back of her hip and lifted her higher. Gasping as he moved deeper, she clawed at his back, chasing her orgasm.

Yara slid a hand between them and pressed hard against her nub, rubbing it as he had earlier. She was so sensitive, she climaxed immediately.

Crying out, she bit his shoulder. He growled her name, moving harder, faster, and she gasped again, welcoming his every thrust. He stiffened, pulling out, and shuddering as his own climax rushed through him.

"Yes!" she cried. "Alec!"

She held him close, wanting to see his face but uncertain what her own showed in this beautiful aftermath. His arms trembled, and he rolled to the side, breathing heavily. She missed the weight of him atop her. Turning, she watched Alec in the dancing shadows. Eyes closed, she rested one hand on his chest, wanting that skin-on-skin contact she hadn't realized she'd crave.

What happened now? Would he stand, dress, and leave? That thought hurt, but she braced for it. But no, he opened his eyes, met hers, and smiled.

Oh. And there went her foolish heart, turning over in her chest and telling her things she had no right to feel.

Alec reached out and tugged her against him. One arm wrapped around her waist, holding her close. Shivering now, she rested her head on his shoulder. She liked this. Better than him standing.

"Cold?" His voice rumbled, its quiet undertone shivering down her spine. He didn't wait for an answer, but reached down and tugged the blanket over them. "I'll tend the fire in a bit."

***

ALEC HELD her tightly as her breathing evened out. He knew this was a bad idea. Knew he'd never be able to let her go. His arms tightened around her, his fingers combing through her long hair.

He would've bet against this. He knew the odds and the chances; he'd gambled with his life and those of his crew often enough. He would've lost this bet.

Somehow, in the space of a week, he'd fallen in love with Yara Conrad.

Oh, he'd tried to convince himself it was lust. Lust he could handle. He wanted her, again and again. This one time wouldn't be enough, but he'd known that before he carried her to bed. Now, he didn't want to move from this position, holding her warm body against his, the scent of her soft skin surrounding him, the feel of her strong, muscular leg sliding along his.

"No regrets?" Her voice drifted through the quiet of the room like a low, forgotten melody.

"None." Never. He held her closer. "You? There are more consequences for you."

"Eh." She moved slightly, and he opened his eyes. The room remained dark save for the single candle and the dying fire. He felt her prop her hands on his chest and shift her warm body more fully onto him. "I'm not ignorant of those consequences."

His eyebrows rose, and he looked down at her in disbelief. "You don't care?"

"I care," she said slowly. "All women care about that, given the way society forces us to care." She leaned her head on his chest again, her fingers drawing random shapes on his chest. "But I'm prepared for them."

"Yara." His throat tightened. "If you're pregnant…"

"Please." She didn't sound angry, merely tired. Resigned, perhaps. "Don't offer me marriage for that and that alone."

Thoughts whirled in his head like a maelstrom, and he wondered if he even knew what he meant. Alec rolled them over so they lay side by side and he could see her more clearly.

Brushing her loose hair from her cheeks, he took another moment and gathered his thoughts, but it was no use.

"Will your family disown you?" The thought chilled him, but he needed an answer.

She huffed a laugh. "No. I'm quite protected, don't worry about that."

He did, though. But with so many wounds now open and exposed, he realized how messy his life had become in a short amount of time. The one person he couldn't leave behind was himself, no matter how he tried.

And Yara. He found he couldn't leave her.

His hand drifted down her back, and he tugged the blanket over them.

"I've been thinking," she said, clearly changing the subject.

He let her. He wasn't sure what more he had to say besides a marriage proposal. Which lay on the tip of his tongue, much to both his surprise and his soul-deep understanding. Not because she may or may not be pregnant. Not because their journey across southern England ruined her reputation.

But because he loved her.

It was as simple and complicated as that. He loved her and did, indeed, want to spend his life with her.

"Always dangerous." He hoped the laughter in his voice defused the awkward confusion of a moment ago. "But do go on."

"You were in Brighton for several months, yes?"

"Four." Suspicion clawed up his throat. "Why?"

"None of your crew contacted you?"

Alec rolled onto his back and stared at the ceiling. Part of him wanted to stand, dress, escape this conversation. But he stayed still and let the guilt and anger seep into his bones.

"No. When I finally searched through the piles of correspondence, I saw nothing from them."

The image of that mound of letters he'd last seen on the

morning of their engagement at the racecourse plagued him. Invitations, business letters from his various enterprises, a few personal missives from women he knew in London. Nothing from the family he'd found over the years.

"That's not right." She sat up, her hair falling over her shoulders, her voice indignant. "Unless you lied, which I doubt, what happened was an accident. The fact they blame you isn't right. You're all grieving."

He reached up and twirled a lock of her hair around his fingers. "I don't know that grief has a right and wrong. It simply is."

"Well." She shifted and folded her legs beneath her. "Aren't you the wise one."

"Wise?" He chuckled but didn't meet her gaze. "I'm not sure about that. I've had a lot of time to think about this."

"And your conclusions, oh not-wise one?" She captured his hand and held it between hers.

It wasn't an erotic gesture, despite their nakedness. Rather, it was a simple act of kindness. Friendship. Alec couldn't figure whether it had a deeper meaning than compassion. The anger that had followed him since leaving his father's house leveled off around her.

He knew why, had discovered the reason during their long week of traversing England. They each suffered from their own disappointments in life. They'd both escaped to Brighton in what was clearly a vain effort to forget those disappointments.

Had he known from that first meeting that she carried her own sorrows? No. He wasn't a mind reader, as she'd pointed out. But she captivated him enough that he forgot all about his.

"I've concluded that, while I'm not to blame for the storm, I was the captain of *The Argo*."

"Your ship is *The Argo*?" She snickered. "I should've known. Go on."

He grinned wider, smiling up at her. They also shared a love of Greek mythology. "As captain, it was my responsibility to see to my crew's safety."

"I agree with that." The words came fast and clipped. "It was. You are not, however, omnipotent. Unless you lied about that, too?"

Shaking his head, Alec sat up and swung his legs over the side of the bed. He stood, stretching well-used muscles, and walked to the fire. Stoking it, he let her words sit between them.

"I'm not," he said softly, watching the fire catch again. "I know that. They know that, too."

Peter. Johnnie. Elis. Jasper. Davey. Noah. Rickey. Giles.

"So they abandoned you?" He heard her move from the bed. She huffed, indignant once more, and the rustle of her dressing gown filled the silence. "I'm not sure they deserve you."

"Grief, Yara." He stood and found his own robe, still neatly folded on the stool by the fire.

"I know." She sighed and tested the tea, but it'd long turned cold. Shifting her attention to him, she held his gaze. "I care more about you than your crew. And in the week we've known each other, I've learned how much responsibility you carry on your shoulders. Do they know?"

EIGHTEEN

*A*lec shook his head and dressed. "More tea?" He didn't look at her. "Or food?"

"Alec." She said his name softly, but she watched him pull away.

His pain hurt her, though she understood what he meant about grief. About responsibility. About why he tried to run from all that and why it hadn't worked. You couldn't run from yourself. A hard lesson she had also learned.

"All of London knows the reason." His words fell flat, and the anger that had accompanied him throughout their time together returned. "We were celebrated when we brought in the goods they missed. Ignored when we didn't. Of course, they never knew what we really did."

"Hilton?" She already knew the answer but whispered his name into the darkened room.

"They wouldn't have cared, and it didn't matter what they thought anyway. We ran the blockades for the money, for the future." Those last words came out so bitter, Yara thought she could taste them.

"It took a while before we returned. *The Argo* had sunk,

broken up on the shoreline. By the time I found another ship, the crew was already grieving. No one spoke; it was like we all lost a part of ourselves. We'd lost men before, but never like this."

She hesitated for only a breath, then she stood. Slowly, quietly, she crossed the room in borrowed slippers and took his hand. He wasn't alone. Even in the scant light, his stormy blue gaze, lost and broken, met hers.

"When we made port, they were waiting. It was our routine, I'm not sure when or how it started. They stood at the dock and waited, sometimes for days."

He stopped, but she didn't comment. Yara knew all too well the way shipping worked. The fickle wind, the tides, even the French.

"When we didn't return with *The Argo*, they knew." He blew out a breath.

"Did they know it wasn't your fault? That you aren't God?"

He shrugged, restless, pacing the small room in long strides that ate up the space, his bare feet silent on the floorboards.

"They blamed me. My fault for sailing there. My fault for taking risks."

"And was it?" She stepped back as he paced around again. "Did you take unnecessary risks? Were you sloppy? Did you put profit over your people?"

"No." He ground out the word and stopped before her. He looked outraged, his voice equally furious. Yara knew him; he wouldn't lie. "Simple trip, in and out. We'd done it so many times before." He scrubbed his hands over his face, through his hair. But his shoulders dropped. Defeated.

"Then they blame you because they're angry. Devastated." She reached for him again, taking his hand and drawing him near. Her heart ached for what happened, what he'd endured. "You're right; people grieve differently, but I've learned that it's easier to blame a person than it is to blame chance or fate or God."

"Maybe." He sniffed hard, and she pulled him closer. He didn't resist when she wrapped her arms around him, holding tight. "So I left. I didn't want to stay in London, where the crew and their families lived. I didn't want the stares and whispers and gossip that hounded me."

She understood that, too. The pieces of one's soul that chipped away with such malice.

"It wasn't your fault." She swallowed around her own grief, heartache for his pain, for the damage done to the man she—

Yara pushed away that feeling. A night of passion, a chance to indulge in her burning need for him. No more.

"Alec." She pressed her hands against his back, bringing him that much closer. "I've never been more certain. You aren't to blame. You're a good man."

She leaned up and kissed under his jaw, nipping the skin along his neck. He shuddered in her arms, all the breath rushing from him.

"If you weren't, you wouldn't have protected me. That's the kind of man you are." Confusing as hell, but honorable.

Now wasn't the time for such clarifications.

That conversation would only lead to her ever-growing feelings for him, and that wasn't what this moment was about. She could go on, rehashing the last week, how he'd listened to her fears for her mother's safety in the wake of Armstrong's death. How he'd ensured her reputation by employing various aliases. How he'd held her and kept her warm.

That was for later.

"Come back to bed." She stepped back, tugging him along with her. Yara untied the sash along her robe and let it fall open.

Alec hesitated for a moment. Only a heartbeat. Then he shucked off his robe and crawled into the bed, eyes dark as they held hers.

His kiss was rough, hard, stealing her breath and her sanity. Yara wrapped herself around him, holding him against her. She might never let him go, and that was the problem. A problem for later. She kissed him back, pouring every ounce of clawing need she had for him into that kiss.

He abruptly pulled away. Startled, her breath coming in harsh gasps, she blinked up at him.

"Beautiful." He shook himself. "Yara." Then he kissed her again.

Yara knew. Words seemed inadequate, too flimsy and small. But his touch told her all she knew he couldn't say. All she couldn't either.

One hand traced along her cheek, her jaw, down her throat. So light, so gentle, she thought she might cry from the beauty of it. His lips followed, taking his time, exploring her taste.

ALEC SLOWED. His arousal burst through him, a clawing need for this amazing woman, but he slowed. He knew once wasn't going to be enough—once more wouldn't be enough, either. It didn't matter. She lay beneath him now, her breath coming in short gasps, her skin flushed.

So he took his time, running his tongue along her shoulder, only to return to her mouth and kiss her again. Yara fisted her hands in his hair and rolled onto her side, one leg sliding along his hips. She shuddered against him, a small whimper of need he knew he'd never get enough of.

Pushing her dressing gown off her shoulders and shoving the material aside, he helped her sit. He didn't want any interference from her clothing. She leaned back, unashamed, her body flushed, her nipples hard, tempting peaks as she watched him. One hand, calloused from working with her animals, from wielding her dagger, trailed down his chest and over his hip.

She stilled and met his gaze, bold, dark, and aroused. Her fingertips brushed over the tip of his cock, and his hips jerked forward. Once more, she stilled, her gaze holding his. A wicked grin crossed her lips, and his cock stiffened at the sight. Jaw clenched, he waited.

Yara wrapped her hand around him, stroking his length. A strangled moan caught in his throat, and Alec fisted his hands in the bedding. In a single, smooth move, she leaned forward and pressed her lips to his belly, her tongue flicking out to taste him.

"Yara." Her name was the only thing he knew, her breath on him, her hands against his skin. Her touch threatened his control. He caught her hands, dragging her against him. He'd never felt so wild, like a schoolboy during his first sexual encounter.

With his mouth on hers, he drew her atop him, settling her legs around his hips. Her hands braced on his chest, her hair falling from its braid and surrounding him. Drowning him? He was already lost in her.

Alec growled; the harshness of the sound surprised even him. He wanted to lavish worship on her. Her beauty, her body, her passion. But he kept his words to himself, afraid of what he might confess.

Instead, he kissed along the tops of her breasts, his fingers trailing up her lush hips, along her waist and belly. Taking one breast in hand, he kissed her nipple, which was already a hard peak, nipping it until she gasped and arched against him. His teeth closed over it, tugging until she whimpered, her fingers scraping through his hair, holding him close.

"Now," she panted, one hand slipping between them. He covered her fingers with his, and together they rubbed her nub. Her eyes closed, and she rocked faster against their joined hands.

"Touch yourself," he ordered, wishing for daylight so he could see her properly.

Or the longest night, as this might never end.

Rolling them onto their sides, he slipped a finger into her as her own touch quickened. With a wordless cry, she fell over the edge of pleasure. She stiffened, gasping as her orgasm raced through her. Oh, but her beauty took his breath away.

He wanted to taste her again, make her sob his name as he pleasured her over and over. But then her fingers once more wrapped around his cock, and his mind blanked. He wanted her like this every night. Spread before him, open to him.

"I want—" Yara broke off and shook her head. "Can we make love with me on top?"

It was not what she originally planned to say, and he knew it. Curiosity burned through him, but more than that, he wanted her riding him.

Alec rolled onto his back, and she straddled his hips. He took her hand, and together they guided him into her. Once he was fully seated, he held himself perfectly still and waited for her to adjust. She moved slowly, her gaze on his, her hands braced on his chest.

"Do you like this?"

He'd like her any way he could have her. Gripping her hips, he urged her faster. "Yes," he ground out. God, yes. Her rising over him like an avenging Valkyrie? He wanted that and more.

"Touch yourself," he managed. "I want to see you orgasm again."

She did as he said, and within moments her orgasm tightened through her. She ground against him, those sounds teasing him as she came. He wanted this every night. Every morning. Wanted to watch her shatter at his touch again and again.

He felt his own climax build at the base of his spine, and he moved faster. Yara's thighs tightened around his hips, and her nails dug into his chest as she gasped his name. His control completely snapped.

He rolled her onto her back and pulled out as he came, his

face buried in her shoulder, breathing in the scent of her like a dying man. His arms gave out on him, and he collapsed atop her. He thought he ought to move, but Yara wrapped her arms about him and held tight.

As if she, too, didn't want this night to end.

Eventually, he rolled onto his side, bringing Yara with him. He held her close and pressed a kiss against the top of her head. With a silent vow, he promised her he'd do everything in his power to see that she was safe. Safe from Samuels, safe from whatever society might say about her.

From himself.

He'd use whatever alias, whatever story he could concoct so she never knew the pain of society's rejection. Yara had already suffered enough, unable to see her dream come to fruition.

Alec held her for a long while after both of their breathing eased. He didn't want to move, didn't want anything to disturb this moment. But he knew it needed to end. They had plans to make and another long day of riding ahead of them.

"I—" She paused, then cleared her throat. "How do you feel about heading to my aunt's house? It's just off Cavendish Square, less than two miles from Horse Guards. Mama will already be there."

"I know you're worried about your mother." He kissed the top of her head again and didn't read too much into how natural that felt.

"I am." She exhaled, her fingers curling against his chest. "And I know heading straight for Hilton is the best idea. But I have resources at my aunt's." She pressed a kiss against his chest. "I like resources."

He chuckled and drew her closer. "Gathering your resources?" He shrugged, unsure of anything at the moment. "Why not head straight for Hilton? We know, or suspect, Samuels is waiting for you. Even if he had the time and connections to discover all your relations in London, or knew them already, why would he think you'd go there first?"

"Exactly."

Confused, he looked down at her. She met his gaze and waited. "Ah. Throw him off the trail, so to speak." He shrugged again, restless to finish this and yet reluctant to leave her arms. "He'll have had time already. Planned something, perhaps gathered his own resources. Would your mother have contacted Hilton?"

"Yes." She shifted, and her head fit almost perfectly against his shoulder. He liked that. "He's a member of the family now."

"What?" Alec looked down but couldn't see anything from that angle. "What do you mean?"

"Not in the traditional sense." She yawned and shivered against him. He tugged the blankets up and reminded himself he should leave.

Lying in bed with her was a terrible idea. One he could grow used to all too easily.

"Landon, Esme's husband. He works for Hilton—or used to, I suppose. I'm not certain about that now. Anyway, Hilton has discovered many resources in Conrad Shipping. My eldest brother, Grayson, has sailed missions for him. And I know my Uncle James knows him somehow. Plus, we adore his wife."

Alec blinked, wondering at the rather convoluted connections between Hilton and the Conrads. He hadn't even known Hilton had married. "You're certain Hilton would've told Lady Conrad about your mission? You said she didn't know."

"He wouldn't have, no. He's too practical. But he'd have told her enough that she wouldn't threaten him." Yara paused, and Alec honestly had no idea what her next sentence might be. "My father still might."

He snorted. "All right." He ran his hand down her back. "If Hilton knows we're taking the long way, and that you have information about Armstrong's spy ring, he'll be waiting."

"So will Samuels," she reminded him.

Alec nodded, but all he knew was that he had to protect her. That was all that mattered.

He stood and began to dress. Partly so he could escape his relentless need to touch her. Partly because he needed to move, sort through the thoughts racing round his head. The emotions crowding his heart.

"We'll leave at dawn." He watched her, still on the bed, face shuttered. "I'll inform Mrs. Bagshaw and have her ready an early breakfast and some food for our journey."

"All right." Her voice carried easily across the room. Stretching her long torso, she raised her hands over her head. Alec nearly bit down on his tongue. He couldn't tear his gaze away from her. "Hmm." She opened her eyes and began to braid her hair. "We should arrive in London sometime in the night."

That sounded like a terrible idea. "No." He grunted and turned for the door. "More highwaymen and little moonlight with these persistent storms? No. We'll find shelter closer to the gates and head into town first thing."

"Another day's delay," she warned him, as if they spoke of a ship sailing on the tide and not her life.

Yanking open the door, he glanced over his shoulder. "In the daylight, I can see better. Protect you better."

She didn't say anything about being able to protect herself. She just watched him. In the daylight, he might remember why he needed to keep his hands off her.

But he doubted it.

"Alec."

He paused and turned.

She chewed her lip, a move that showed her uncertainty. It twisted through him, but he had no idea how to ease any of the tension between them.

"One more day." She nodded, her face revealing nothing. "The roads are a mess, I agree."

"Then we'll head for Horse Guards. Let Hilton deal with Samuels." His lips twitched. "He has resources, too."

She smiled, a slow, soft one that made his heart thud. "All right." And the trust in those simple words made him weak in the knees. She laughed and rubbed her forehead. "When I suggested we continue on to London and not head back to the Brighton townhouse, I honestly hadn't realized how, ah…what's the word."

"Adventurous? Wet? Long?" He grinned but silently added, *Indulgent. Happy. Passionate.*

"Those are good words." She nodded sagely. "I accept them all." But she sighed and added seriously, "I had only wanted to keep my mother, the entire household, safe. It wasn't one of my better plans; I admit that now."

"You wanted to keep the people you love safe," he said. "There's nothing wrong with that. It's what most people want."

"Hmm. But I've dragged you into this. I have no idea if Samuels went after Mama, and by now it's been so long I don't know…"

She trailed off, and he closed the distance between them. He knew. "They're safe. From what you told me of your mother, I'm sure of it. As you said, she has resources in London. Was it better to leave her and ride separately?" He shrugged and kissed her fingertips. Reaching behind him, he felt along the floor until he grabbed her dressing gown and gently covered her. The fire kept the room warm, but he knew she detested the cold and damp. "I've no idea, but don't apologize to me. It's been a most interesting week."

Head tilted, she studied him. Her hand tightened around his before she slipped her arms through the robe. "Interesting, yes. That is a good word, too."

Alec kissed her forehead, tempted to climb back into bed with her and forget about Samuels, Hilton, and the rest of the world.

"I'll be back with more food and another pot of tea. Anything else?" She silently shook her head. At the door, he looked back.

Every day. He wanted this every day. But he tamped down that wish.

"Check on Alastor." Her voice caught, and he wondered what she wished in that moment.

"Yes, ma'am." He bowed and disappeared out the door.

He knew what he wanted. The problem was, after all his pushing her away, did she want the same?

NINETEEN

*O*nce more.

He couldn't get enough of her.

He doubted he'd ever get enough of her, no matter what he told himself or what he told her. Lies, all lies. Her fingers tangled in his hair, dislodging his hat, pulling him closer.

They hid in a small copse of trees less than an hour's walk along the main road into London and the mad dash they agreed they needed. The sooner they arrived at Horse Guards, the better for everyone. Even this early, the steady roll of carts filled the predawn air. Alec didn't care. He lifted her against the tree, shoving her skirts out of his way.

Alec knew he had to stop. Stop kissing down her neck, stop his fingers as they found her wet heat. Stop pretending this was less than it was.

"Yes," Yara whimpered, but he heard more in that wistful sound. In the desperate way her nails scraped along his scalp.

Once more. Just once more.

Fumbling with the fall on his trousers as she giggled against his mouth, Alec finally sank into her. One more time. Awkward as it was against the tree, her dagger heavy in her pocket, he didn't care.

Yara surrounded him. Her breath hot against his neck as her fingers found her nub. The way she tightened around him as her pleasure moved through her. Her teeth sank into his shoulder, and Alec growled, tightening his hold on her.

His knuckles scraped the tree, and he wasn't entirely certain his knees wouldn't give out, but he chased the euphoria Yara gave him.

Her fingers slowed on her nub as her lips pressed against the side of his neck. "Alec." She chanted his name, voice soft and commanding, and he grasped the sound as he did her body. Completely.

His orgasm raced up his spine, sharp and hot, and he only managed to withdraw at the last moment before his knees gave out. They crashed onto the wet leaves, breath knocked out of them both.

Breathless, sated, he blinked up at her. She laughed down at him, her face flushed, her eyes sparkling with joy. And that emotion he refused to name. The one neither uttered. But then her lips pressed against his, and he drowned in her essence.

They kissed slowly, as if they had all the time in the world. As if they shared a passionate tryst in the wood and nothing more. As if this wasn't one more time. She sighed against his lips, and he tasted her regret. Not for their early morning time together. But because once the sun rose, it'd be at an end.

"I was wrong." She pulled back and rested her head against his chest.

He found her hand and twined their fingers together, holding them against his heart. "Hmm?" he asked, his eyes closed against the rain that dripped from the leaves overhead. He kissed her fingertips. He didn't even mind the damp seeping into his trousers. "About what?"

"Sex against a tree."

His eyes shot open. "What?"

She sighed, a mix of utter contentment and humor, but she didn't move from her position. "I wasn't certain how that could possibly happen, but you proved me wrong."

Laughing, he closed his eyes again. One more moment together. Here, on the uneven ground, with a root poking his hip and the wet mud seeping through his trousers and Yara's pleasurable weight atop him. He never believed he'd be so torn between duty and a woman. But he'd never held a woman like Yara in his arms.

She tore every shred of constraint to hell. He'd crawl through glass, naked, for this woman.

That thought sobered him, settling in his bones like a vow. No matter how true it was, he shoved that feeling, and those words, deep inside him.

Alec opened his eyes and reluctantly sat up. He didn't know what, but something urged him to move, and now. Fear, perhaps. Fear of his feelings for Yara that pounded through his heart and crowded his tongue.

"We should go."

They were still bound by duty, and time's inexorable countdown moved toward zero. She held him close, as if she, too, knew that. She wrapped her arms and legs about him as they sat on the cold ground.

"Alastor is waiting," she whispered against his neck.

Her voice held that strong, even note she employed whenever she hid her true emotions. Alec wondered what she was hiding now. If he asked her outright, what would she tell him? Did he have the courage to tell her?

Kissing the top of her head, arms tightening around her once more, he knew the answer to both questions. All those words neither had the courage to speak.

Yes, he'd tell her.

They righted themselves, cleaning up the best they could

given their trek through the English countryside. She shrugged out of his jacket and smoothed the simple braid that hung down her back. In the gown and heavy cloak they'd bought from Mrs. Bagshaw, she looked small and fragile.

But he knew better. Yara stood strong and capable like the fiercest of warriors. The words danced on the tip of his tongue, but he swallowed them.

"This cloak is warm." She stepped from him, putting a distance he didn't want between them. He wasn't sure she wanted that distance either. The fact it was for the best meant nothing. "But what I wouldn't give for a lovely fire and a good, hot cup of coffee."

He took her hand, an automatic gesture now, and led her toward Alastor. The horse eyed them, as if he knew what they'd been up to. Considering their activities these previous days, Alec would bet he did. Luckily, Alastor wasn't telling.

"I doubt Horse Guards offers the sort of coffee you're used to." He helped her onto Alastor and took up the reins. "Where did you find it?"

"We import it." She settled in the saddle and lifted her hood, covering her hair from the elements and her face from any suspicious men looking to kill her. "Directly from the Egyptian growers. We have contacts the world over, and we purchase directly from them."

"What's the flavor? It's not sweet like sugar."

She wrinkled her nose. "We don't use sugar. We don't use anything from the Americas, where they have slaves."

Alec's eyebrows shot up. This puzzle piece slotted in cleanly with the rest of those he'd spent the last week fitting together.

"It's cardamom. Adds a bit of extra flavor to the coffee."

He nodded, not entirely certain he'd ever had cardamom before he tasted the coffee at her townhouse. Where he had first discovered he couldn't quite leave her.

Alec met her gaze, pushing their intimacies from his mind.

Or trying to. "Well, I'm certain there's a fire somewhere." He frowned, remembering his visits to Horse Guards. Fires, yes. Of course they had those—how else could they heat the place? "Does Hilton still have that cupboard for an office?"

"I've no idea. I've never been inside." She broke off, her teeth worrying her lips for a fraction of a beat. "He came to the house," she reminded him.

"Ah, yes." She had vaguely explained how she knew Hilton. It was still a bit convoluted for him, but then, he wasn't certain of all the players. She had a large extended family.

Alec shoved aside his jealousy and the loss of his own extended family and started for the road, where villagers already traveled into town with their market goods. He knew his next step: get Yara and her letter implicating Lieutenant Robert Samuels to Hilton at Horse Guards. After that? He had no idea.

THE DRIZZLING rain dripped from her hood, slipping down her cheek. Tired of the rain, the chill, and the constant uncertainty, she forced her mind away from her current situation.

Unfortunately, that meant remembering their more pleasurable interlude in the wood long before the sun rose.

Her skin tingled, and her nipples ached for his touch again. The pull of his teeth as his fingers slipped into her, tightening that pleasure until she cried out. Yara bit her lip, hands fisting around the reins. Not the path her thoughts needed to take. Definitely not.

Alastor shook his head and looked over his shoulder. "Sorry," she muttered, leaning across to pat him along his neck.

"What happened?" Alec peered up at her, squinting against the rain.

"I wasn't paying attention," she said truthfully. "Pulled too hard. I'm sorry, Alastor."

Alec frowned at her, as if he knew she lied. Well, stretched the truth. But telling him her exact thoughts wouldn't do either of them any good. Not as they followed the mostly silent crowd of farmers with their early vegetables and livestock. The crowd took up the entire road, and she wondered how any coach made its way in or out of London so early in the morning.

Adjusting her hood, she tried to keep the rain off her face. It was no use, but at least the material hid her. They needed to keep their identities secret, after all. Yara adjusted the hood again and kept her head down. Her khanjar lay awkwardly at her side. The pockets of her new gown weren't made for the length of it, but she hesitated to wear it openly. Discretion was key, after all.

"I owe him a long rest." Alec's quiet voice held a note of laughter. Perhaps his thoughts paralleled hers, and he, too, grasped for a distraction. "First I ignored him, then this." He shook his head, his hand giving her leg a gentle squeeze. "I'm sure he's angry with me still."

"He's been fantastic this last week," she agreed. She ran her hand along Alastor's neck again. Better that than reach for Alec. *No more touching.* She reminded herself of that. "But I'm still angry with you for ignoring him so long." She peered down at Alec, wanting his hand on her bare leg.

Her own thoughts didn't even shock her anymore. She craved his touch, his taste. The feel of him moving inside her, his body warm and large surrounding hers. Yara jerked away and looked ahead.

"Anything?" The word squeaked out far louder than she'd intended.

Focus, Yara. Focus on making it to Horse Guards, and Hilton, in one piece. She still wasn't certain that was the best destination. She'd rather head for Aunt Nadia's townhouse, where she had allies and resources to thwart whatever attack Samuels had planned.

Alec was set on heading directly for Horse Guards, but she wasn't completely convinced. Yes, Hilton had resources, too, and yes, it'd be easier for him to arrest Samuels then and there.

Yara liked having reinforcements.

"No." Something in his voice made her look down. He shook his head, rain dripping off his hat. "I don't like the pace," he said quietly.

"Hmm." She wanted to say more, but the road was crowded already, and, as neither of them had any idea what Samuels looked like, caution seemed the better option.

With Armstrong dying in her arms, Yara hadn't thought to ask about Samuels's features. She'd been far too busy comforting Armstrong and worrying about her next step. Had he seen her at Whitehawk? Or only when she met Armstrong in Preston? Did he even follow her now?

Alec insisted no one was following them, and Yara believed him. Wherever Samuels had been when he confronted Armstrong, he hadn't followed Alec and Yara as they raced from the field. Yara believed that, but she worried.

She pressed cold, wet fingers against her eyes. This was not her best plan. Not by a long shot.

"Can you see ahead?" He peered up at her again. "Any opening?"

She looked, but the predawn remained gloomy, the shadows moving along the road in monotonous precision. The sun peeked above the horizon, just barely lighting the road, but with the clouds and rain, she doubted it'd brighten the day.

"No, not without detouring off the road and around the crowd." She frowned, picturing that scenario. "In the darkness, I'd not wish risking Alastor's footing."

Which was why they'd stopped last night; the soggy ground muddled their progress and made every step treacherous. Two long ditches paralleled the main road, and one wrong step meant disaster.

Stopping had nothing at all to do with being unable to keep their hands off each other. Nothing whatsoever.

She rubbed her nose, which was cold and wet, and tried to think of a plan. One that would break them free from this crowd, keep them all in one piece, and didn't require any more fantasies about Alec's hands.

"It's still another half hour or so." He didn't sound happy as he urged Alastor faster despite the cart ahead of them, which they quickly passed. "Once inside the city, we'll ride."

Arousal shot down her spine. Yara swallowed hard, suddenly flushed despite the cold spring morning. She might never get enough of his arms around her, his hard chest pressed against her.

"Not a great way to stay undetected," she reminded him. She sighed and added, "Not that you could remain undetected." She grinned. "You are quite tall. And muscular."

Tall, handsome, distinguished with his sharp features. His walk, confident and sure, ate the distance between him and his target. She could watch him walk for hours on end, especially with the way his trousers hugged his thighs. She very much enjoyed his muscular thighs.

Alec snorted and shrugged. "I'm more concerned with survival at the moment." He met her gaze, his blue eyes grave in the uncertain predawn light. "Yours."

They walked in silence for a while. She tried to look around in the growing light but couldn't see much beyond her hood. Still, unease danced over her skin. As much as she wanted to attribute it to Alec's presence, and his constant touch on her leg, she could not.

The cold sensation chilling her to the bone was far from the pleasant warmth she felt around him. No, this was something telling her that making their way to Horse Guards was a mistake. Samuels knew who they were—who she was, at least.

As much as Alec's arguments for doing just that made sense, Yara had a feeling he was wrong.

"Where does she live?" His voice startled her, and she frowned down at him.

He glanced up, met her gaze, and nodded. Yara waited as they passed another cart. A dozing boy leaned against the rear gate as they made their plodding way into town. Even Alastor danced anxiously, hurrying along the road, snorting and tossing his head.

"Who?" But she knew.

Alec peered up at her from beneath the brim of his hat. He'd come to the same conclusion, then. "Aye." He nodded, as if they'd spoken of this new plan aloud.

"Cavendish Square." She barely heard her own words, but he had.

"Let's go." He urged Alastor faster, and long before they crossed into London, Alec swung up behind her.

His strong arms settled around her, warm and comforting. His solid presence warmed her back, and once more she found herself leaning against him despite her best intentions.

"Is anyone following us?" she asked.

"I don't think so, but it's impossible to tell." She felt him shake his head, and his arm tightened around her. "They'd have had to wait at this specific road and post sentries at all hours."

"It is the main road from Brighton." It was a conversation they'd already had. And she'd agreed with him that this road was the fastest way into London and the best way across town.

"I won't let anything happen to you, Yara."

"I know," she said, hoping her tone conveyed all she could not speak.

His promise settled in her heart and made her want things she knew she couldn't have. Perhaps retiring to a country cottage was her best option. Isolated, just her and her animals and no further heartbreak. Swallowing her rage, she reminded herself she'd agreed to a simple night of pleasure.

Their simple night had turned into multiple nights. And mornings. And afternoons. There was nothing simple about the passion between them. It burned hot, scorching her soul and binding her to him. But he didn't feel the same, and her heart physically ached from that knowledge.

"I have a plan." His voice rumbled against her ear, shivering over her skin.

"Am I going to like it?"

He chuckled and held her tighter as they made their way past the carts and into London proper. "I have a feeling you're going to hate it."

"Then why are you suggesting it?" Her hands settled on his around Alastor's reins. His gloved hands covered hers, warming them as best he could.

She missed her riding gloves—any gloves, for that matter. Those she'd worn to the races nearly a week ago had been stained with grass, mud, and Armstrong's blood. She couldn't remember what happened to them, but they were hardly gloves for an English spring. She hadn't thought to ask Mrs. Bagshaw about a new pair, too preoccupied with exploring this passion with Alec.

"Because I have nothing else." He wrapped himself tighter around her, warming her, protecting her. "And this is the best way I can think of that keeps you safe."

Yara didn't even care if his touch was more for show than anything. A way they could speak of this new plan without being overheard. She still yearned for a future with him. Foolish girl.

"All right." She sighed but didn't move. "I'm listening."

TWENTY

Alec stopped two blocks from Yara's aunt's house near Cavendish Square. He dismounted, caught Yara, and didn't care who might be up at this early hour. He kissed her. One hand holding Alastor's reins, the other cupping the back of her head, he kissed her as if it were their last.

He didn't think on that, just poured every word he couldn't say into that kiss. Promises he couldn't make; oaths he'd spend a lifetime keeping with her. How could he ask her to spend her life with him when he'd made a mess of the one he had? He had bridges to mend first. Alec might have been a rogue, but he couldn't leave her without one final promise.

Breaking apart, breathing heavy, he met her gaze. "One hour."

She nodded, her cheeks flushed. "I'll be there."

"Be careful. Don't bring the armada." His lips quirked up at the face she made, scrunching her nose but nodding. He stepped back. The words were there. Right there. "Be careful," he repeated. He swung back into the saddle and held her gaze. "I love you."

Her eyes widened, and her mouth fell open. "What?"

He wheeled Alastor around and raced for Horse Guards. Alec didn't look back, but the image of Yara's stunned face would remain with him for the rest of his life. He had no idea what happened next, nor what sort of reception she'd give him at their next meeting. But he looked forward to it.

It wasn't far to Horse Guards from Cavendish Square—not quite two miles, though he'd never ridden it. This early in the morning, he easily traversed the distance.

He thought of nothing save Yara's blank expression in the face of his confession.

Heart still thundering in his chest at his admission, he boldly strode into Horse Guards, boots clacking on the stone, great-coat flapping around him. He knew what he looked like: taller than average, travel-worn, determined as he crossed the floor, ignoring those who tried to stop him.

Even at this hour, the building teemed with people. War didn't sleep.

He knew where Hilton's office sat, the small cupboard they'd stuffed him into when they finally admitted they needed his particular expertise. Alec never knew if they'd gifted him the hole in the wall because he maneuvered spies like chess pieces, or because they truly had run out of space.

As a betting man, he bet on both.

He didn't knock, just pushed open the door. No one followed him now. None of the military bureaucracy tried to stop him. Either that meant Samuels didn't know him and his reasons for being here, or the man wasn't here.

But Alec didn't believe that. Samuels was here, waiting. Spying on Hilton's meetings somehow or another.

Yara was safe. She was with family, allies. He didn't want her to be alone, no matter how excellent she was with her dagger. The vise around his heart tightened, but Alec stayed with the plan.

"Are you alone?" he asked Hilton, who looked as exhausted as Alec had ever seen him.

"Von Stein?" Hilton shook his head and ran a hand down his face. "What are you doing here?" His eyes narrowed. "Are *you* alone?"

Hilton's tone set off a thousand warning bells in Alec's head, but he gave a curt nod. He knew. Yara had been right when she said her family would contact Hilton. "Are you?"

Spreading his hands wide, Hilton gestured around his cramped office. Every surface overflowed with papers. "Where is Miss Conrad?"

Hilton knew they'd escaped Whitehawk together. Alec nodded, a brief movement of his head, then stilled.

Were those footsteps? Alec moved a half step closer to the door and listened hard. Not Yara's, not yet. She wouldn't come alone, which eased that vise around his heart, but not enough that he could relax. When she did arrive, he knew Samuels would as well. This ruse, his stalling, all of it, was solely to protect her.

"I'm afraid Miss Conrad fell off my horse two days past." He hadn't been convinced about that particular part of their lie, but Yara had insisted Hilton would understand.

For one precious moment, Hilton's face was comically blank. His eyebrows shot up, and then his eyes immediately narrowed. "Yara...fell off a horse?" he repeated slowly.

Ah, yes, he clearly knew Yara and her horse-riding capabilities. Half expecting a drawn pistol from wherever secret hiding place Hilton kept one, Alec paused. When no shot came forth, he nodded, keeping his face blank.

"I'm afraid so. She disappeared into a river." An embellishment he probably needn't add.

"I see." Hilton silently closed the distance between them. Alec eyed him warily, braced for an attack, but apparently Hilton trusted him. "And the papers she carried?"

Alec reached into his pocket. One door was against his back, and he blocked it fairly well. No windows for anyone to spy on the spymaster. But he'd bet his fortune that a peephole of some sort existed. Hilton must've known or suspected it, too, because he angled himself in front of Alec. He handed Hilton the note Yara had scribbled, the materials borrowed from one of the shop owners as they raced through town.

Lieutenant Robert Samuels

"Lost with her," Alec lied, but he already knew Hilton didn't care about his answer. He had what he needed.

"I'm sorry about Miss Conrad," Hilton said, stepping back. The paper disappeared into a pocket with a flick of his wrist. "I'll pass my condolences on to her family."

Alec listened again but heard only the distant shuffle of people in the halls. He had no idea if this plan would even work. Samuels might not have waited for them here, or he might've overheard Alec telling Hilton about Yara and left, thinking himself safe.

Though one way or another, Hilton would've learned of Yara's return. Samuels would've followed him, which would've been easiest. No one else need enter this calculation—he could spy on Hilton from within Horse Guards and no doubt learn more secrets than he could in a year at Preston. Then he could've easily followed Hilton when Yara returned.

It made sense. Alec knew it, which was why he'd insisted on this plan.

"I'll be off." He eased a step back. "*The Argo* sails at the end of the week. I'll be in Calais if you need me."

Hilton's eyes narrowed, and his cheek ticked up. Alec had never seen such an expression on the man. Usually reserved and collected no matter the circumstances, he never let his emotions break through.

Alec braced for that pistol shot again. Then again, Hilton had heard of *The Argo* and its murky fate. Alec hadn't told him specifically, but Hilton would have heard, either through proper customs channels when they returned on another ship or some other way. Knowing Hilton, most likely both.

Had it been an hour? Yara should've been right behind him. He'd drop her off, she'd find her aunt, explain what was happening, and meet him here. She'd be safe with plenty of others surrounding and protecting her.

Except him. His palms became clammy with the distance. With not knowing what happened.

"I'll meet up with you before then," Hilton said, his words dismissive. He didn't move toward his desk, just stayed still, watching.

Alec waited, taking another half step toward the door and listening. "Good." Nothing yet. And he had a feeling he'd hear Yara and her entourage when they entered. "I've spent far too long on land; I need to get back out...."

His last words trailed off. Ah, yes, there she was. A dark, fierce grin spread over his face. Hilton must've picked up on it, because he'd already stepped for the door.

Head held high, her bedraggled cloak trailing behind her, Yara walked down the hallway as if she owned the building. Behind her, two couples followed, each looking as fierce as she. And Godred. Alec blinked. What in blazes was he doing at the townhouse? Men scattered out of their way, some scowling and muttering, but none trying to stop her.

Alec stepped fully into the hall and watched. He had no interest in the everyday officers here. Only one person concerned him. Hilton walked beside him as he stalked down the long hall toward Yara.

One man actually offered a semblance of a bow. Alec wondered who he was and which member of her entourage deserved such respect.

"Ah, I see Mr. von Stein has slightly exaggerated," Hilton said.

Alec met Yara's gaze. They stood only a few feet apart, close enough he could touch her. Instead, he curled his hands into fists at his sides. She raised her chin, lips tilting upward. Her dark eyes met his with a warmth he tried very hard not to think too much about.

"Only slightly," she acknowledged with another partial smile. To him, she asked, "Anything?"

He shook his head. "Let's get into his office." His gaze flicked around the hall, where even more people watched now. "We're too exposed here."

Yara stepped beside him, and he rested his hand on the small of her back. He only realized the intimacy of it after the fact. Pistols at dawn—so be it. Not that they'd be necessary. He wouldn't ruin her reputation.

Pushing those thoughts aside, he ushered her inside Hilton's cramped space. Somehow, all eight of them fit in here, though Alec couldn't have explained how. Standing behind her, he gripped his own dagger and waited.

<hr />

"Fell off your horse?" Hilton cracked a small grin. "As stories went, it was believable."

Behind Yara, her father snorted in disbelief, but she didn't turn. She hadn't gotten round to that part of their plan. There'd been a lot of rushed explanations in the cramped carriage ride.

"We needed a story you'd know was false but Samuels would believe."

She looked over her shoulder, but Alec shook his head. No Samuels sighting yet, which concerned her.

Yara produced the letter from Sergeant Armstrong she'd kept safe and dry during their trek across Southern England as well as the packet her mother had, indeed, packed up. She handed Major Blackwood's missives over first, which Hilton added to the precarious pile atop his desk. She carefully unfolded the bloodstained one from Sergeant Armstrong and handed him that one as well.

"Armstrong lists his proof for suspecting Samuels," she told Hilton. She didn't lower her voice; the entire point of her entrance was to capture Samuels. "He questions Blackwood's loyalty but offers no proof of anything else. He also lists several others with questionable gambling debts, though I don't think that alone makes one a French spy. Merely unlucky."

Alec's strong presence relaxed her. She hadn't realized how much she relied upon him these last days. With only the two of them—well, and Alastor—it'd been simple to do so. Even with her family there and ready to protect her, Yara found herself standing near Alec.

"And Samuels?" Hilton asked, skimming the letter.

She didn't reach for Alec, though with him so close that temptation beckoned. Instead, she curled her hands into fists and did her duty.

"Gambling debts, mostly," she continued. "Samuels has been disciplined numerous times, demoted." She slipped a hand into her pocket, where her khanjar lay. Now that the end was near, she couldn't help but expect the worst.

"I'm surprised he wasn't drummed out," Hilton muttered.

Yara suppressed a grin. Alec had said the same thing, but with more colorful wording. "According to Armstrong's list, the French paid well enough that he did what he could to stay."

A commotion outside the office stilled her tongue. Khanjar in hand, she slowly turned. The entire room chilled, everyone now armed in the too-tight space.

"Yara," Alec whispered, taking her left arm.

"I hear it." But she didn't know what *it* was.

"Bomb."

Yara's gaze whipped to Uncle James, Aunt Nadia's army colonel husband. He spat the word, grabbed Nadia, and pushed her out the door. Before Yara could take more than a step, Alec physically lifted her and rushed out behind them. He flattened her against the wall, covering her body with his.

In the space between Alec lifting her and the device going off, Yara closed her eyes and reveled in this one final touch. She still didn't know what to make of his confession on the street corner after that fantastic kiss.

When she saw him again in the hallway, his expression gave away nothing. Of course, this certainly wasn't the place for such conversations, but she'd hoped for something. A look, a touch, a whispered word of affection. Now, with his large body pressed against hers, his arm across her chest, holding her as if he'd never let go, Yara allowed herself a moment.

Just one. Just long enough to hope for a future.

She expected a loud sound, a rush of air. She'd never been so near such an explosion before, and she braced herself against the wall and Alec's body. The explosion shook the ground and the wall, but Alec remained immobile.

Rubble rained down on them, and dust and smoke thickened the air. Coughing, she swiped at her eyes, ready for an attack. If Samuels had gone to all the trouble of setting such an incendiary device, he was also prepared for an attack to finish the job.

"You all right?" Alec asked, pulling back.

His stormy gaze, worried and angry, held hers. She nodded, coughed once, and stepped away from him. "Yes. Alec—" Her hand reached for his, squeezing it in that uncertain moment.

He held her gaze another moment, then straightened. "You see him?"

Anger vibrated through his voice, low and piercing in the sudden cacophony of sound as the rest of the building realized what had happened. With so many soldiers swarming their location, it'd be more difficult to find Samuels.

She turned, back against the wall, and peered through the dust and debris. "No."

"Yara?" Her father's voice pierced the hallway, and she turned toward the sound.

"I'm all right, Papa."

"Keep everyone back," Alec growled. "Not yet."

She'd explained their plan, such as it was, on the way from Cavendish Square. Her parents and aunt and uncle, and even Godred, knew what she expected here. They were prepared.

Then it happened. A figure emerged from the chaos, wielding a pistol and a knife.

Yara readied herself. Alec stood by her side, snarling at the man, ready to take him down with a single swipe.

"Stupid hell-born bitch," the man snarled.

"Samuels, I presume?" she asked coolly. "I'd say it's a pleasure, but I don't lie."

Except to herself. Except about her feelings for Alec. But that wasn't the point.

"I'm going to kill you," Alec said evenly. The cold words startled Samuels, who glanced at him.

That was his mistake. He took his eyes off Yara, angered Alec even more, and didn't know who to strike first. But Alec did. He disregarded his knife and tackled Samuels, who was clearly more of the sneaky, spying sort than the fighting sort.

They crashed against the ground, shaking already precarious walls. Yara jumped out of the way, keeping to the side and searching for any others who Samuels might've brought with him. Her family kept the rest of the building at bay, and Hilton disappeared into whatever remained of his office.

The fight didn't last long. Alec unleashed his fury on Samuels, who tried to fight back but was no match.

"Alec." Yara eased around them, getting his attention. She wasn't foolish enough to touch him or interfere in any way— that would surely only see her harmed. Fall in love with him? Yes. Get between him and his opponent? No one was that foolish. "Alec!"

Fist raised for another punch, he stopped, pulled back. Samuels, clearly still alive, breathed heavily as he lay on the ground. She searched for a quip about how this was anticlimactic, or something about her hero. But words dried up when he met her gaze.

"You're unharmed?" He stood looming over her, hands cupping her shoulders. Then he let her go and flexed his fingers, anger still coating his words. "He didn't touch you?"

"I'm unharmed." She watched him wipe his knuckles on trousers that had definitely seen better days.

She had so much she wanted to say. She wanted to thank him, ask if he meant his words on the street corner. Figure out what happened now. She didn't know what came next and didn't want to ask.

"Yara!" Her father's voice cut through the hallway.

With far too many words left unsaid, she turned. "I'm fine," she reassured her parents. "Completely unharmed." Physically.

From the corner of her eye, she saw Alec haul Samuels up by his shirt and drag him down the hall into Hilton's office, where he dropped him into a corner. Samuels didn't even open his eyes, just collapsed onto his side.

"Let's help Hilton before he loses years of work." Her father's blue-green eyes narrowed at her. "And then perhaps you can introduce us?"

She offered a small smile that felt as artificial as it probably looked. Introduce Alec as what? Her defender? An escort who saw her from Brighton? Her lover? Former lover?

Probably not that. Though by the way everyone looked at her, she figured they already knew.

"How did you know it was an incendiary device?" Alec asked as they scooped piles and piles of papers from the office onto a wheelbarrow someone had found.

"Oh, he's very good at such things." Aunt Nadia winked up at her husband, who merely grinned back.

It hadn't been a large bomb; it certainly wasn't large enough to take down Horse Guards. One wall partially collapsed, and a small fire smoldered in Hilton's office. From his muttering, it sounded as if he'd lost several piles of paper, though they managed to cart out the rest before the fire spread.

The buckets of dirt they threw onto the fire added to the dust that was already heavy in the air, and Yara was grateful when she and Alec stepped outside. They stood beside Alastor, who looked tired from their days-long adventure.

"Yes, you're a good boy." She didn't look at Alec as she petted the horse. "You'll see he's taken care of? You can use our stables; he deserves nothing but the best."

She didn't mention Alec's stables or the fact they'd returned to London. There was much she didn't mention, but Yara didn't know how to begin.

"I won't ignore him again," he promised. "I learned my lesson. We'll be heading home."

"Will you return to the townhouse?" she asked. The sky had brightened. A strange sort of hazy day had dawned while they'd dealt with Samuels. "Breakfast maybe?"

Breakfast, meeting her family, one more moment together. She swallowed those words and kept her gaze on Alastor. Once more, Yara pushed her emotions down, deep inside her heart, where she kept all her disappointments.

Except he had said he loved her...where did that leave them?

"I don't think so." Alec looked left, where a man with an impressive mustache and an even more impressive scowl stood with his arms crossed. Godred, his friend. "I think I've put this off long enough."

Godred sauntered over, his gaze not on Alec but on her. "Are you going to introduce us, Alec?"

Alec sighed, but a thread of humor returned. "Godred, this is Miss Yara Conrad. Yara, my first mate, closest friend, and sometimes valet, Cillian Godred."

"We met briefly, at Aunt Nadia's." Yara nodded, smiling slightly. It was all she could manage. "A pleasure. I've heard all about you, I'm afraid."

Godred laughed, the smile splitting his face. He slapped Alec on the back. "Good." He leaned in and said conspiratorially, "Your mother is terrifying." He looked toward the carriage, where her family waited. "I think I'm in love. Any chance she'll leave her husband and run away with me?"

Shocked, Yara snickered. "I doubt it, but it can't hurt to ask."

"Excellent!" He clasped his hands together, grinned, and sauntered back toward the carriage and her mother. Her family pretended they didn't watch her and Alec.

"He was at your aunt's townhouse?"

"Apparently, after the chaos at the racecourse, Mama found him at your townhouse. They traveled back here, sent for my father, and planned to give us until the end of tomorrow before they sent out a search party—or possibly only Micki, I'm not sure. Everything was very rushed after you dropped me off."

After that kiss.

"Ah." He cleared his throat. "I'm sure I'll get an earful then."

They stood in awkward silence for another long moment. Yara thought she might explode. And when he swung onto Alastor, she did.

"That's it, then?" She glared up at him. Tired, cold, hungry, exhausted. And so very confused. "You'll just leave?"

"Yara, I—"

"You what? Didn't mean what you said?"

He opened his mouth, snapped it closed, and shook his head. "I meant every word."

Oh. Her heart raced, and all those hopes she dared not look at too closely soared with his words.

"Then why are you leaving?"

TWENTY-ONE

"You still deserve better." Alec meant it, even as his heart told him to shut up and kiss her. He held up a hand, forestalling her obvious protests. This wasn't the place for such a conversation.

Also, if he remained in arm's reach, he knew he'd do something scandalous.

Kiss her, propose in the middle of Horse Guards, all of the above.

"I need to make things right with the crew. See where I stand with them."

He had a lot of amends to make. Godred, the crew of *The Argo*, Alastor. Christian and Sabine. He held her gaze. Yara. He owed her so much. She'd shown him so many things this past week, he knew he'd never be able to properly thank her for everything.

Or tell her all he wanted to say.

"All right." She offered a slow nod. Her voice had cooled, that same tone she used whenever she hid her emotions. "I'm not waiting around for you."

Her words hit him like a punch. Alec swallowed and called

himself all kinds of a fool. But he knew what needed doing, and he'd put it off for far too long.

He nearly told her she shouldn't wait for him, but at the last moment he swallowed those words. He wasn't that stupid. "I have a lot of people to apologize to. And your family needs to know you're all right."

"I see," she said in that same tone that ripped out pieces of his soul. "You're leaving for me."

"No." Damn it, this wasn't how he wanted this conversation to go. Him on Alastor, her standing before him, a horde of onlookers gaping, as if this were the latest drama at Drury Lane. "I'm leaving now because your family is worried, and I have to find what's left of mine and make things right. Whatever happened with my crew, I owe them my presence. No more running."

She held his gaze in the hazy morning light. People streamed in and out of Horse Guards as if no incendiary device had exploded and nothing unusual had happened. The town was waking up, calls from the street vendors echoing even here. And still Yara watched him.

Alec held her gaze, willing her to understand.

Finally, she nodded again, her face softening. "For the record, I love you, too."

With that, she turned and walked away. Mouth agape, Alec watched her and thought he might be the most foolish man on the planet. Letting the beautiful woman he loved, and who loved him, walk away after such a revelation.

He nearly leaped off Alastor and raced after her. His life was a mess, and now that Yara was safe, fixing it was his first priority.

"Let's go home, Alastor."

He turned his horse in the direction of his own townhouse on Harley Street. Not as fashionable as Cavendish Square but still highly respectable. Alastor, however, refused. Alec didn't look behind him to where Yara stood. No doubt she laughed at Alastor's antics. Sighing, Alec leaned over and patted the horse's neck.

"I know." He scratched between Alastor's ears and decided he wasn't above bribery. He'd bet Alastor wasn't above taking a bribe, either. "I know. I have a lot to atone for. Give me a couple days, and we'll see her again."

Alastor shook his head and snorted.

"You need a nice rubdown, I agree. And all the apples you can eat. Carrots, too. What else? A good rest, I promise, but not too long." Alec shook his head though the horse couldn't see him. "Not like before. No, a good exercise after this last week of mud and rain."

Alastor looked over his shoulder, as if weighing Alec's promises. Eventually, he moved. Alec didn't look back, though he knew Godred would give him an earful for abandoning Yara.

With every step Alastor took, he cursed himself.

Maybe not a couple days. He already missed her smile, the way she fit in his arms. The warmth of her kiss first thing in the morning and the sigh of her breath along his cheek as they settled into sleep.

Urging Alastor faster, he turned onto his street and planned his next step. He all but leaped off of Alastor, raced up the steps, and startled his butler into his next life.

"Sir?"

"Thomas." Alec nodded at the man, who gaped at him in surprise. "I'll need a bath, a fresh set of clothes, and the locations of my crew." He paused, one foot on the first step. "And make sure Alastor is pampered—apples, carrots, a good rubdown. All of it. It's been a long couple of days."

Mind racing, he detoured for the kitchens. Ignoring the surprised looks of the staff, he snagged a chunk of bread and a bit of cheese, then took the steps two at a time. Willoughby, his valet, stood at the door. His real valet though Godred made an excellent stand-in for a man more suited to life at sea. Willoughby now wore such a severe frown, he wondered if he should add the man to his ever-expanding list of apologies. Probably.

"I see you aren't dead," Willoughby said with a haughty sniff.

"Ah." Alec cleared his throat. "No." He offered a small smile and shrugged. "Not dead." He eyed the tub and wondered if it contained freezing water in retaliation. "Is that a hot bath?"

Willoughby sniffed again. "I debated a freezing one."

Alec stripped off his muddy, wet clothing and dipped a finger into the hot water. Perfect. Lowering himself, he eyed his valet. "I owe you an apology, too. For disappearing like that." The hot water seeped into his muscles, and he sighed.

If Yara was still speaking to him after all this, he definitely planned on taking a hot bath with her. Perhaps he'd have a larger tub installed in the master suite so they could comfortably enjoy such luxuries.

One step at a time. Hadn't she told him that?

"You worried the household," Willoughby said, lifting a bucket of water. Alec eyed it and braced himself. Just in case. But the warm water cascaded over him rather than the ice bath he anticipated. "If it wasn't for Godred, we wouldn't have even known where you disappeared to. Or if you were still alive."

Alec sat upright as he scrubbed his hair. Oh, but it felt amazing to clean away two days' worth of mud and sweat and rain. "Godred?"

He hadn't even thought about that. Of course his friend would tell the household staff where he'd gone. Probably told the crew, too, which meant none of them had tracked him down. He'd told Yara that, but it hadn't fully sunk in until now. Alec didn't know what to make of that, but this wasn't about him.

"I do apologize." He turned toward Willoughby. His valet

looked unconvinced. "It won't happen again. I have amends to make, things to sort out."

Alec liked and respected Willoughby, but only Yara knew his reasons for disappearing into Brighton. He supposed he'd need to tell the crew and their families what happened, or a portion of it, but the anger and melancholy he'd felt these last months, he'd share with Yara and Yara alone.

He'd share his guilt; they'd expect that. And he'd apologize for not being there when they needed him most. Everything else, he'd share only with Yara, who understood him far better than he had any right to expect.

"Ah, there you are." Godred strode in as if he owned the place.

Alec merely rolled his eyes. "I thought you returned to Cavendish Square with the others."

"I did." He eyed Alec, who braced for a tongue-lashing about abandoning Yara. "Quite the family, that is. I admire them."

"Thinking of transferring to Conrad Shipping?" Alec raised an eyebrow and braced once more as Willoughby poured another bucket of water over him. Still warm. Alec relaxed.

"Trying to convince the lovely and utterly terrifying Lady Conrad to run away with me." Godred sighed dramatically. "Alas, she seems devoted to her husband. More's the pity. You should see her with that dagger." His eyes widened with envy. "A true thing of beauty." He stopped and scowled. "But you!" He jabbed a finger at Alec, who expected it, even naked in the bath.

"What happened after the racecourse?"

"You mean after you and Miss Conrad disappeared?" One of Godred's red eyebrows raised, but he didn't smirk. No, he looked dead serious.

"As I'm sure you've heard, there was a mob. And some sort of explosion." Alec never discovered what that was from. Rising, he dried off. "Do you know what happened?"

"Munitions explosion I think, but we didn't investigate. We left immediately after Lady Conrad arrived."

"We escaped," Alec said, hurrying the conversation along. He had far too much on his agenda today for dawdling. "It was a madhouse, and I was concerned for her safety."

"Aye. Bennett and Una explained as much. Said you and she disappeared, and they expected you at the townhouse."

"There were complications." Alec toweled off his hair and mentally urged Godred to get to his point. He wouldn't share anything about Yara's mission in Brighton, even if Godred had been there at Horse Guards. "Go on."

"Aye, well, Lady Conrad seemed to know about those *complications*. By the time she arrived—"

"How?"

"How what? Did she arrive?" Godred frowned. "Carriage, of course."

Alec rolled his eyes. "How did you know something happened? How did Lady Conrad find you?"

"Cap," Godred sighed, his annoyance clear. "Everyone knew what happened at Whitehawk. Within an hour, news spread over Brighton. The servants told me, but before I could head for the Conrad townhouse, hoping you were there with Miss Conrad, Lady Conrad organized everyone like a military commander. Within another hour, we left."

"You along with them." Alec nodded and dressed, reveling in clothes that fit him, clothes he didn't worry he'd rip if he stretched too far. And they were clean—he'd never fully appreciated that before. Pausing, he narrowed his eyes at Godred. "How did you convince them to let you travel with them?"

Godred looked sheepish. "Lady Conrad, have I mentioned she's beautifully terrifying?" Alec nodded, not at all certain where this was headed. "She held me at dagger point. Threatened to skin me alive if I didn't come, and I believed her." He rubbed his neck. "Still do."

Alec opened his mouth, then snapped it closed. Laughing, he ran his fingers through his damp hair.

"It's not funny," Godred muttered.

He'd seen Yara use her dagger with deadly precision. Not only at their first meeting in the alleyway, where she'd pretended to be her friend, but also on the road. Those highwaymen would never forget her anger or her dagger.

"What did you say that convinced her otherwise?" Alec dreaded Godred's next words, but he needed to know what he was up against. He already half thought Yara would hold him at knifepoint when he found her, but now he wondered if she was the only person he needed to worry about.

Pistols at dawn, indeed.

"Well…" Godred drew out the word and scratched at his cheek. "I said something along the lines of how honorable you were, and possibly how infatuated you were with Miss Conrad. Then she muttered something about how Gretna Green was the more preferable problem, which I still don't understand."

Alec laughed again. He shrugged on his jacket and laughed and laughed.

"Oh, sure, laugh at my help." Godred scowled. "I risked life and limb for you—quite literally! And this is the thanks I get."

Alec crossed the room and slapped his friend on the back. "I'm grateful." He paused and said more softly, "I am, Cillian." Godred winced at his given name. He preferred Godred, as it came from an old Irish king. "I don't deserve all you've done for me, not only in the last week, but these last months. And I'm grateful."

"Well." Godred sniffed somewhat dramatically. "You're welcome."

Alec held his friend's gaze another moment, then turned to his valet. "Willoughby, I'm not sure when I'll be back. You have the list of the crew's locations?"

"Thomas will have it when you leave," his valet promised.

"Excellent." Alec didn't appreciate his staff as much as he ought, and he vowed to remedy that. "Thank you." Turning back, he gestured Godred out the door. "Tell me the rest while we walk."

Godred didn't say anything as they walked down the stairs. Just as well. Alec needed a moment to plan his visits. Learning what happened while he and Yara traveled from Brighton was all well and good, but he had apologies to make and bridges to mend. He wasn't certain how one went about mending bridges that had been thoroughly burned to the ground, but Alec was determined.

"Lady Conrad seemed to think Miss Conrad would head toward London, and no one argued with her." Godred eyed Alec as he turned toward the kitchens. "What are you doing?"

"Eating," Alec said, deflecting while he organized his thoughts. "Haven't had anything since last night. That cheese didn't count."

"Don't be obtuse."

"I have a lot planned," he admitted as they rounded the corner. Alec nodded at Cook, who silently set a plate before him.

"And do any of your plans have anything to do with the lovely Miss Conrad?" Godred sat beside him and snagged a chunk of bread and a piece of cheese. He wiggled his eyebrows. "A courtship, perhaps?"

"Godred," Alec warned. "Don't say a word about my future wife."

The room stilled, and Godred choked. "Courtship." He pounded his chest. "Courtship, I said." He grabbed a tankard and swallowed down its contents. "*Courtship*. It's been a bloody week!"

Smiling around his bite of meat, Alec raised his own tankard in salute. "First things first. The crew. Have you heard from them?"

Scowling, Godred finished his roll. "You mean all that correspondence you ignored?"

"Anything." He looked at his plate and counted off the names of his dead crew. *Peter. Johnnie. Elis. Jasper. Davey. Noah. Rickey. Giles.* He hadn't seen a letter from anyone, but he also hadn't thoroughly looked through the pile.

"Nothing," Godred admitted quietly. "I'm sorry, Cap."

He'd expected that. He had. It only made him all the more determined. He finished his meal, thanked the kitchen staff, and turned for the foyer.

"Thomas." He nodded at the butler.

"Your list, sir."

Alec took the list of his crew and their last known addresses. "Thank you."

First on his list, Chloe Jones.

"What are you going to do if they won't talk with you?" Godred asked as Alec shrugged on his coat.

The weather had not improved, but his mood had. Amazing what a bath and a good meal could do for one's constitution. And a plan. Yara liked a plan, and he didn't blame her. Figuring out his next step and seeing it through settled something in him.

Standing in the foyer, just he and Godred, Alec admitted his fear. "I don't know," he said quietly. "I abandoned them when we needed each other the most."

"What happened was an accident, Alec." Godred repeated the words he'd said only a week ago.

A week. Alec shook his head at that. So much had happened in that time, it felt like a year. He looked out the door, watching the drizzle mist in the air. Was Yara warm by a fire? Had she enjoyed a hot bath as well, a cup of Egyptian coffee? Micki would be by her feet, of course.

He stepped for the open door, determined to see this through. For himself, for Yara, for their future. Most of all, for the friends he left behind.

"An accident, I know," he agreed. "But you were right. We needed each other afterward."

The crushing guilt had nearly destroyed him. Yara understood, but she wasn't here. Still, seeing his crew, his family, was worth the time he'd spend away from her. Even if they never sailed together again—even if he never sailed again—he needed to make these amends in order to take that next step.

The one he wanted with Yara. A future, marriage. A family, perhaps, though he'd honestly never thought of such a thing. With Yara? He'd take it all and then some.

Would his crew, the family of those lost, understand? Understand his own grief? He'd said everyone grieved differently, but would they know how deeply he mourned the loss of his men? The loss of the lives they'd all built? The laughter and joy and family he treasured?

Only one way to find out.

Alec stepped out the door.

TWENTY-TWO

It took Alec ten days. He wasn't certain what he'd expected, how quickly he thought he could meet with the crew he'd abandoned four months ago. He couldn't meet with everyone, apologize, and plan for their future in a single day. That wasn't feasible.

What had Yara said about his expectations? Something about being reasonable, but Alec had no idea what his expectations had been. So he had nothing, reasonable or otherwise, to go on.

He'd managed it. Mostly.

He didn't find his crew and make amends because of Yara, but if it hadn't been for her, he wasn't certain he'd have taken that first step.

"Come on, Alastor." He urged the horse faster. "We're almost there."

Every day away from Yara made him want her more.

He didn't know what he expected there, either. The fierce love he had for her to fade? That the memory of her would simply disappear, and he'd get on with his life as if their week together had never happened?

Neither one of those things was possible.

The sun shone down on him from high in the sky as he outpaced his carriage and Godred, who was most likely sleeping inside. The stable lad at the coaching inn they'd stopped at late last eve had eyed Alec. The boy clearly found him wanting, but he begrudgingly offered directions. They left hours before dawn.

As if Alastor knew they were nearing Yara, he picked up even more speed. They turned onto the manor's drive, and he admitted he was impressed with its length.

Finally, he rounded a corner, and Nelda Hall spread out before him.

Alec didn't examine it; he didn't care what it looked like or how large it stood. Now that he'd arrived, all he cared about was finding Yara. He debated where she might be midmorning, whether he should visit the stables first or the second barn he spotted in the near distance.

He needn't worry about finding Yara. Given the lookouts the manor possessed, by the time he dismounted Alastor, the court-yard was crowded with people, all eyeing him as if he'd appeared from the depths of Hades. Alec patted Alastor's side in silent reassurance.

Or perhaps he reassured himself.

"Ah, Mr. von Stein." Paul Conrad walked confidently through the crowd, who parted for him without a word. His hair grayed at the temples and curled along his collar, making him look dangerously distinguished. Alec braced himself, but he stopped just out of arm's reach and nodded. "How nice to see you again."

Alec nodded in return and waited for more—anything more. A mocking statement about being late, a more inquisitive one about his intentions. Pistols at dawn.

"I apologize for not sending word of my arrival."

Conrad shrugged and waved Alec's words away. His gaze, a most interesting blue-green, held his, and Alec changed his mind. If Conrad wanted him harmed, he'd have never made it up the drive.

Impressed, and undeterred, he offered a grin. "I'm looking for Yara. Is she in one of the barns?"

Conrad's mouth twitched. "The stables." He tiled his head toward the appropriate building. "With the mares."

Alec nodded and strode in that direction, keenly aware that the entire courtyard was watching him. Let them watch. He entered the stables, and it took him less than a heartbeat to find Yara.

She stood just outside the second stall, cooing at the horse inside. Micki sat obediently and quietly beside her.

"What a pretty foal you are."

"Yara."

She stilled and slowly turned. Her dress had seen better days. It was clearly something she wore specifically around the stables. Her braid hung down her back, half falling out of its plait. Her hands were smudged with dirt, and she looked as if she hadn't slept in days.

His heart stilled. Her beauty captivated him, making all the words he'd planned out completely vanish.

"You came back."

His footsteps faltered, but only for a moment. Closing the distance between them, he took her hand. The feel of her skin against his grounded him—it also ensured she didn't swing at him. She had a mean hook. "Did you think I wouldn't?"

She shrugged, watching him with that curious caution she often displayed. "I wasn't sure," she admitted.

Alec frowned. "Do you think I tell—" He broke off and looked around. He didn't want an audience for the most important conversation of his life. Thankfully, Godred rode in the carriage, still a mile or so behind him. "Are we alone?"

She nodded. "I presume your arrival caused the commotion

in the courtyard. The lads raced out to see what all the ruckus was about."

"You didn't?" He eyed Micki. Her tail wagged happily, and she tilted her head up at him but didn't otherwise greet him.

"Erato was foaling." She glanced at the horse and her foal. "I couldn't leave."

He squeezed her hand, bringing it to his lips. "My beautiful, compassionate Yara. Of course you couldn't."

She watched him, her face closed off, but she didn't pull away. "Did you see your crew?"

"I did. And I'll tell you about it later." He kissed her finger-tips, and her fingers curled around his hand, tightening just the slightest. "Why did you think I wouldn't come back?"

He had a good idea why. She'd been hurt, ignored, tossed aside, and forgotten. Praised for her way with animals and her inheritance, but never for being herself. Still, Alec thought she understood him better than that.

"It's not that I didn't," she hedged.

"Do you not believe that I love you?" He drew her closer, and she didn't resist, which he took as a good sign. "That I'd tell you such a promise and renege on my vow?"

"I—no, I don't believe that." She frowned harder. "You left."

"I did." He kissed her cheek. "I'm sorry. I was in the wrong. But before anything, I needed to get my life in order." He kissed her other cheek. "You were right; it was a mess. And one of my own making, or at least partially so."

"And now that you feel your life is in order, you've returned?" Her voice wobbled, a clear sign of her hurt, and it cut right through him.

"No. I realized life isn't meant to be completely in order. That's a lie we tell ourselves to delay things." He pulled back and met her gaze. "Things like, 'I'll marry my beautiful Yara when I ensure my crew don't hate me and my life is what it was before.' Which will never happen."

Her breath stopped, but she nodded, as if that was the expected thing to do in such situations. Nod. "And what—" She broke off and took a shuddering breath. "And do they hate you?"

He wasn't surprised she'd asked that question rather than acknowledge what he'd said. Alec gathered her closer. "Some still do. And if I never have the life I did before the storm and the accident, then that's all right. That life didn't involve you. That life would never have led me to you. Even if we'd met, I wouldn't have been in any position to realize the wonderful, magnificent woman you are."

She licked her lips, a rare sign of hesitation. "I see. What do you plan now?"

"Beyond convincing you we ought to marry?" He kissed her forehead, fingers tangling in her braid. "Beyond promising to never leave you again?"

"Not even for the sea? Not even for Hilton?"

He shrugged dismissively. "Even if he needs me for a mission, that doesn't mean I'll leave you behind."

"Oh." She swallowed again. "Is that your promise, then? You won't leave me behind?"

"My promise." He kissed the palm of her hand, dirt and all. "I promise I'll love you even when you threaten me." Probably especially then. He'd never realized how attractive a woman holding a knife in righteous anger could be. "I promise I'll never take you for granted. I'll listen, and not only about the animals." He twined their fingers together. "I promise you'll be in charge of all the animals on whatever estate we purchase, and my stables in London, and whatever else you wish."

He kissed her gently, testing the waters, but she kissed him back, her hand tight around his. Her body remained stiff and still, but the passion they'd shared on the road from Brighton burst forth.

"And I promise," he added, with another kiss to her nose, "I'll never leave you again. I'll love you until my dying day."

"THAT'S A LOT OF PROMISES." Yara's heart beat so loudly, she was surprised he didn't hear it. Surprised it didn't leap from her chest. "I like the one about the animals the best."

She evaded the real question, and she knew it. Alec's raised eyebrow told her he knew it, too. Mind racing, Yara tried to step back, but he held her securely. If she really wanted loose from his embrace, she knew he'd release her, but it'd been ten days. She missed him.

She also needed space, distance between them, despite how much she enjoyed being back in his arms. Plus, she doubted she'd have a clearer head with distance. Over two weeks, and she still couldn't clearly understand the hot rush of emotions—love and passion and trust—she felt for this man.

"We spent a week together," she said, repeating the excuses she'd told herself during the days he'd been gone. "That's hardly enough time to know if what we shared might last."

The rest of her life both terrified and intrigued her. Beckoned her toward him.

"You're right." He didn't move away, which gave her confidence that they might work through this. "We might end up hating each other after a few years."

Not what she wanted to hear. Expected to hear, yes. Hoped to? Not at all. Then again, she didn't know what she hoped to hear.

He'd already laid out a very impressive list of promises.

"You believe that?" Yara kept her voice even, calling on years of practice in doing so. "That in five years—or three, or seven—we'll have drifted apart?"

"No." He kissed her fingers again, still uncaring about the grime that coated them. The stormy blue of his gaze drew her in, and Yara felt herself falling. "If anything, I think these last months have taught me that things require work. Building a fortune, keeping that fortune, earning trust, keeping that trust. Love." Another fingertip kiss, accompanied by that half smile that curled her toes. "Keeping that love."

A band around her heart eased, and she breathed more freely. Hard work she knew all about and accepted.

"Those are a lot of promises," she repeated. "I intend to hold you to every single one."

Alec laughed and kissed her again, a quick, hard kiss that sparked the fire burning within her. In the last days, she'd wondered if perhaps she imagined the passion between them. If that passion had burned itself out during their week together. It hadn't.

"You haven't answered my question." His lips moved gently against hers.

"I don't recall a question," she teased, pressing him against a beam. Micki offered a low yip but didn't otherwise move. Good girl that she was.

"Will you marry me?"

"Yes."

The word, giddy and breathless, burst from her, and she nearly laughed. But then Alec kissed her again. His body warmed her in the cold, damp barn, and his mouth sent fire through her veins.

"I didn't expect I'd fall in love with you," she admitted, breathing hard and trying to remember why decorum might be important. "Let alone in a week."

"I know. Then again, I never expected to fall in love at all. It wasn't something I saw in my life." He pulled back and looked around. Erato was busy with her foal, a wobbly-legged, gleaming brown mare. "What did you say her name was?"

"Erato," Yara said.

He choked on a laugh. "The Greek muse?" She smiled in agreement. "And her daughter?"

"I'm thinking Cleophema, of course." Cleophema being the

daughter of Erato and…some king Yara couldn't recall at the moment. "Cleo for short."

"Of course." He easily lifted her, so reminiscent of their time together, and carried her the few steps to the tack room. Sitting on the stool, he set her on his lap, and Yara wound her arms around his neck and kissed his cheek.

"What happened with your crew?" She pulled back, one finger brushing down his cheek. His eyes darkened, but then Micki came in.

"*Mestrih*, Micki." Yara reached down and scratched Micki behind one ear.

"She's much calmer here."

Eying Alec and his obvious attempt at evading her question, Yara merely shrugged. "She knows she has to be cautious by the mares. Especially now, when they're foaling. Otherwise, she can't stay with me, and she doesn't want that."

Alec reached down and scratched her along her back until Micki whined in pleasure. "What does *mestrih* mean?"

"A loose translation is 'at ease.' Relax. Stand down. It means Micki can be her usual exuberant self." She waited, then asked again, "What happened with your crew?"

"Four months was a long time," he admitted, gaze still on Micki. "Two of my men cut all ties and signed on with other ships, but I found everyone."

She waited, but he shook his head. All right. She'd accept this shortened version. For now. The fact that he'd taken her advice and sought them out, had accepted responsibly for deserting them, was huge despite everything.

"They accepted your apologies? Your reasons for staying away?"

"Chloe Jones did, yes. She was grieving the loss of her husband, and I know that." He shook his head.

It still hurt him, she knew. The accusations, the blame. The fact he grieved, too.

"Holly? Walter? Ian?"

"Holly refused to speak with me." Alec sighed and rubbed his nose. "Slammed the door in my face. But Walter, Peter's brother, he let me in. Ian, too." He shrugged, but she knew Holly's reaction had hurt him. "It'll take more than these last days for things to right themselves, and they'll never be the way they were. I know that."

Yara couldn't understand how his family hadn't embraced him after all this. No matter what kind of arguments she and her siblings got into, Yara knew they'd always welcome her back. Perhaps it was a matter of time. Perhaps his crew didn't think of him as highly as he did them. Yara didn't know.

"And Christian? Did you speak with him?"

"No…I sent a letter."

Frowning, she narrowed her eyes at him. "You sent your brother a letter?"

He offered her that lopsided grin. The one that made her heart turn over and her mind go pleasantly blank. "I wanted to find you," he admitted.

She wasn't mollified, though she liked the order of his priorities. Liked being first. "And this letter says…?"

"Only that I want to mend things. Try, at least." He shook his head. "It's been three years since the old earl died. Longer still since Christian and I spoke. I'm not sure how that's going to pan out, but since I was righting everything else, it seemed like the time."

"And Sabine?"

"Sent her a letter, too, though I doubt she'll even read it." He sighed and ran a hand down his face. "I didn't attend her wedding, and I'm not sure she's forgiven me for that."

"All right." Yara would accept that. Nothing happened in a day. Or even ten days. "What happens now? Are you getting the crew back together? Running blockades again?"

She didn't necessarily mind the danger, though now that

she'd found Alec, Yara preferred him here. Still, danger lurked everywhere. In the fields between Brighton and London. In the constant rain and the permanent chill it could cause. A fall from a horse, even one as beautiful as Alastor or her own Masika.

"What do you want?"

Yara blinked at him. "Pardon?"

"Do you want to run blockades? Sail on my ship? It'll have to be new, I suppose." He frowned and sighed. "I loved that ship. Perhaps one named *Salaminia*."

Her lips twitched. "I do love sailing. And Greek Mythology." She tilted her head and frowned. So few people had asked what she wanted. "That's a lot of decisions to make now."

"We have time." His arms tightened around her. "Though I suppose starting a family might hinder any blockade running."

"Family?" She blinked at him again.

Alec laughed and kissed the corner of her mouth. "After we're married." He paused and peered at her, eyes narrowing. "Unless you're already pregnant?"

"No." Mouth dry, she shook her head. "No, I'm not."

He nodded, face revealing neither relief nor disappointment. "Another thing I learned these last weeks. Better to take things one step at a time."

She laughed, combing her fingers through his hair. "Whoever told you that gave you good advice."

"She's brilliant, I admit. Beautiful, too."

"Clever, witty, bold," Yara added. She rested her head on his shoulder. "Whatever happens now, we'll walk it together."

He held their joined hands over his heart. "Together. I promise."

"I like that word," she whispered.

"Good. Because I promise we'll face the future together."

Eventually, Yara stood and held out her hand. "I think we've stayed here long enough." She let out a long-suffering sigh and glanced toward the still-empty door. Peeking around the corner, she didn't see anyone in the stables, nor hovering at the barn doors, but she knew her family well enough.

"I'm actually surprised no one's come knocking." She sighed again. "Or sneaking up and eavesdropping." Which was more likely.

Alec stood and kissed the top of her head. "Godred should be here by now, too."

"Godred? He's coming?"

"Aye, he followed in the carriage. We left before dawn, and I had Alastor." He grinned and chuckled. "I outpaced him by a mile at least."

Snickering, a most unladylike sound, Yara started for the door. He stopped her and took her hand. She liked that, the promise of it. Together.

As they neared the barn doors, she clearly heard Godred. "Ah, Lady Conrad. A pleasure."

From across the courtyard, Yara saw him offer an ornate bow to her mother, but he was just out of arm's reach of her father. She stifled another snicker.

"I was just telling your husband about Alec's wild journey." He shook his head, red hair gleaming in the sunlight. "No respect, that man, I tell you. Dragged me across the country, got me up hours before dawn, then left me behind!" He paused when he spotted them. "Ah, Alec and the lovely Miss Yara."

"Godred." Alec scowled, but Yara squeezed his hand in warning.

"I take it, since you walked out of the stables without a dagger sticking out of you, that all is well?" Godred asked innocently.

Her mother snorted, and from the corner of her eye, she saw her father cover his own laughter with one hand.

"Is that what you think of me?" She shook her head. "That I'd leave my khanjar *in* him? I'd never leave behind evidence like that."

Godred's mouth dropped open, and he laughed, big, boisterous sounds of joy. "You're a dangerous woman, Miss Yara. I like you."

"I'm glad to hear it."

"Godred," Alec growled. "Shut it. Or we won't invite you to the wedding."

In the silent moment between his announcement and the congratulations, Yara smiled up at him. "You do know how to make an announcement."

But then her mother was hugging her. "I'm glad you didn't run off to Gretna Green."

"It's still an option," she muttered. Alec had the audacity to laugh.

He ginned over the crowd of well-wishers and winked at her. Maybe Gretna Green was still an option. He mouthed *I love you*, and her heart pounded faster.

"How long does it take to plan a wedding?" she muttered.

"We'll be quick, darling." Her mother kissed her cheek as her father hugged her tight.

"You're happy, Yara?" he asked, his piercing blue-green eyes holding hers.

"More than," she promised. Alec found her hand and squeezed. "But I still think Gretna Green might be the faster option."

THANK YOU FOR READING!

Thank you for reading!

If you enjoyed this book, I'd really appreciate it if you helped others enjoy it, too. Reviews are precious and help persuade other readers to give my romances a try.

Sign up to my VIP list for a short story, *One Day with You.* This story, along 3 additional short stories about Louise and Malcolm, are only available to my list. https://bit.ly/ 3kSzMjI

I send weekly newsletters with things like new releases, special offers, pictures of my dog, recipes, and other exciting news about my stories, preorders, research, and travel that I hope you'll enjoy as much as I do.

STAY CONNECTED

ckmackenzie.com
instagram.com/ckmackenzieauthor
facebook.com/ckmackenziebook
tiktok.com/@ckmackenzieauthor

ALSO BY C.K. MACKENZIE

Kaya and Paul: The Conrad Chronicles:

Husband of Convenience

Sins of a Rogue

A Lover's Promise

Conrad Legacy:

The Lady's Marquess

The Lady's Pirate

The Lady's Rogue

coming soon...The Lady's Risk

Nadia and James: Part of the Conrad Chronicles

Smuggler's Captain

Her Captain's Honor

www.ingramcontent.com/pod-product-compliance
Lightning Source LLC
Chambersburg PA
CBHW030431160726
47991CB00005B/1687